**AND FOR AUGUSTUS ALVIN YORK
ELECTED NOVEMBER 4, 1980
IT IS THE ZERO HOUR....**

ELECTED TO
A LIVING NIGHTMARE . . .

York was seized by a numbing sense of dread. Twice in less than a year he had been the target of total strangers out to murder him. If two had already tried, how many hundreds—thousands—of others were out there waiting to kill him? How many thousands more lunatics and fanatics were gnashing their teeth at this moment in uncontrollable hatred for *him*? He shuddered. All of these people were unknown to him, never seen, never heard by him, yet all of them were obssessed with *murdering* him. It was a realization as frightening as any nightmare he had suffered as a boy. Yet it was real—and it was irrevocable. Someone was stalking him. Someone would always be stalking him as long as he was President. . . .

THE ZERO FACTOR

WILLIAM OSCAR JOHNSON

PUBLISHED BY POCKET BOOKS NEW YORK

Another *Original* publication of POCKET BOOKS

POCKET BOOKS, a Simon & Schuster division of
GULF & WESTERN CORPORATION
1230 Avenue of the Americas, New York, N.Y. 10020

ISBN: 0-671-83261-1

First Pocket Books printing March, 1980

10 9 8 7 6 5 4 3 2 1

POCKET and colophon are trademarks of Simon & Schuster.

Printed in the U.S.A.

Prologue

It is a phenomenon well known to many that for the past 140 years no President of the United States who won election in a year ending in zero has left office alive. Seven in a row have died or been murdered:

William Henry Harrison. Elected to first term November 3, 1840. Died April 4, 1841. Cause: pneumonia.

Abraham Lincoln. Elected to first term November 6, 1860. Died April 15, 1865. Cause: gunshot wound.

James Abram Garfield. Elected to first term November 2, 1880. Died September 19, 1881. Cause: gunshot wound.

William McKinley. Elected to second term November 6, 1900. Died September 14, 1901. Cause: gunshot wound.

Warren Gamaliel Harding. Elected to first term November 2, 1920. Died August 2, 1923. Cause: stroke.

Franklin Delano Roosevelt. Elected to third term November 5, 1940. Died April 12, 1945. Cause: cerebral hemorrhage.

John Fitzgerald Kennedy. Elected to first term November 8, 1960. Died November 22, 1963. Cause: gunshot wound.

Augustus Alvin York. Elected to first term November 4, 1980 . . .

Chapter 1

Morley was probably very drunk, but York couldn't be sure. Sometime after midnight he had lost count of the number of Jack Daniels he had finished himself. Morley's deep voice rattled on in his usual assured staccato. Drunk or sober, he maintained the same tone, patrician and authoritative. York squinted at the campaign manager. Morley sat in a big shabby armchair across the hotel room. The place was lighted by one small lamp and the silent flickering television set, and his figure was obscured by the darkness.

"We're into no-man's-land now," Morley was saying. "The 1980s: The dread decade. Mankind commits suicide with its own technology. Chaos, crisis, the beginning of the end. . . ."

He sounded like an oracle hiding in the shadowy corner of the room. York knew Morley was wound up and could continue talking like this for hours, spinning theories, weaving ideas, listening to his own voice, entranced by his own rolling language. It would hardly matter at all to Morley if York were paying attention to him.

York glanced at the newspaper lying at his feet. His picture was on the front page, a large photograph ten inches deep and four columns wide, taken the night before at the last rally of his presidential campaign. The camera had caught him with his arms raised over his head, fists locked in a gesture of triumph that he had not felt. The early edition of the Louisville *Courier-Journal* carried an eight-column headline over the picture:

GOV. YORK ENDS WHITE HOUSE RUN HERE; INCUMBENT FAVORED ON ELECTION EVE

York pushed the paper aside with his feet and glanced toward the silent image on the television. He saw his own figure there, too. His left arm chopped the air as he spoke. He saw himself grin and wink and wave. The crowd was rhythmically waving "We Love York" signs that Morley's men had routinely distributed before the rally. As he watched, York could hear again the wild cries of the crowd. He could feel the wind, bitter and wet with the coming cold rain as it ruffled his hair and bit his cheeks. The floodlights had blinded him, bathing him in harsh, brilliant light which brought no warmth to the raw night. He had felt exposed, naked, and more lost than he had ever been in his life. But none of this showed as he watched himself on television.

Morley droned on. "Ever read Auden?" His voice took on a chill tone. *"In the nightmare of the dark, all the dogs of Europe bark. . . ."* York could not focus on the words, but the sound of the voice alone raised a sharp sense of fear in him. He got up from his chair. "Andy, you are depressing the hell out of me." His words were slurred. "We leave at six-thirty in the morning, right?" He looked at his watch. "Christ, that's only three hours. I'm going to bed."

"Six-thirty, Gus." Morley coughed. "We meet the terrible decade. The first election of the Eighties. It's like one of those guys said—maybe Kafka. This is the

decade of the evil sleepwalker, sleeping chaos . . ."
Morley laughed, a metallic cackle. He was definitely
drunk, very drunk.

York crossed the parlor to the bedroom. He imagined Morley might go on speaking to the empty room,
but when he closed the bedroom door behind him the
campaign manager fell silent. York undressed quickly
and crawled into bed beside Milly. She did not move,
but York was fairly certain she was awake. He passed
into a drunken coma that lasted an hour, then awoke
and lay rigid in the bed, his brain heavy with the
whiskey. Suddenly he began to shiver. Milly rolled
toward him and put her arms around him. "Cold,
darling?" she murmured sleepily.

York mumbled that he was. Then he dozed in Milly's
arms. It seemed like moments later when the phone
rang and Morley announced cheerfully that it was six
A.M., Election Day 1980.

At that hour, in the lobby of the aging hotel,
Appleton and McCarthy, Secret Service agents, were
conferring. The cavernous chamber was draped with
red, white, and blue bunting. Bright-colored campaign
signs hung from the pillars and the walls. Suspended
from the ceiling were a dozen huge smiling billboard-
photographs of Governor York. The lobby remained
somber despite these decorations.

Appleton, the Secret Service man in charge, felt a
sudden chill as McCarthy held out an envelope and
said: "Another one. They found it in a mailbox at the
main post office."

Appleton took the envelope from him and held it
gingerly, as if it were a snake. The address on it was the
same as the others, a cramped color-crayon scrawl that
said:

HON. GOV. A. A. YORK
C/O STATE CAPITOL
FRANKFORT, KY.

He asked McCarthy, "You had the fingerprints checked?" The agent nodded and Appleton pulled the message out distastefully. As with the others, it was written on the rough, blue-lined paper of a child's composition book. Each word was made with a different color crayon, seven rows of rainbow characters that pronounced a death sentence on the Republican candidate for the Presidency:

YORK: SHIT HEEL NIGGER LOVER. FUCKING NIGGER KISSER. BULLET HOLES IN YOUR NIGGER-SHIT BRAIN. TODAY! TODAY! NOV. 4, 1980! YOU'LL BE BLEEDING BULLET HOLES ON YOUR NIGGER-SUCKING FACE! DEATH! TODAY!

Madness shimmered in the bright crayon colors. Appleton sighed and looked at McCarthy. "For ten straight letters he talks about doing it 'today.' I hope he has it wrong again."

"Me, too. There's something in these that goes beyond your average racist weirdo, isn't there?"

Appleton shrugged. "Maybe. Maybe not. He gets the dates right and he spells the words right. You can't tell how irrational he is. We have to assume he's going to try it one of these days."

Appleton handed the letter back to McCarthy and said, "Send it to the lab with the rest of them." He strode through the hotel lobby and out the revolving door. At the top of the hotel steps he paused for a moment and gazed down beneath the canopy into the drilling rain. He did not bother to remove his tinted aviator-framed spectacles. They made the day markedly darker, but he did not lift them, for these were as much a part of the persona of Appleton as the muted gray tweed suit, the black wing-tipped shoes, the white button-down shirt, black knit necktie, and stern, chiseled face. He tried to recall how many election days in the twenty-three years he had been in the Secret Service had been made as entirely of gloom and rain as this one was. He found that he could not clearly remember a single one. He did remember the weather on Election Day 1960, however. He had been at Hyannis with the Kennedys, and that day had been one full of sunshine and ocean breezes, a glistening Cape Cod day. Well, he *thought* he remembered. . . .

Appleton himself had been so excited by everything in those years, with every nuance and intimacy he discovered behind the imposing façade of the Presidency that, now, he could not really trust his memory. In those days of the late Fifties and early Sixties, he had imagined he could feel the throb of power in the very carpets at the White House. He had even glimpsed power in the turf that clung to Eisenhower's golf clubs, seen glory in the bits of lint on John Foster Dulles' Homburg, heard grand strategies and high purpose in the squeak of Sherman Adams' plain black shoes. Then came the Kennedys, and he had been bathed in the glamor and arrogance of Camelot for a short while. The rainiest days had seemed sunny to Appleton, but no more.

He spoke into the walkie-talkie in his hand: "Is Right End on the way down?"

A voice sounded crisply: "Still in the room."

As he began to descend the hotel steps, the chill of

the morning hit him and he shrugged into a trenchcoat. He examined the faces of the four dozen people crowded under the dripping canopy. They were a motley group—the campaign press crowd, bored newspaper reporters, wisecracking photographers, preening network correspondents with coteries of technicians who were wired for sight and sound and plugged into twenty million homes even at this ungodly hour of this ungodly morning. Most of the faces were familiar to Appleton, for they had followed wherever the campaign had gone.

This was his *sixth* presidential Election Day, November 4, 1980. And as proof of the terrible transiency that had shaken that august office during Appleton's years at the White House, he was now serving his *sixth* President. There was not a certifiably great one among them: Eisenhower, Kennedy, Johnson, Nixon, Ford, and the incumbent, who was running today for election to a second term. Mediocrity, mendacity, or murder had served to reduce them all.

* * * * *

A tall, thin man stood languidly in the queue to passport control in Tokyo International Airport. Occasionally he rubbed the straw-colored stubble that had appeared on his jaw during the flight from San Francisco. A clerk flipped open his American passport, which was made out to one Darryl Michael Hagerty, born in 1929 in Dallas, Texas. None of these facts was true, but the photo matched the tall man's face perfectly—a long, sharp face that was as full of planes as if it had been sculpted by Lachaise. His features were all the more arresting for the deep pockmarks in his cheeks. He wore his dark blond hair in a Prince Valiant cut with thick sideburns. His eyes were the color of black coffee.

It was impossible to tell that the hair was a wig and the irises were contact lenses.

Customs in Tokyo were relaxed, and he moved through the airport quickly. He wore a double-knit tan suit and vest with a gaudy necktie and zipped black boots. That, plus the vaguely foolish haircut, made him look exactly like the heavy-machinery salesman that his business cards and identification papers indicated "Darryl Michael Hagerty" to be.

He took a taxi to the railroad station in downtown Tokyo and boarded a midafternoon bullet train to Kyoto. Once there, he took a cab to the Daichi Holiday Inn, where he registered as "Hagerty." He left his passport at the desk, as is the custom. In his room, he tipped the old Japanese bellman who carried up his two bags and thanked him in a deep Houston drawl, though the man clearly spoke no English. He double-locked the door with the chain, pulled the curtains across the window, and then sat down in front of a mirror above a dresser. He removed his wig and sideburns to reveal a fashionably short-cropped head of brown hair. When he removed the coffee-colored contact lenses, his eyes proved to be a strikingly light blue. With cold cream from his shaving kit, he rubbed off a thin coat of makeup, changing his complexion from the faintly ruddy color of a heavy drinker to a lighter, healthier-looking hue. He pulled gum wads from behind each ear and they returned to a flatter position.

Then he stripped off the Texan's double-knit suit, the gaudy tie, and shirt, then showered and shaved the stubble on his cheeks. He dressed in a soft navy turtleneck, light tan corduroy jeans, and desert boots. Stretching his long angular body in front of the mirror, he casually examined his face for new lines and wrinkles of middle age, then took out a small tape recorder from his first suitcase and switched it on. A string quartet was playing Mozart. He removed several books from the suitcase and arranged them on the dresser. One was a French edition of Levi-Strauss' *Tropique,* another was a copy of Rilke's early poems in German, a third was a collection of Chekov's short stories in Russian.

He put the books down and opened the second suitcase. It contained a suit of hard gray material, cut in the lumpy fashion of clothes made in Eastern Europe. He took out three starched white shirts, each frayed at the cuffs and collar, a pair of scuffed black shoes, ankle-high with laces. He took out four neckties, each a different muddy color, each with a stain or two. He piled this seedy clothing on the bed, took a razor blade from his shaving kit, and carefully cut the lining on the lid of the suitcase. He reached into the space there and took out a lump of clay-like material the size of a doorknob which was wrapped in a plastic bag. He removed a small flat metal case which he opened to reveal an assortment of delicate wires, electronic plates, and tiny cadmium batteries of the type used in certain mini-computers. He then removed a double-stitched piece of canvas the length of a cummerbund. It had a zipper which he opened to reveal the delicate wiring and switches concealed inside.

Carefully, he placed these items on the dresser top. Then he removed a wallet from the space inside the lining, opened it, and examined the contents. It included an East German passport and identification documents made out to Klaus Steinbugler, a Communist Party member from Leipzig. There was a letter of introduction in German from a high Party official to one Imai Hitsu, who was identified in the address as the Secretary-General of the Red Independence Party of

Japan. The R.I.P. had earned many headlines in recent months for alleged acts of terrorism as well as for a fanatical campaign to unionize workers in Japan's major industrial corporations. The letter introduced "Steinbugler" as an official government representative and emissary from East German laborers who wished to throw their support behind the efforts of Imai to "free the masses of Japan."

The letter, the passport, the other documents were, of course, forged. The photograph in the passport was of a thin, bland-looking man in his fifties. His hair was gray and cut in an old-fashioned combed-back style. He wore steel-rimmed glasses. His complexion was pallid and his expression grim.

"Hagerty" took a gray wig from the suitcase and placed it on his head. From his shaving/makeup kit he took a pair of yellowish contact lenses and inserted them over the light blue of his irises. The amber cast to his eyes gave him an oddly wolfish look. He put on a pair of steel-rimmed spectacles and studied himself in the mirror. He was now a close approximation of the photograph of Klaus Steinbugler, and he said in gruff German, "Good day, Herr Steinbugler. And did you remember to bring your explosives all the way from Leipzig? Are you ready for your job?"

* * * * *

Chapter 2

Appleton was not guarding the President this Election Day, nor had he been for the past thirteen weeks. His responsibility was the life of one Augustus Alvin York, the governor of Kentucky and currently the Republican candidate running against the incumbent President. Appleton was chief of the Secret Service security detail for York, a job he had held since the last blistering week in July at that suicidal Republican convention in Detroit, where York had won his party's nomination for the Presidency by default. Given the chaos and indecision in Detroit, it was not surprising that what followed was a frenzied, panicky campaign, marred by disorganization, confusion, and, worst of all, an enervating sense of futility. Now a pervasive aura of fear also existed because of the crayon letters which had begun to arrive two weeks before.

Mail from similar crazies was not unusual during a presidential campaign. Yet Appleton was more unnerved now than he could remember being in any previous campaign. In mid-October, as the polls showed York falling further behind the incumbent, the pressure within the campaign had risen. The campaign manager, a high-strung, fast-talking Harvard man named Andrew Jackson Morley IV, who was as celebrated for his heavy drinking as for his brilliance as a political theoretician, had pressed for more and more public appearances by the candidate. It was his belief that York was simply not well enough known. Thus, he sent the whole entourage dashing about the country in the final three weeks, visiting dozens of crucial precincts where Morley felt the election would be decided. The candidate and his wife were seen in person by perhaps three million people, and they shook hands with a hundred thousand or more. It was Andrew Morley's theory that though television had to be the primary means for impressing Governor York's personality on the nation, the impact of a personal appearance made a far deeper—and more favorable—impression on voters. If the election was close (which no one expected), the relative handful of voters who had actually had personal contact with Gus York could make the difference.

Though he liked Morley and respected him, Appleton had begun to believe that the campaign manager was being purposely diabolical in his disregard for routine security, that he was concocting the most nightmarish conditions in order to expose the candidate to danger. Of course, this wasn't true, but there *had* been an unusual number of walking tours along crowded city streets, parades with York perched on the back seat of a convertible before milling crowds. And Appleton had seen the gleam of rifle barrels in every open window, the bulge of pistols beneath every coat. He had tried to convince Morley that he was exposing the governor to unnecessary risk. Morley disagreed, but when the first of the color-crayon letters arrived, the campaign manager promised to reduce the candidate's public appearances—somewhat. The reduction proved so inconsequential it seemed inevitable to Appleton that something violent would happen.

When it did, it was not at all what Appleton might have imagined. A week before the election, on a radiant October day in Danbury, Connecticut, Governor York was charging through an excited curbside crowd gathered for a rally in front of city hall. Appleton had followed at York's shoulder, trying to stay between the candidate's back and the crowd behind, at the same time scrutinizing the mass of faces swarming in front of the governor. A thicket of outstretched arms reaching to shake York's hand obscured Appleton's view of upcoming faces, but suddenly he glimpsed amid the arms a woman glaring fiercely and fixedly at the candidate.

He saw the light of rage and lunacy flare suddenly in her eyes. She began digging in her purse and a glint of metal flashed as she withdrew her hand. Appleton slammed into York's side, shoving the candidate away from the crowd so that he stumbled out into the street. Then he sprang toward the woman, bringing the edge of his stiffened hand down fiercely on her right shoulder. He felt her collarbone snap and heard a single shriek as she dropped to the pavement.

When he knelt by her, Appleton found the steel-rimmed spectacles she had been removing from her bag. The look of madness he had imagined was merely the blankness of myopia. She was, it turned out, a checkout clerk at a supermarket; she waited only two days before she filed a $2,000,000 suit for damages.

Appleton received a stinging reprimand by phone from Watson, the chief of the Secret Service. Yet Morley supported Appleton's attack. "I saw her, too, and you did the right thing," he told Appleton. "She looked crazy and dangerous." He had phoned Watson, and Appleton was quite certain that Morley had saved his job in the York campaign, and he was grateful—

though now he had come to see it as a distinctly mixed blessing.

Appleton's walkie-talkie spoke: "Right End is in the elevator."

"Good," he said.

Suddenly he was struck with an almost dizzying sense of disorientation. He squeezed his eyes shut behind the protective brown lenses and concentrated for a second. Ah, yes, Louisville, this was Louisville. In the next few minutes he and Governor York's party and the whole crowd of press and TV types would whirl away together in a motorcade, bound for a forsaken wide spot in the road, deep in the Appalachian mountains. Jezebel, Kentucky. The hamlet where York had been born. Once there, they would perform that hoary bit of Election Day theater: Candidate Returns to Humble Hometown to Vote for Self as President of United States. Then they would come back here, to Louisville, to await the election returns.

Appleton peered down the steps into the rain. Directly at the end of the canopy, two long black limousines sat with their motors purring. Behind the limousines a silver Greyhound bus was parked. Its motor growled, pouring exhaust fumes onto the street. A red and yellow banner on its side proclaimed:

YORK FOR PRESIDENT— CAMPAIGN PRESS BUS

Behind the bus sat two TV station vans, one yellow, one chartreuse, both decorated with signs identifying them as "News Cruisers."

All of this was relatively drab compared to the six squad cars of the Kentucky State Police parked at the curb. They were painted Day-Glo orange and black, and their dome lights rotated slowly and made flickering reflections off the wet street. Like old-fashioned cavalry troops at the bridles of their horses, a dozen troopers stood at parade rest by the fenders of the cars. They were thick-shouldered and grim-looking, dressed in uniforms of robin's-egg blue, belted and strapped in black leather and wearing knee-high black boots. Rain sluiced off their hats and soaked the shoulders of their uniforms, but they stood as stiff and obedient as military school cadets working off demerits. The troopers were not only armed with holstered .45-caliber pistols; they carried sawed-off shotguns and high-powered rifles slung over their backs.

The revolving door rattled. Appleton looked up expectantly and scowled in disappointment. A stocky, heavy-bellied man with a craggy face the color of sand came out of the hotel. He was wearing a baggy gray overcoat and a tan felt hat with a wide brim. His black shoes were long and wide and scuffed; he planted them like flatirons at the top of the steps. A trooper with bright yellow sergeant's stripes on his sleeve looked up questioningly from the street, and the stocky man signaled with a slash of his hand. Then he descended the steps and spoke to Appleton in a deep, confidential drawl. "They comin'. They on the way down."

Appleton said with a breath of sarcasm, "Thanks, Commissioner. Are your boys ready for him?"

"Yup, they ready. We all ready."

Appleton sighed and spoke softly so nearby reporters could not hear him. "Seriously now, Commissioner, won't you change your mind about all this firepower? It looks damn dangerous to me."

"Like I said, son, we got to make a show of it. We want whoever's writin' those goddarn color-crayon letters to get scared off." He gestured toward the troopers. "They enough to scare off any baboon fool enough to try an' get the governor."

Appleton tried to keep his distaste out of his voice, but his tone was bitter and hard. "I can't order you to do a damn thing. You know that. But with so many guns around, someone is bound to get hurt."

The commissioner looked at Appleton and his small eyes burned from deep pale folds of skin. "These men was born with guns. They are trained law officers. We ain't takin' *any* chances that the governor is in jeopardy while he is in his own state on his own presidential Election Day." He hesitated, then lowered his voice to a tense, hoarse whisper. "The only president this sovereign state of Kentucky ever come up with, son, was Abraham Lincoln, an' we all know what happened to him. It ain't goin' to happen again. Those boys got *bullets* in them guns to keep it from happenin' again."

The revolving doors rattled once more and Appleton looked up to see Mikkelson emerge and pause to examine the crowd, the waiting cars, the wet street. Appleton turned his back on the state police commissioner and moved toward Mikkelson. "Are they in the lobby?" he asked.

Mikkelson ignored the question and peered over Appleton's shoulder. "Is everything under control?"

Appleton spoke with unconcealed irritation. "Christ, Mick! Do you see anything *out* of control?"

Mikkelson had joined the York campaign five days before, detached from the President's Secret Service detail. Appleton was still officially in charge of York campaign security, but Mikkelson had let it be suspected that he was a troubleshooter sent to smooth things out. He was an abrasive, nakedly ambitious man. A few years earlier he had made the abject misjudgment of hooking up with Spiro Agnew on the assumption that Agnew had the best likelihood of becoming President of the United States after Nixon. Through an unctuous approach to his superiors, an unswerving capacity for undermining his colleagues, plus a plow-horse willingness to work all hours of the day and night, he had been put in charge of Agnew's security detail at the age of thirty-one. Thus, when Agnew went into exile, so did Mikkelson. He had been forced to work his way back up in the echelons of White House security details. Though Appleton did not want to believe it, there *was* a possibility that Mikkelson had been sent here to report back to Washington on Appleton's performance.

Mikkelson spoke briskly: "Right End is doing a tour of the lobby. Be another five minutes, I guess." He looked at his watch. "Six-thirty on the button. God, he's punctual."

Appleton murmured, "Comes from playing football. They fine them when they're late for practice."

Mikkelson checked the revolving doors, which were quite still. "I hear we got another letter."

Appleton did not want to discuss the subject and he began to turn away. Mikkelson grabbed his arm. "What is it—eight of them?"

"Ten."

"Jesus. Any reason to think he'll try for a hit today?"

Appleton was brusque. "Who knows? None of it makes sense."

Mikkelson nodded. "It's like trying to figure out a wild boar. You don't know if it'll charge you or run away."

"What the hell do you know about wild boars?"

"Not a thing." He looked at Appleton with a small

supercilious smile on his lips. "Which is the same *you* know about lunatics who write threatening letters with color crayons."

Appleton snapped, "Go back inside and come out the door ahead of him. Make sure he is covered on all sides." He was not only angry, he was frightened— about the prospect of an assassination attempt, and about his own capacity to react to it. He adjusted his dark glasses and checked again to be certain that his agents were properly positioned.

Billings and Neil stood beyond the canopy scrutinizing the roofs and upper-story windows. Rain dripped from their hats. They looked as bleak and tense as a pair of wet alley cats. When the candidate appeared, they would turn their attention to spectators along the street. At the moment, there were no spectators. Morris was at the wheel of the candidate's limousine, staring through the windshield. He was depressed, Appleton knew, because of the middle-aged cocktail waitress he had taken to bed the night before. "She never even took her glasses off, " Morris had moaned to Appleton. "Said she wanted to *watch*." Next to Morris sat Wheeler, engrossed, as he was at any free moment, in the stock market quotations of *The Wall Street Journal*. When the candidate appeared, Morris and Wheeler would leave the car and stand like living shields at each side of the rear door as Governor York and his party entered the back seat.

Once more the revolving door turned. Mikkelson came out, followed by Augustus Alvin York. Though Appleton had seen the man hundreds of times in the past thirteen weeks, he was again struck by York's appearance. It was monumental. He stood six feet, five inches tall, with a broad chest, straight back, and shoulders almost as wide as a doorframe. His three-piece blue suit was rumpled, as his suits always were, and his tie was askew, but this only added a relaxed air of manliness to his appearance. His hair was wavy and copper-colored, salted with white. As usual, it was tousled. His face was a map of seams and creases, as full of gulleys and ravines as an Appalachian mountain-side. He had a blunt jaw and a broken nose that was the scarred badge of twenty-four years playing football.

York's expression was grim. Behind his campaign tan, his face was pale. The corners of his mouth drew down, and the curving slash of a frown mark between his sandy eyebrows cut deeper than ever.

York looked down on the press. Photographers' cameras and TV snouts pointed up at him, a cluster of Cyclopean eyes. As if on cue, York raised his long arms and linked his hands together in a huge double fist over his head, the traditional gesture of a prizefighter's triumph. For a moment, his expression remained weary and sad. Then he smiled and it was as if the sun had burst across his face, the transformation was so complete.

He spoke in a drawl, his voice light for a man so large: "Mornin', folks. Great day for ducks."

The press responded with desultory greetings. "Morning, Governor. Morning, Gus."

York began to move down the steps. As he came closer, Appleton felt a surge of pity for him. During the chaotic campaign he had driven himself so close to the far edge of fatigue that he was near collapse. Appleton was sure it had all been for nothing. When York raised his linked hands over his head in that boxer's gesture of triumph, what Appleton saw was a political Primo Carnera, an innocent and inept giant wheeled in to make the champion look good by falling hard in an early round.

Just behind York was his wife, Milly, a tall brunette. Her pale, oval face was stiff from weariness. She was beautiful, missing a kind of classic perfection only because of lips a trifle thin and a slightly prominent chin. Her eyes, a clear brown with long lashes beneath arching dark brows, were her most notable feature. Today Appleton saw that her eyes were full of anguish. It was a look he had seen in other women caught in the maelstrom of presidential politics. It was common at the end of a fierce campaign, especially when defeat seemed inevitable, as it did now. It was also common during days of trouble at the White House. Appleton had never seen this look so constantly and pitiably displayed as it had been in the eyes of Pat Nixon during the final days of her husband's demise. Milly York showed only a trace of the despair that Pat Nixon had exhibited, but Appleton sensed that, for the moment, at least, her spirit was broken.

At the top of the steps, York gently held an arm around his wife's waist. Though she was tall and well proportioned with ample breasts and womanly hips, she seemed childlike next to him. They descended past Appleton, slowly and formally, down to the cameras, the microphones, the waiting notebooks.

Behind the Yorks came Andrew Jackson Morley IV. He was lanky and he peered through his horn-rimmed glasses, picking his way down the stairs like a heron on legs so long and thin that his trousers flapped when he moved. Appleton moved to Morley's side and spoke softly to the campaign manager: "Will they be okay? They look ready to crack."

Morley's voice was deep; his staccato inflections

contained the slight lockjaw drawl of his upbringing via Groton and Harvard. "They haven't slept two hours any night for three weeks. They're tired as death. It's nothing a week of privacy and sunshine won't cure."

"Today and it's over."

"Thank God," said Morley. "Anything new on the maniac letter writer?"

"We got another letter this morning. You haven't told the Yorks anything, have you?"

"Jesus, no! Are you kidding, they'd really crack if they knew some deranged son-of-a-bitch was out there in the rain stalking them."

York and his wife stopped, confronted by a bouquet of TV network microphones. The CBS man spoke first. "Good morning, Governor. Can you tell us how you feel about your chances today? They say the weather is bad all across the country. Does that bother you, sir?"

York gazed down at the man. The question, obvious and banal as it was, seemed to have caught him by surprise. After a few seconds, he said with a deadpan face, "It's a real nice day for ducks, Bob. But like my daddy always said, 'Ducks don't vote Republican.'"

His radiant smile transformed his face again. The CBS man chuckled and a rattle of laughter rose from the press. York went on: "Seriously, Bob, we have lots of loyal people out there waiting to vote for us, rain or shine. Bad weather doesn't keep good Republicans down."

The NBC man said, "The last polls out yesterday showed you trailing the President by six percentage points, Governor. That's a lot."

York's smile disappeared. "Yes, but there were lots of undecideds, and I never saw a poll yet that was carved in stone—or even in soap."

Another wave of laughter rose and subsided. The ABC man stepped forward. "Governor, do you have any comment on the new fighting in Tanzania?"

York frowned, then replied, "We gave you all a position paper on Africa two weeks ago. I'll stand on that, I believe."

The ABC man persisted. "But this is a different situation, Governor. You didn't cover this in your position paper. Certainly you're aware of that."

"I don't think I have been briefed on the situation, then." His eyes glinted and his expression was grim. "We have to be going. They're waiting in Jezebel."

Gently guiding his wife ahead of him, York moved through the crowd of journalists who were scattering through the rain to board their bus. Appleton's agents gathered at the car to shield the candidate as the Yorks climbed into the back seat. Morley began to join them, then turned to Appleton once more, his voice sharp: "You have advance men out there in the bushes? They've checked out that two-bit post office where he's going to vote?"

"Two men went down yesterday. It's been checked."

Morley frowned. "Do you think that nut would try it down there in the mountains? Does that make sense?"

"I don't know. There's nothing in it to make sense."

Morley scrambled onto the limousine jumpseat and Appleton trotted through the rain to the Secret Service limousine. He leaned against the back-seat cushions, but he could not relax. Appleton rubbed his eyes behind his shaded lenses. Then he bolted upward in alarm as a banshee scream split the morning.

A trembling second or two passed before he realized that the unholy shriek came from the five state police cars, their sirens turned to peak volume as the motorcade rolled away from the hotel. As they sped along the gleaming streets, Appleton noted that every stop light on the route had been switched to green and that there was a policeman or a squad car at every major intersection.

The show of force was impressive. The question was whether it would make an impact on the wild mind of the writer of those ten letters that promised the murder of Governor York.

* * * * *

"Hagerty-Steinbugler" stared grimly into the mirror, examining his disguise. Then he quickly removed the wig, the spectacles, the contact lenses. He flickered his long tapered fingers briefly, as if in the warming-up exercise of a concert pianist. He rubbed his thumbs across the balls of all his fingers as if to further sensitize them. He picked up the clay-like material and unwrapped it. For a moment he held it gently in one hand, caressing it sensuously with the fingers of his other hand.

The material felt almost as smooth as ivory to him, yet his expert touch also told him that its slight graininess guaranteed its volatility was superb. Plastique. It was an amazing material, soft and pliable as a sculptor's clay. Yet for all its lovely tactile qualities, plastique was a powerful explosive, a murder weapon of terrorists and assassins for years. When the proper charge of batteries and detonator was molded into a hunk of plastique, it was transformed into a device of roaring instant death, a burst of flame and thunder. The power of a fifty-pound bomb could be contained in a hunk no larger than a woman's compact. Properly placed, it would tear off a man's head, blast open his torso, leave him a bleeding hunk of flesh with no more humanity than a slaughtered steer.

He held the plastique in front of him, poised as if it were a huge gem on the points of his fingers. He gazed at it for a moment, then said in German, "Death brings a high price in Japan, Steinbugler. Inflation and greed are terrible companions." He spoke softly to the hunk of plastique: "You are a million-dollar creation, my pretty thing."

He set about the intricate work of assembling his bomb. The radio-activated detonator of cadmium batteries and a wired-spark device had to be molded exactly so inside the plastique. Equipment for the detonating radio beam itself had to be assembled inside the canvas cummerbund which he would strap around his waist on the day of the assassination of Imai Hitsu.

He had produced such a bomb many times before, a remote-control weapon that was foolproof at relatively close range—the perfect instrument of death for an absentee assassination. He could activate the radio signal in his belt, and, from as far as fifty feet away, it would detonate the battery-embedded plastique, turning any target into the devastated remains of a man.

"Hagerty-Steinbugler" had successfully used such a bomb no less than seven times in the past five years. Indeed, the similarity of his technique, the repeated deadly perfection with which he killed and then vanished, had once caught the attention of a couple of alert Interpol men investigating three bombing assassinations that had occurred in Europe over an eighteen-month period. They had applied the code name "Le Bombardier" to the mysterious killer or killers. (The authorities could not believe that one man alone had done them all.) But when the crimes remained unsolved, the name remained in musty filing cabinets and was heard no more.

Yet this was Le Bombardier himself in Kyoto. He had grown quite rich at his profession over the years, and now glorious prosperity had blessed him once more, for the Bishi Corporation of Japan had agreed to pay $1,000,000 for the extermination of the trouble-maker and terrorist, Imai Hitsu. It was a secret agreement arrived at through the murky channels that Le Bombardier had developed to keep his business of assassination alive and thriving. He killed for profit, and he was as meticulous about keeping his contracts as he was about constructing his tidy little bombs. To kill the terrorist Imai was a commercial transaction to him, as abstract and as lacking in moral question or philo-sophical doubt as the balance sheet of a corporation.

Now he set to work in earnest at the motel dresser to make a device for killing Imai. His delicate fingers were as steady as a jeweler's, tender as a lover's as he married the small array of electronic bits to the lovely plastique. His face was serene, his concentration total. He had thirty-six hours to complete his bomb. Then he would introduce himself, as arranged, to the Red Independence Party leaders, including Imai. He would ask to be seated on the platform when the fiery agitator appeared before several hundred Bishi workers assem-bled for a union rally in a municipal Kyoto auditorium. As Klaus Steinbugler, a warm and supportive friend from the German Democratic Republic, a place of honor on the podium would certainly be in order.

A few moments after Imai stood at the lectern to speak, the plastique would explode, and a million-dollar assassination would occur before the shocked and frightened eyes of an audience of several hundred—a macabre and theatrical touch that Le Bombardier liked to repeat in his assassinations whenever possible.

* * * * *

Chapter 3

York gazed out the window without seeing the passing land. He was tired of social pretense, of unmeant courtesies, enforced niceties. All through the campaign he had paid empty compliments with phony enthusiasm and received the same with artificial gratitude. He had laughed at bad jokes, traded warm handshakes with men he detested, spoken sweetly to women he thought sour and mean-minded. He had grinned when he felt angry, chuckled when he felt sick, shouted in triumph when he felt only the grim certainty of onrushing defeat.

He looked at Milly. She sat with her head pressed back against the seat, her eyes closed. The skin beneath her eyes showed a purplish tint now, and the lines at the corners of her mouth were taut.

York looked at Morley on the jumpseat; his fingers sorted swiftly through a sheaf of papers. He was a man racked by tension, consumed by nerves, yet he had been the dynamo, the mind, the soul of the campaign. To York, it had all seemed blurred and confused, extemporaneous, often out of control. But Andy Morley had always at least pretended that there were logical, even imperative, reasons behind every speech, every parade, every rally, specific points to be gained from every factory-gate reception, every five-minute TV interview, every church-basement pep talk.

York sighed. The logic of the campaign had long ago eluded him, and this trip, home to Jezebel, Kentucky, seemed almost more bizarre and unrealistic than the rest of the campaign. Home? Of course, it had been home for the first sixteen years of his life. His roots ran deep into the flinty mountain soil, yet he had returned no more than half a dozen times once he left. He had not been back in twenty years. His father and mother were both dead before they turned fifty. His brothers, both older, had left home before he did, and they never did return. They might even be dead; he didn't know. Neither would waste his painful, precious ability to write on something as frivolous as a letter home. In fact, York was the only one in his family with a high school diploma, let alone a college degree. He would have liked to have credited this to his intellectual tenacity and his moral fiber, but he knew better. It was his very bigness, his physical toughness, his talent for controlled violence that had given him his education, his career as a professional football player, lawyer, and politician—including this strange and baffling role as a candidate for President of the United States.

That he was here at all, speeding along in this limousine past the familiar raw rock and dripping bare trees of these poor mountains, seemed almost a matter of black magic. It was as if some dark and secret ritual had transformed him from the former Gus York, a simple, honest Kentucky football star turned simple, honest Kentucky politician, into this Gus York, a grinning tin god who had suddenly laid claim to the grand capacities and superhuman insights necessary to be the most powerful man in the world.

Whatever he might not know about power and the Presidency, he certainly was no stranger to the occult. His boyhood memories were stamped with the recollection of his father and his mother speaking in low voices on moonless nights about the ghosts and spirits and cold walking souls that inhabited the swamps and hollows of the still mountains. Traffic in the dark arts was common around Jezebel during York's childhood. Gypsy bands, snake cultists, and fire-eaters; spiritualists and hot-eyed old men who claimed to speak in tongues came through town. There was one sinister old woman who said she could make a bird die as it sang on a tree limb a hundred yards away—and did. There was a blind woman who claimed to have cohabited with the devil and thus, having seen Satan's penis, was no longer allowed to look upon God's lovely world. There were inexplicable cures for incurable diseases, séances by kerosene lamps, miraculous visions of the future which came true.

It was all accepted as a form of life beyond real life, the wandering dead and the aberrated living gifted with "the powers." Now as the presidential motorcade rolled farther into this bleak land, York felt a familiar boyish awe at all the unknowable things that existed in nature—out there, just beyond the comprehension of ordinary men.

He turned away from the rain-streaked window and looked toward Morley on the jumpseat. He decided to break the odd mood that had taken him. "Andy, can you tell me what the hell that ABC man meant about Tanzania? Is something going on there today that is really so different?"

Morley turned around, his blue eyes wide behind the thick glasses. "Nothing is different, Governor. That son-of-a-bitch was baiting you."

York said drily, "What are they going to do without Gus York to kick around anymore?"

Morley laughed. "They've been pretty good, Governor. A lot of those guys like you—personally, if not politically. The press could have been more vicious."

"I suppose."

Milly York spoke. Her voice was low and throaty. She did not open her eyes, and her teeth seemed to be clenched. "More vicious? The *Times* called you 'a mediocrity.' The Chicago *Sun-Times* said you were a man with 'backwoods smarts, but no uptown class.' The *L.A. Times* said your politics were 'blurry,' and the *Boston Globe* said you were 'a political accident looking for a victim,' whatever that means. Not vicious?"

Morley said calmly, "Well, it was tough, really tough. But remember when *New York* magazine ran a cover picture of Gerald Ford as Bozo the Clown? Now, that's really *vicious*."

Milly's voice had an edge to it. "Telling the truth is not as vicious as this has been, Andy." She opened her eyes now and turned to gaze at York. "God, they started printing your obituary before you started campaigning, Gus."

Milly closed her eyes again and York turned once more to the rainy landscape rushing by outside the window. He would face this day and finish it, make a few more requisite public appearances—voting this morning, TV interviews tonight, the concession speech. By tomorrow morning at this time, he would be a free man again, released from this maniacal charade in which he, Gus York, was supposed to be a man who contained the stuff of Presidents.

He sighed noisily. "Damn! I really wonder what I'm doing here. I'm the biggest phony going."

Milly put her cool hand on his. "No, you aren't and after today, darling, it won't matter."

Morley spoke with his customary staccato authority.

"Gus, you and Milly are both too damn exhausted now to see anything positive in this whole frantic mess. But you've grown. Presidential politics is like one of those steel blast furnaces: either it consumes you, or it tempers you and makes you stronger than you ever were before."

York said softly, "Andy, I've never felt more consumed in my life. The truth is, the whole thing should never have happened."

Milly's hand tightened on his. She said nothing. Then Morley spoke. "You're right, it shouldn't have. When it started, that convention was set on an unalterable course. Reagan should have wrapped it up on the first ballot. It was his for the taking."

Milly murmured darkly, "That damn Peg Ironwood . . ."

York nodded. "Damn Peg Ironwood is right. I still can't believe she let it get out of control. I thought she was one of the toughest women I ever saw. But she sure wasn't tough when she got up there with that gavel."

"A candy battle-axe," said Morley, chuckling. "Any time the party has a shot at knocking over an incumbent, it seems to turn on itself and commit some kind of terrible self-immolation . . . a hundred million people watching on television. It was one of the nastiest, cruelest prime-time bloodbaths since the Friday Night Fights. Black delegation versus white delegation. Undiluted barbaric racism versus smug, shining liberalism on horseback. The Democrats couldn't have engineered a more devastating situation if they'd written a script for it. God *damn* Peg Ironwood. . . . "

York closed his eyes. It seemed years since those sweltering scenes of anger and argument on the convention floor in Detroit. The one image that stood out in his memory from the chaos was that of the party chairwoman, Peg Ironwood, banging her gavel again and again as the sound of furious debate rose from the agitated delegates. Soon her hair was soaked with sweat and frizzed out on her head like the snakes of Medusa. She sobbed and she ranted and she pounded her feckless gavel, but no one listened. She had lost control during a crucial floor fight over a platform plank on equal opportunity. Delegates locked tight on opposite sides and no candidate could break the deadlock. Finally the Republicans slogged through the nineteenth ballot without a nominee for President. The delegates sat limp and pale, exhausted. Suddenly, Peg Ironwood collapsed at the podium. It was three in the morning and the convention was adjourned until the following noon.

That same morning at seven, Peg Ironwood had recovered enough to phone a dozen party leaders and demand that they assemble in her suite. She spoke to them in a quavering voice, "The party's a shambles. The election is lost. But we have to have a candidate— someone, anyone." That was all Peg Ironwood managed to say before she began to weep uncontrollably and left the room.

Everyone was so exhausted by the convention disaster that a dozen powerful and intelligent men sat in confused silence for almost ten minutes. Then one of them, a longtime senator from Kansas, rose and said quietly, "We need someone bland and respectable, someone who won't be irreparably damaged in the future by a horrendous defeat—which is inevitable."

After discussing a dozen possible candidates, they finally agreed on York, Kentucky governor and former pro-football star. At the twentieth ballot, his name was to be the only one allowed into nomination. When Peg Ironwood was told the identity of the new Republican candidate, she was furious. "Gus York, shit! You might as well nominate Donald Duck!"

"He's neutral," responded the senator from Kansas.

"He's neuter!" screamed Peg Ironwood, as she burst into tears again. Arrangements were made immediately for her to check into a hospital. Another convention chairman more eager to please and receptive to the deal was selected. Then someone realized that Gus York had not yet been informed or consulted about his impending nomination.

The phone rang in York's hotel room at about eleven A.M. The senator from Kansas declared that York had been selected as the G.O.P. standard-bearer for the upcoming presidential election. Would he accept?

York at first assumed that the senator had been enjoying his famous prediliction for morning drinking, but the bass-voiced drawl sounded sober enough over the phone, and when the senator came to the room precisely half an hour later, York saw that he was indeed dead sober—and dead serious about York's running for President.

Milly asked anxiously, "Will anyone in this country vote for someone nominated on the twentieth ballot?"

The senator said, "Warren Harding wasn't nominated till the thirty-second ballot, and he won going away. There is precedent. But I would be misleading you if I told you that I thought you had a real good chance of winning. You don't."

"Who will run with me?" asked York.

"Naturally, you have the choice of your vice-presidential mate." The senator paused. "But we think that Browning Dayton of California would be a fine young man. He's smart, Governor, and he's been in the Senate long enough to be developing a good reputation."

The decision, of course, had already been made. And so had the decision on campaign manager. Andrew Jackson Morley IV, former *New York Times* political reporter and now a valued advisor to the Republican National Committee in Washington, would be in charge of the York-for-President campaign. Morley was known as a hard-drinking man with a bad temper. But he was also a man who knew the needs of the media along with the intricacies of polling.

The worn-out convention delegates, docile as lambs, dutifully nominated the governor of Kentucky as their presidential candidate. They cheered him halfheartedly and waved a slapdash forest of hurriedly painted York–Dayton signs. York felt a certain exhilaration despite the tarnish of the prize he had won. The hurrahs were pleasing to his ego, as were the interviews with famous network anchormen and national news reporters whose bylines were far better known then the name of the presidential candidate.

But the good feeling did not last long. Peg Ironwood signed herself out of the hospital the day after York was nominated. She went immediately to *The New York Times* and spoke for quotation: "Gus York is a hillbilly nonentity, and two years from now his name will be one of the favorite trivia questions of the day." After a spate of thumbnail biographies reviewed York's long and bruising football career, people inevitably recalled Lyndon Johnson's famous jibe that Gerald Ford couldn't walk and chew gum at the same time because he had played too many games with his helmet off. Democrat-instigated bumper stickers soon appeared, which read: YOU SHOULD HAVE WORN THE HELMET, GUS. Few presidential campaigns had ever been launched with less promise.

The weather had taken a turn for the worse as the motorcade wound deeper into the mountains. Mist rose like gunsmoke in the pine trees along the highway. Ahead and behind, sirens wailed. Now the caravan fled around a curve and passed a small highway sign that said: JEZEBEL, POPULATION 142.

"Home, sweet home," York said.

"Looks a little clammy." Morley gazed at the black, dripping trees and the rain-slicked highway.

"Always clammy in November," York said. "I never remember once being warm, really warm, between Halloween and Easter."

The motorcade slowed. The two leading police cars and the Secret Service limousine bounced off to the right and into an open space that was rutted from decades of auto wheels. A pair of rusty gas pumps stood together a few yards from the one building that was, from that vantage point, the only visible structure in Jezebel, Kentucky. It was a long one-story lumber structure with an unlighted neon beer sign in the one large window. Painted letters, long ago faded on the window, said: POLLOCK'S STORE. Over the screen door a weather-scarred sign indicated that this was also the U.S. Post Office for Jezebel, Kentucky.

The driveway quickly filled with vehicles. The sirens fell to an ominous moan, but the dome lights still revolved on the squad cars, flashing across the tree trunks and into the shadows of the woods.

Troopers sprang from their cars, rifles and shotguns slung over their shoulders, and moved quickly to a series of prearranged points. The police commissioner stood by the fender of one squad car and scrutinized the movements of his men like Napoleon dispatching cavalry units.

The screen door of the store swung open and two men emerged, wearing hats and tan raincoats. "Secret Service," said Morley. "At least we're in the right place."

"I wonder what the hell they found to worry about in Jezebel," said York. "Anyone around here wants to fix a thieving politician, they tie him to a tree and tar and feather him, then cut him loose—free to run for office another day if he's a mind to do it."

"Sounds civilized," said Morley.

"That's politicians. When it comes to federal agents, revenuers, and tax men, they tend to disappear real quiet. No violence, no fuss; they just don't show up at the office again. Ever again." York smiled.

"That sounds less civilized," said Morley.

"Maybe not civilized, but practical," said York. "Those revenuers got back at us, though. They came back as ghosts all over the countryside. In one swamp there was a man sitting on the ground, still as stone except for streams of blood running down his face. On nights of a full moon he'd moan and you could hear him for miles. Another dead revenuer lived in the steeple of an abandoned church. You could see his face, white and still with bright red eyeballs that never blinked, in the steeple where the bell used to be. Whole country's full of ghosts and spirits, of men dead by foul play or revenge."

The screen door swung open and a bone-thin man wearing a faded blue shirt and baggy black pants peered out. He cocked his head at the array of vehicles, the rotating dome lights, the grim cadre of troopers.

"Amos!" The governor opened his car door and

leaped lightly over the water-filled ruts, running toward the man at the screen door.

All four doors of the Secret Service limousine sprang open and the agents hurried after York. The thin man in the doorway watched suspiciously. Then suddenly his face softened almost imperceptibly. He was smiling.

York reached out a hand and said, "Amos, how are you?"

"Hidy, Gus," the man said shyly.

York grabbed the man's hand and began to pump it vigorously. But the hand felt dry and frail as twigs in his huge paw, so he held it gently. He examined Amos Pollock's face and saw a man twenty years older than himself, though they had been born less than a month apart. One eye gleamed strangely. York scrutinized his old friend. It was as if he had to penetrate a mask in order to see beyond the parched skin and the static, staring eye—to see another face, the best friend's face that he had once known better than his own. He could not find it, and suddenly York's mouth felt dry. He said, "Got an Orange Crush for me, Amos?"

The old man chuckled and the black void of his mouth shocked York. "Betcha." York followed him inside the store.

Two Secret Service men accompanied York, and Appleton conferred with Thomas, who had spent the night in Jezebel. "Any problems?" Thomas shifted uneasily. "Yesterday, there was hardly anyone around. Only that old gink with the glass eye, the postmaster. But, Jesus, this morning it was hardly light and all these people started creeping down out of the woods."

"What people?" asked Appleton.

Thomas gestured toward the mist and trees beyond the store. "Those people. And, goddammit, some of them have got guns!"

Appleton looked into the woods and was startled to see that there was indeed a silent assembly of people, perhaps fifty or sixty of them, standing motionless among the tree trunks. They seemed as indigenous as stones and stumps. "Who *are* they?" he gasped.

"They're okay, uh, I'm ninety-nine percent sure they're okay," said Thomas.

Appleton grabbed Thomas by the arm. "Who do you know here who really belongs here? Any of York's relatives?"

"No. But there's a kid who is the son of the postmaster. He's over there by that tree."

Appleton barked, "Get him to stand next to you and identify every goddamn person in that crowd. Start with the ones with the guns. Anyone who the kid doesn't know by name, grab him. Get those gorilla cops to help you if you have any trouble." Appleton shoved Thomas toward the boy, then turned toward the store.

Milly, York, and Morley had disappeared through the screen door. Behind them, the press was picking its way hurriedly through the mud. Television crews had erected portable lights to illuminate the gloom. They bleached the scene to a shadowless flatness that made the old store look as artificial as a studio set for *Tobacco Road*. The TV lights did not, however, reach into the woods, and the effect was of two separate worlds: one an artificial and agitated island of searing man-made whiteness; the other still and primeval, full of an almost supernatural gloom.

Appleton watched warily as the mountain people in the woods moved almost imperceptibly over the spongy ground, sidling past tree trunks until many of them stood at the edge of the darkness only a few feet from the lighted open space. At least a dozen men carried rifles. Appleton called anxiously to Thomas, who stood conferring with the spindly son of Amos Pollock: "He knows them all?"

Thomas nodded. There was relief in his voice. "Every one."

Appleton headed quickly toward the store. Behind him the NBC man faced a camera and raised his microphone to speak to millions of people tuned into the "Today" show: "Tom and Jane, I'm here in the Kentucky village of Jezebel, birthplace of Governor Augustus York. He's inside Pollock's Store right now, voting for the man he'd like to see as the next President of the United States. These people behind me . . ." he gestured toward the woods and the camera swung in that direction—". . . are residents of Jezebel, childhood friends of Governor York. . . ." The NBC man stepped confidently toward the woods, his microphone at the ready. As he drew closer, the spectators slowly retreated, receding like wraiths into the trees. "They don't seem to have anything to say," said the NBC man with a light laugh.

Inside the store, York sipped Orange Crush. "Looks like business is right prosperous, Amos," he said. The place was badly lighted. Cereal boxes were stacked against packages of mousetraps and a faded display of stove polish stood between some jugs of root beer and a loose pile of work shoes.

Amos squinted around the store as if he was checking to see if York was correct. "Ain't a real big moneymaker." He paused, "Ain't a real little one, either. We get along."

"Like always," said York. The place was amazingly familiar after so many years. The fragrance of the store was one of the best memories of his boyhood—apples, tobacco, leather, and woodsmoke from the stove. York's father had come here in the evening and on

Sundays with the other men from the mountain hollows to talk. During these conversations their gaunt faces lost some of the sadness etched there by the terrible poverty of their lives. York remembered the smell of tobacco smoke and the reek of sweat. This was the only place York ever saw his father laugh.

Morley and Milly came to the counter where York and Amos Pollock stood, and York took Morley and Amos by the arm, speaking more bombastically than he meant to, trying to bind together this unlikely pair. "Amos and I threw our first football together, Andy." Amos bobbed his head, his good eye shining at the recollection.

"Any old friends still around?" York asked.

Amos shook his head. "Lots o' people gone; lots o' people dead. Lots o' people disappeared."

"They don't come back?"

"You never come back much, Gus. For your Ma's funeral that once, twenty years back. Just that once. Until now when you come back to vote for the TV." Amos was staring at the floor, embarrassed for speaking at such unconscionable length about such an uncomfortable subject.

York nodded his head. "Old friends aren't always good friends," he said. He clapped his hand on Amos' bony shoulder. York heard whirring and clicking behind him, and he turned to see a dozen camera lenses trained on him and Amos.

Morley looked at his watch. "Governor, we better get on with the voting. The TV people are waiting. NBC and ABC want live pieces for 'Today' and 'Good Morning, America.'"

York shrugged. "I know it. Sorry, Amos, we should have time for a real good chance to chew the fat. But not today."

"You have the ballots, Mr. Pollock?" asked Morley. Amos put two slips of paper with two stubby pencils on the counter.

A loud voice sounded from the press assembly: "Hold up the ballots, Governor." York did. "You, too, Miz York." Milly did as she was told. "Again, Governor, do it again." And he did. When the photographers stopped snapping their shutters, York turned to write in his vote.

He held the pencil stub, no longer than a cigarette butt, poised over the paper for one or two seconds, deliberating. Then he quickly, almost reluctantly, scribbled his own name. He stepped back and Milly let her ballot fall through the slot, too. They turned automatically and smiled at each other, stiff public smiles, part of playing the game, like casting the votes. Just as mechanically, York reached out to shake Amos' hand vigorously, pumping it up and down as cameras clicked. Finally, his old friend twisted out of his grip and slipped away, embarrassed, pretending to straighten a row of dust-thick Lysol bottles that had not been moved for years.

Amos kept his eyes cast downward as the press people crowded out the door. York did not return to shake his old friend's hand before he left. He knew that there had already been too much gratuitous handshaking for Amos. He waved and said across the cluttered shelves, "Luck, Amos. I'm coming back, y'hear?"

Outside, he stepped off the front porch into the rain. Morris held a black umbrella over him and two other agents moved in close, almost touching his elbows, as York paused for questions from the press.

"Stay back up on the step there, Governor, can you?" shouted a television man.

York stepped back up and towered over everyone by almost two feet, his copper hair a beacon above the clusters of black umbrellas. Appleton closed his eyes in resignation at York's exposed position.

York squinted into the TV lights, then held out a hand to test the driving rain. He shuddered, grinned and said, "Jezebel weather."

The ABC man stepped forward and said, "Governor, how did it feel to return to Jezebel as a candidate for President?"

York spoke slowly, his drawl more pronounced than usual. "It makes me proud to come back where I started and be one of only two men on earth who has the chance to be the next President."

He looked over the ABC man's head for another question, but the correspondent pressed on, the trace of a sneer on his bland face. "Let me put it this way, Governor, maybe you could say something a little more specific than 'real proud?'"

York glared at the man. He felt his temper flaring as he spoke tightly. "You say that 'real proud' doesn't measure up. Then, how about this? I feel humble. *Real* humble, my friend, because I am sure there are nowhere near enough Republican ducks *or* human beings out there to bring this ticket in a winner. I also feel tired and I feel beaten and, now that you mention it, I don't feel 'real proud' at all."

York glared a moment longer at the correspondent, then said gruffly, "No more questions."

He plunged through the reporters, his hands in front of his face pushing umbrellas out of the way. Then as he approached the trees, one of the spectators shouted, "Hidy, Gus!" A few began a desultory clapping of hands. It was a frail and alien sound, and it soon vanished in the gloom of the woods, yet it warmed

York, as if he had been folded in an embrace. These were his people; he was home.

He began to push roughly through the startled reporters so he could move closer to the spectators gathered just inside the edge of the trees. They stood there shyly, like children watching an adult party after bedtime. He cried, "Hey! Who's out there?" They held back at first, then began to move toward him, pale and specter-like in their faded denim. A tall hawk-faced man approached him. York reached out to shake his hand. Then to his own immense surprise, he wrapped his arms around the man and hugged him. He did not recognize the person, but it did not matter. The man walked off, shaking his head as he revealed a grinning display of bad teeth. Others drifted down through the wet trees. They shook his hand. Some names sounded familiar, but he recognized no faces, and he merely greeted them over and over again.

A Secret Service agent tried to keep an umbrella over him, but York gently pushed him away. The exhilaration he felt was almost painful. Rainwater coursed in streams down his face and he was grateful because it concealed his tears.

York plunged farther into the woods. He moved along the soaked ground up the hill about twenty yards until there were no more people in the trees, except for one lone person standing where the tree trunks grew closer together and the gloom thickened.

She stood by a stand of pale birch trees, a tiny woman, less than five feet tall. She wore a shapeless black coat that was too large for her, and on her head, nearly concealing her pinched face, was an old-fashioned sun bonnet knotted in a bow beneath her chin. In the shadow of the bonnet, he could see the shine of her eyes, and the thin, purplish line of her lips.

He said hello, but she did not move. He began to reach for her hand. A man down the hill said, "That's Esmerelda Culp, Governor. She was the snake girl."

York hesitated and involuntarily drew back. The Culps. Snake cultists who in the years of his boyhood had been almost as frightening as the specters of dead revenuers. He remembered a moonless night as a child when he and his father had come upon a gathering at a small hollow, perhaps a hundred people, silent as the hills themselves, seated on rocks up the hillside. Below, illuminated by kerosene lanterns and the headlights of a pickup truck and mainly by the moon, the Culps were performing their strange and captivating ceremonies.

Snakes coiled familiarly, almost affectionately, it seemed, around the arms and necks of the Culps as they shouted wild praises to God. There were perhaps ten in the family, each as impervious as the other to the coiling forms on their bodies, each equally fevered in his or her ravings to the Lord.

The star of the show had been Esmerelda, a hollow-eyed waif, not yet in her teens. She had reached into a barrel of rattlesnakes and brought them out one at a time and put them around her neck and over her frail shoulders, brutes as thick as a man's ankle, until her bony little body was draped with reptiles. York recalled that her flowing black eyes had seemed to be the only part of her not covered by snakes. They must have weighed more than she did. Their rattles chattered like castanets in the silent night.

Esmerelda Culp stood like a goddess, never flinching, never bending beneath her writhing cape of reptiles. York's father had leaned over and whispered, "Powers of the damned, boy. She got 'the powers.'" For weeks afterward, York had awakened whimpering with fear, certain in the knowledge that Esmerelda Culp and her snakes were in his room, writhing silently toward him in the dark.

Now she reached forward and clutched his wrist with a hand as thin and dry and powerful as a hawk's claw. Her voice was scratchy and hoarse. "Black dreams comin'. Mad and fearsome times."

The mouth closed and became almost seamless. The claw loosed its hold on his arm. York suddenly felt a flash of cold. But she said nothing more, and York could only turn away and walk down the hill toward the blinding TV lights beyond the trees.

When he emerged from the woods, he felt strangely refreshed. In the confrontation with Esmerelda Culp, he had contacted something oddly comfortable, a touchstone with the superstitions of his boyhood.

But when he climbed into the limousine and saw Milly, he became anxious again. Her face was a mask of despair and exhaustion, and York was momentarily alarmed. "Milly, are you all right?"

She nodded slowly. "Yes. I'm just so tired."

York studied her face and felt a stab of grief seeing her so transformed. He reached over and put his hand on hers. It was soft and cool and smooth, as soothing to touch as Esmerelda Culp's chapped claw had been disturbing. "You can sleep all day, love," he said as he took her in his arms. She began to sob.

The limousine door opened and Morley began to climb inside. When he saw the Yorks, he quickly backed out. "I'll ride with the Secret Service," he said. "Is she going to be all right?"

York nodded. "Tell the goddamn troopers to keep their sirens off, Andy. She has to get some sleep."

Morley slammed the door and York's limousine

leaped forward through the puddles onto the road and sped toward Louisville. The engine rose to a soothing purr and Milly soon stopped sobbing and her body relaxed in York's arms as she slept.

* * * * *

Chapter 4

Morley stared through the rear window of the limousine as Jezebel vanished around a curve. "How do people survive in a place like that?" he asked Appleton, seated next to him.

Appleton said nothing. He was rubbing his fingers deep into his eyes behind the dark glasses. Morley turned to look at him and said, "You ought to get some sleep, Appleton. You have to stay sharp."

"Sleep? What the hell is that?" Appleton let his head flop back against the cushion. He hadn't been able to sleep more than an hour at a time for the past week.

"You should probably take the afternoon off. Get some rest for tonight."

Appleton said tightly, "I can't."

"How seriously do you take those letters?"

"Seriously."

"They're all definitely from the same guy?"

"Absolutely. Handwriting is all the same crazy scrawl, every word with a different color crayon. The wording's always similar, the spelling's perfect. We ran all of them through the F.B.I. lab. Graphologists say the handwriting is unmistakably the same. Same fingerprints are all over all of them, same cheap tablet paper, even the same package of Crayola crayons. The prints aren't on file, and you could buy all that stuff in any dime store."

"All the postmarks from Louisville?"

"Yes."

"You've done everything you can?"

Appleton sighed in exasperation. "*I* can't think of anything else. We ran the usual security checks on the hotel people. They all have the usual daily change of pins to identify themselves. We'll have guys on all the roofs, and that moron state police commissioner has got more firepower around than there was at Pearl Harbor. It's just a matter of time before one of those apes shoots somebody."

Appleton had detected the fragrance of whiskey when Morley spoke. Morley's reputation for drinking was legendary, but in the thirteen weeks Appleton had been close to him, the man had never been obviously drunk. Appleton hoped this would not change today.

Morley leaned forward and clapped a hand on Mikkelson's shoulder, who sat in the front passenger's seat. "Turn up the radio, will you?"

A newscaster was saying, ". . . a report from Brushton, Maine, with eleven eligible voters. This village makes it a habit to be the first polling place in the United States to count its votes on Election Day. The polls in Brushton open at midnight and close fifteen minutes later, when everyone has voted. Today, the vote was nine for Governor Augustus York, two for the President. For the record, Brushton has voted Republican for the last fourteen elections. Now, for the weather . . ."

Morley said, "I have an odd sense about this election. It's not going to be the runaway they predicted."

Mikkelson spoke brightly from the front seat. "You think the governor might actually win, Mr. Morley?"

"No. I wouldn't be so rash as that. Not without a

more thorough computer system to predict it. There have been so many things against us. That madness in Detroit—and no one had ever heard of Gus York outside of Kentucky and the National Football League before the campaign. Of course, who's to say that playing end for the Chicago Bears for sixteen years isn't a great qualification for being President? Goddamn football has probably had more effect on the national psyche in the last twenty years than religion, politics, or sex."

Mikkelson had turned to watch as Morley spoke, and now he said admiringly, "That's a fascinating theory, Mr. Morley. About football."

Morley gazed at him a moment, his blue eyes wide behind his horn-rimmed spectacles. "Is it?" he said sharply. "Not very original." He paused, then went on. "Another thing going against us is Gus York's own perception of himself. He doesn't believe he's big enough to be President. Doesn't have the ambition for it; never did. Too damn much humility." He paused. "That's against us. There's the damn weather. Also against us. And . . ."

Appleton stopped listening. He did not feel the weather was against his purposes at all. Quite the contrary. It meant there would likely be a smaller crowd at the hotel for the election returns that night. A smaller crowd meant fewer faces to scrutinize, fewer chances that the color-crayon writer could melt into anonymity and make an unobserved attack. The election would be over earlier than if there was a large voting turnout, and that meant York would retire earlier, and that meant there was a chance for more than one hour of sleep for Appleton.

As Morley's comments ran on, Appleton heard the clink of metal on metal and he knew that Morley was opening the flat silver flask he carried. The campaign manager drank and the pungent fragrance of bourbon bloomed in the car. Morley offered the flask to the Secret Service agents. Mikkelson said, "No, sir, not on duty. But, thank you, all the same."

Appleton did not reply. If he took a drink, he would only start seeing more gun barrels in the shadows. Only once in his life had he been truly, blindly drunk—on the dense and mournful Saturday of November 23, 1963, the day after John Kennedy was murdered. Appleton had been in Dallas during the assassination and he had been on *Air Force One* for the stricken flight back to Washington on Friday the twenty-second. The next day a chilling rainstorm settled in, and his grief was so profound that Appleton began drinking whiskey at noon. He drank, speaking to no one in a seedy bar on G Street, and wound up at twilight vomiting in a gutter, rainwater sluicing past his head, cleansing away the sickness of the whiskey but having no effect at all on the numbing fear that gripped him.

Fear, not grief, drove Appleton to drink himself into oblivion. And the fear sprang from his fresh recognition of a terrifying truth: the murder of a President— any President, *all* Presidents—was totally beyond the protection, the management, the control of the Secret Service or any other human agency. Appleton had seen the blood and brains of John Kennedy splattered over the bouquet of roses that Jackie Kennedy held in the back seat of the motorcade convertible. In that mad juxtaposition of violent death and delicate beauty was the truth of his profession: only absurd good luck lay between a live President and a dead one. Nothing mere man could do would keep a President alive if luck— capricious, stupid, unpredictable, blind *luck*—was running wrong.

Appleton and the rest of the Secret Service White House detail had been as naïve as alter boys about what they had assumed to be their own unquestionable capacity to keep a President safe—*perfectly safe*—from harm. Once Kennedy was murdered, these men were never the same. They were shaken to the roots of whatever faith in whatever powers they may have come to depend on.

Appleton had been in the Los Angeles hotel kitchen when Robert Kennedy was killed on the night of June 6, 1968. He had not gotten drunk after that, but his mind went oddly blank for several days. He was thirty-six that year, but he felt as if he were seventy and senile. He wanted to quit the Secret Service, but Appleton could think of nothing he was qualified to do besides guarding politicians who seemed to wind up dead.

Appleton had stayed on with the Secret Service White House detail because he had no choice. It was at this time that he took to wearing dark glasses indoors and out. He told himself his eyes were strained and often sore, but he also liked the way the tinted glasses provided a muted look to life. That same year his wife left Appleton to live in an Alexandria development house with a systems analyst from the Navy Bureau of Supplies and Accounts. Appleton had felt nothing much about that, either. . . .

Mikkelson spoke sharply. "Where the hell is the governor's car?"

Appleton bolted up in the seat. The road ahead was empty. Morris, at the wheel, said, "I think they just got a little ahead of us."

"You *think!*" snapped Appleton. His voice was flat and metallic, but he felt the familiar cramp of anxiety in his stomach. Morris stepped on the accelerator. The limousine surged over the crest of a hill. The other limousine was only a hundred yards ahead. Appleton sighed and closed his eyes for a moment. His heart was pounding: he felt chill sweat between his shoulders.

* * * * *

In Kyoto the tall East German known as "Stein-bugler" crossed his legs and gazed benignly out at the audience of Bishi workers. At his left, fifteen feet away, the self-proclaimed terrorist and agitator, Imai Hitsu, was well into a lengthy harangue, spewing forth a torrent of angry Japanese which Le Bombardier assumed was a predictable assault on the oppressive ways of the Bishi Corporation toward its employees.

Le Bombardier watched the man gesticulate in fury. His passion was contagious, and the audience sat in rapt attention when he spoke and applauded noisily when he paused. From time to time, Le Bombardier applauded, too, with slow and ponderous slaps of his hands. He felt no excitement, however, no involvement with the speaker or the listeners. He eyed Imai, a stumpy man with a large, round skull and a bull neck. His victim. The man, so energetic, so savage in his gestures, so intense in his speech, would be dead in five minutes, perhaps less. All that vitality and anger, the raging eyes, the wagging mouth, the pounding, clenched fists—all would be silent and bloody, shred-ded and stilled by the blast that Le Bombardier would soon trigger.

* * * * *

Chapter 5

In Louisville the limousines rolled into an alley at the rear of the hotel. They had received a report that the lobby was crowded, and Milly was still red-eyed from weeping, so York ordered his driver to use the rear entrance. The Secret Service car pulled up right behind them as York and Milly were ushered toward the hotel. York saw Appleton coming toward him. The agent's face was grim and tense, as usual. The man's tightness made York especially nervous, but then he had always felt uneasy under the surveillance of Secret Service agents. They served as mainly a reminder to York that the presidential political environment was fraught with unknowable dangers and inexplicable passions that threatened him in a way no ordinary man would ever be threatened. He had been thrust into a supercharged atmosphere of public exposure, stripped of privacy, and set up as a focus for every warped mind and lunatic whim. He was now a convenient, perhaps irresistible, object for hatred and attack.

The entourage moved quickly into the back halls of the hotel, past the hot, food-smelling kitchen. York stopped at a rear elevator that stood open. Appleton spoke quickly to York: "Not here, Governor. It won't stop at your floor. We have to go to the lobby."

York looked at Milly's face. "Mrs. York would rather not be seen by a lot of people."

"It's security, Gus," Morley said softly. "They have only one elevator that runs express to your floor. It's in the lobby. It's fixed so it can't stop at any other floors. All the rest are set so they can't stop at your location. Just security."

"Dammit! You'd think we were criminals. Can't we do anything like normal people?"

Milly touched his arm. "I'm all right, darling. "I've got dark glasses in my purse.'"

They moved quickly through the lobby to the open elevator. The crowd saw them and set up an excited ripple of applause. Reflexively, York grinned and called out, "Hello! Thank you!" The elevator door closed and he slumped against the wall. "Thank God," he said, "it is almost over."

Morley said, "You did your duty, Governor. A noble effort. You can rest now because it *is* over."

York replied, "You're right, Andy, I did do my duty." He sighed and spoke absently, as if to himself. "My daddy could hardly read all the words on a calendar, but when he spoke, he usually made sense. Right now he would've said, 'Hey, boy, you got that sissy Republican ass whupped offa you for President. Now git on back to bein' a common, ordinary ever'day human bein', which is all you was in the first place. President! Hah!' "

The whooshing sound of the rising elevator filled the car. York put his arms around Milly and hugged her, wishing she could have been spared this. At the twentieth floor, the elevator came to a stop. York and Milly followed Appleton and Mikkelson into the corridor. Four other Secret Service men stood as plainclothes sentries at the ends of the corridor. Six gaudy giants from the state police stood at attention along the corridor walls, as imposing and ornamental as any Buckingham Palace Coldstream Guards.

Milly and York entered their suite alone. She sank onto the bed and lay with her head on her arms, breathing in long, jolting sobs. York gently ran his fingers up and down her back. He arranged her tangled hair, took off her shoes, and held one stockinged foot in his broad hand. He could think of nothing else that was useful to do, so he went to the window and watched the rain. Then he slowly lowered the windowshade. He sat down in a chair beside the bed, listening as Milly's deep sobs slowly faded. She turned over, and he said, "Will you be all right, Milly? Can you sleep?"

She was silent for a moment. Then she sighed and said, "Come help me undress."

York unbuttoned her blouse from the back when she sat up. She stood while he helped her with her skirt, and raised her slip to remove her panties. She sat on the bed again, looking up at York. Her voice was so hushed he barely heard her speak. "Gus?"

He bent toward her and she raised her tapered fingers to caress his face. One hand moved to the back of his neck and gently pulled him to her. Her kiss was shy at first, a moist and warm touching of one corner of his mouth, then the other. Lightly, she covered his lips with hers. He sat next to her on the bed and put his arms around her. She wore only her slip, and he felt the warmth and the softness of her breasts against his chest. Her hand moved down his spine, around his hip, onto his thigh. Her kiss was urgent now, and her hand flowed lightly over his inner thigh and moved upward slowly.

He felt her desire in that motion, the excitement, the potential for escape, and he felt how much they needed it. Sex, a lovely immersion in its pleasure. But he could produce no feeling, no physical surge that allowed him to join Milly in her desire. It was a familiar deadness, and he knew she was aware of it. He waited. She moved her mouth to his ear and whispered, "Darling? Will you try? Come to bed with me?"

York swallowed. A powerful sense of loss swam over him. He shook his head slightly, a movement almost imperceptible to himself. But Milly felt it and she knew.

York felt her dejection. Her arms slipped off his shoulders and she lay back. He rose and murmured, "I'm sorry. I'm . . . it's as if I were dead."

She lay motionless on her back, her eyes closed. "I'm so damn tired. I'm so damn sick and tired of what has happened to us."

York took a blanket from the closet and spread it over her. He kissed her cheek and said, "Don't worry, darling. Everything will be like it was." She reached up a cool hand to caress his face, but she said nothing. A minute later when he paused at the door to the living room of the suite, he heard her breathing turn deep and steady. She was sleeping at last.

He shut the door quietly as he entered the parlor. It was permanently imbued with the shabbiness that infects old hotels. The carpet was a nondescript gray and blue pattern that showed a minimum of dirt and lint. The furniture was upholstered in a mottled design intended to conceal the traces left by numberless traveling salesmen and wayward transients over the decades. Today, the furniture—a sofa, two easy chairs, a TV set—had been arranged like a theater facing a large television camera. The floor was a tangle of cords and cables, and the room was littered with floodlights. He would spend election night here, watching the returns on the television set while the nation watched him. The pain of his defeat, he thought, would be no more private than the fiascos that led to it.

York sat in an old easy chair and tried to relax. But he could not.

He and Milly had not made love since the second week of the campaign, more than three months ago, and it had not been for lack of time or place. York had simply and suddenly become impotent, and nothing he or Milly, loving Milly, tried could change that.

He suffered these failures in grim, sweating silence: ashamed, frightened, angry. He had always found sex a romp and joy, a constant excitement in his life. When he played football, sex had been an extension of the physicality of the game, as well as a prize for his heroics as an athlete. Sex was a reward, a repeating proof of manhood, as well as a manifestation of tenderness that countered the violence of the game.

When he met Milly, he was in his mid-thirties and almost at the end of his football career. Their lovemaking became a revitalizing force that nourished and comforted him when he was rocked by the intimations of failure that followed his realization that he was too old to continue to play.

Gus York was not a particularly speculative man, but he had come to suspect lately that his impotence might represent some kind of ultimate symbol of his moral weakness as a man. In truth, he realized that he had had no accurate idea what kind of man he really was before the campaign began. He had believed himself to be honest, decent, untempted by corruption, capable perhaps of an occasional lie or a sometime deception. But never a man of constant hypocrisy and enduring deceit. Now he wondered who he was.

He had been a simple product and stern disciple of the hoary church-school which preaches that sport builds character and competition develops morality. Football offered an ultimate criterion, York believed, almost as revealing as war when it came to measuring a man's true supply of courage and capacity for heroism. York had played the game for twenty-four years—in high school and at the University of Kentucky, and a bruising, joyous sixteen years with the Chicago Bears. He prided himself on being a rough player but not a dirty one, prided himself on his endurance, his immunity to pain, his unwillingness to give up even in the most hopelessly lost game. Those had been simpler—and poorer—years in professional football, and later York even convinced himself that he had possessed a special Spartan purity because he played the game before TV commercialism poisoned it with avarice and opportunism and easy millions.

Even politics, before he was ushered into this arcane and killing world of presidential politics, was more or less an extension of his simplistic perceptions as a football player: you are what people say you are. Public adulation for his public performance served to give him an inflated idea of his own honesty, his own morality, his own worth. He had returned to Kentucky a celebrity from his salad days with the Bears. He was nicknamed on every sports page "The Kentucky Gladiator." Small boys worshiped him with dream-filled eyes and old men guffawed in pleasure and embarrassment when he gently clapped his big paw on their bony shoulders.

Though he displayed the expected mannerisms of modesty over the praise he received, Gus York had had no doubt that all those nice things said about him were true.

He had then worked hard to earn his law degree at night school in Chicago. Once home again in Kentucky, he joined a law firm in Paducah, where it became only natural for him to use his fame and sterling reputation to run for public office. In 1966, he won the mayoralty of that small city by an overwhelming margin. He set about to clean out a clutter of minor embezzlers and cheaters in some city hall offices. He began an investigation that ended with the city clerk, a longtime leader in York's own Republican Party, going to prison for a year after he was found guilty of bribing state legislators to award a highway contract to a firm owned by his relatives. The papers called York "Honest Gus," and he served as mayor for four years, then went to the State Senate. He became the Republican leader there, ran for governor in 1974, won, and was re-elected by a landslide in 1978. As governor, he had been an efficient administrator, he was convinced; honest and straightforward, he was sure. "Honest Gus" they called him again and he believed it. He had become convinced that in politics he could trust his reflexes, just as he had been able to trust them in football.

That had all changed with his first immersion in the tumultuous cold water of presidential politics. He had found that he possessed few of the insights and almost none of the instincts required to survive, let alone thrive. Even worse were the hundreds of ways the daily campaign revealed that he was really no different from other weak and opportunistic men. To his dismay and continuing surprise, he found that he was more than willing to bend with almost any wind, obey any whim or compromise that seemed expedient to advance his candidacy.

Early in the campaign, a professional media consultant, a small effeminate man with an air of impenetrable self-confidence, began shadowing York. He scrutinized him during his public appearances as if he were a very interesting biological specimen in a special laboratory culture. He filled notebooks examining York as he spoke to a crowd, as he shook hands at a factory gate, as he sipped punch at a precinct reception. When York told Morley he was irked by the man's constant presence, Morley said, "The guy's a genius at packaging an image. He is studying your habits, little things about you that might be wrong."

"Wrong? Like what?"

Morley shrugged. "We don't know yet, but he's the guy who remodeled the man who upset the incumbent for the Senate in Michigan in 1976. He made him change his contact lenses to a darker shade of blue and stop wearing bifocals in public. It made him look years younger."

York shook his head as Morley continued. "Times change, Gus. This same guy set up a famous photograph of Ronald Reagan on his horse—rugged individualism. He got Jerry Ford to start wearing three-piece suits—more statesmanlike." Morley paused, then grinned embarrassedly. "It's all merchandising, Gus. At, at a certain level, no one can avoid it."

"I suppose not. I wonder who the guy was who thought up the gimmick of Lincoln splitting rails. A packaging genius, too?" Morley gave a brittle chuckle.

But York wasn't sure enough of himself in the presidential maelstrom to ridicule or refuse to accept the ideas of the master image-maker. In Des Moines, after he had arranged for York to stand on the hood of a tractor and address a gathering of several hundred farmers in a corn field, the image-maker drew him aside. "Governor, that was a great photo opportunity," he said, "but you *have* to stop standing with your hands in your pockets when you make speeches. Just get out of that habit right now!"

York blinked and said, "Why? I never knew I did it."

"You do it all the time, Governor, and it looks like you're *playing* with your *balls!*"

York was speechless for a moment. Then he felt himself blush. "Well, uh, I'm not," he said.

"It doesn't matter what you're actually *doing*, Governor. The point is, if it *looks* like you're playing with your balls, people will assume that you *are* playing with your balls. And what kind of an image does that put forth for a man who wants to be President of the United States?"

"I really don't know."

"Well, think about it."

York didn't want to think about it. Nevertheless, from then on, whenever he started to relax by putting his hands in his pockets, he yanked them out as if his pockets were filled with burning coals. There was, of course, the problem of what to do with his hands when they weren't in his pockets. After watching him closely during an impromptu speech from the steps of a bank in Ketchum, Idaho, the image-maker took York aside again. He was very excited. "Governor, the problem of what to do with your hands is solved! You've kept them out of your pockets like a good fellow. But now you tend to put them behind your back or clasp them in front of you. That looks like a child reciting in Sunday school."

York closed his eyes in exasperation.

"The solution is that you put your right hand in your coat pocket—not pants, *coat* pocket. Then, with your left hand, you use a chopping gesture, like John Kennedy."

York used John Kennedy's chopping gesture. The image-maker also insisted that York develop the habit of winking whenever he grinned. "There's a vague resemblance between you and Will Rogers, and if you wink when you grin, it's emphasized." York winked like Will Rogers when he grinned. The media consultant suggested that he put a dab of rouge on each cheek in the morning to give him "the ruddy, rugged look," that he exaggerate his mountain drawl when he was in the South and far West, but try to eradicate it almost completely in the Midwest and Northeast. York cultivated a ruddy look and modulated his drawl. The expert insisted that it was important for the campaign that York emphasize his kinship to Sergeant Alvin York, the sharpshooting hero of World War I. York protested that there was no such kinship, but the next day a press release was issued declaring that Governor York was a "shirttail kissin' cousin" to the heroic Sergeant York of Tennessee.

Gus York had let that stand, too. There was, it turned out, damn little he wouldn't do when he was told to do it.

York did not invent or insist on dubious practices, but he went along. When Andy Morley and other men, more seasoned and surely more cynical than he, told him that he should be friendly with certain influential men that he did not like and did not trust, York obeyed. He grinned and shook hands and told them mountain jokes as if these men were his pals and confidants.

He was not entirely unaware of what was happening to him. The pressure of hype and hysterical hard-sell was everywhere throughout the campaign. Morley yammered constantly at staff advance men because they had not produced a large enough crowd at rallies—as if such crowds were only like so many cattle to be driven to a certain point as esthetic background for a Marlboro Man commercial.

In Lincoln, Nebraska, York listened as Morley angrily denounced a distraught staff man who had failed to produce several thousand people at city hall for an important speech by York on agricultural policy. After the harangue, York said to Morley, "Why the hell can't you let it all just *happen?* Why can't it just be natural?"

Morley's blue eyes widened in surprise and then he spoke with deadly seriousness: "Gus, there is one thing you absolutely can*not* be in national politics—and that is *natural.* You can be dumb, dishonest, conniving, naïve, vicious. But you cannot be natural. People's expectations must be met. They expect big crowds for a successful candidate. So we produce big crowds— unnaturally, if necessary. Letting things take their natural course is tantamount to leaving things to chance. And that, Governor, is the most dangerous thing you can do in politics today."

York realized that his own natural personality had been slipping away from the first day of the campaign. As he was polished and molded and finally packaged to fit people's expectations of a presidential candidate, he was so exhausted by Morley's heartbreaking twenty-hour daily schedules that he could do little more than comprehend and obey whatever orders he was given. Being natural seemed so alien and pointless in the frenzy of the campaign that he actually welcomed the rouge, the calculated drawl, the Kennedy chop, and the Rogers wink as dependable symbols of what he had come to perceive as himself. Even his ongoing impotence seemed oddly in keeping with his new persona.

Wearily, York closed his eyes and listened to the rain drill the windowpane. He dozed off and when he heard a door open and the sound of footsteps across the floor, he thought it was a dream. Startled, he opened his eyes and saw a figure in the shadow across the room. York started to rise from his chair when a powerful light snapped on. Blinded, he stumbled forward into the cables and nearly fell. "Who's there?" he bellowed.

There was silence. York was alarmed. "Who are you?" he shouted.

A high-pitched voice cried out beyond the light. "It's me. Tony, from CBS."

York stared helplessly into the blazing light. "Turn the goddamn thing off!"

The high voice almost squeaked. "Governor, I didn't know you was here. Honest." The light went off. York found himself unable to see anything but shimmering purple circles. He rubbed his eyes.

"It's okay. Now please get the hell out. I want some privacy." York could see now that the TV technician was a little man; his eyes bulged and his face was pale from the shock of York's presence.

"Governor, okay, but we got to check out this equipment sometime."

"Not now, please."

The door from the corridor opened and slammed sharply, and Morley's crackling staccato sounded: "What an abomination this place is." He picked his way through the snarl of cables and past the floodlight stands. Stumbling and catching himself, his face turned bright red and the tendons in his neck stretched taut. He shouted at the CBS man, "You cretins pollute everything you touch! Now get out of this room, or I'll shove the microphone down your throat!"

The little fellow started to protest. Morley leaped toward him, cursing furiously. He grabbed his arm. The technician wrenched out of his grip, ripping his shirt, and the CBS man scuttled out the door.

Morley's shoulders slumped and he said tensely, "Sorry, Governor. Those network people act like they're royalty, even the two-bit technicians. I just couldn't take it anymore."

York had seen Morley's temper before. To him, it was nothing more than a brief, harmless explosion, and probably therapeutic. "It's over," he said. "You better sit down and have a drink with me."

Morley loosened his tie and picked his way through the tangle on the floor. "I'll get it. Sit down, Governor." He went to a cabinet and took out a fresh quart of Jack Daniels, pouring two tumblers half-full.

They sipped gratefully. York set his glass down and began to untie a shoe. His voice was thin with fatigue. "I'm going to get myself barefoot." He stripped off one shoe and a sock. "In Jezebel they used to say that one bare foot lets more cooling refreshment and good news into your body than taking off every stitch you got on."

Morley drank another half-inch of his whiskey. "My mother never did let us go barefoot."

"You were one of those deprived rich kids, Andy. Never got mud between your toes, never skinned a squirrel. Hell, you probably never even got to go swimmin' bare-naked."

"Not a chance. I'd have been sent to reform school

for being a public nuisance if I'd taken my shoes off where I lived. You didn't go around barefoot when you had the British ambassador for dinner."

York smiled. The whiskey was doing wonders to his state of mind. He sipped again. "I've never felt so tired," he said. "No football game ever came close."

"It's been a rough and bitching time, Gus. I've seen these things up close before. My father was involved in Tom Dewey's campaigns—twice—and I covered Goldwater during '64 when I was still with the *Times*. But even McGovern in '72 didn't take as much all-around personal punishment as you."

"I don't have anything to compare it to, thank God. But I'll tell you, Andy, I'd a lot rather swim the Australian crawl up and down the Ohio River in the month of December than go through one more day of this campaign. And Milly . . ."

"She's strong, though, Gus. I can't think of another woman I know who could have come through under this punishment."

"So why was it so goddamn tough for us?"

"You were new. You had no foundation, no national support around the country. You were strangers to the establishment—in *both* parties. The power brokers and the big money didn't know you. They resented you. There was a quality of hazing to the whole thing. And you never learned to pace yourself, Gus. You went as strong as some third-rate little kaffeeklatsch in Keokuk as you did for a ten-million-dollar benefit at Madison Square Garden. You never understood that sometimes you should come on at half-speed—or less."

"That's from being a dumb hillbilly football player, Andy. I never did know how to put out less than everything. Even with the Bears. I used to get myself so worn out that I'd be sobbing after a game we lost by six touchdowns."

"That do-or-die-spirit stuff is pretty out of date, Governor. Perfect for Norman Rockwell paintings and rhyming doggerel."

York chuckled. "I always thought Norman Rockwell was the greatest painter in the world, and my favorite poet actually was Grantland Rice. You remember— 'When the Great Scorer comes to write against your name, he'll not write if you won or lost, but how you played the game'? It was carved in stone over the door at our high school gym."

Morley said, "The Great Scorer is more of a cynic than he used to be, Governor. He doesn't write how you played the game anymore, but how much you got paid."

The phone rang and Morley answered. York closed his eyes and listened absently to the campaign manager's voice. "Lined up around the block . . . ? Honest to God? In *Boston* . . . ? Damn! I'll be down in a minute after I finish this, uh, conference with the governor."

Morley hung up the phone and picked up his drink. He was frowning as he studied his legal pad of notes from the conversation. York asked, "Anything wrong?"

"No, no." His tone was puzzled. "Some figures from Boston and a couple of places in Texas. I'm not sure what's happening."

York sipped his drink. He felt the unfamiliar sensation of total relaxation begin to spread through his system.

Morley snapped, "Damn! If they'd given me the computer capability I wanted, I could check even these puny numbers off against the base. I'd know *exactly* what's going on. This way, I have to guess. Goddamn budget-cutters! Anyway, Gus, I'm beginning to think that if it hadn't rained and snowed and dumped damnation all over the country today, you might have had an excellent chance of sneaking past the President."

York shrugged. "Not me." He sipped the dregs of his whiskey, debated having another, and set the glass down. "There's no chance. You know that. But, dammit, Andy . . . there *was* a time when I honestly believed I had a chance to win. What a fool . . ."

Morley said quickly, "Not necessarily. Everyone who ever runs thinks he has a chance to win. Every Vegetarian and Socialist Progressive, every Right-to-Lifer. It's plain old human nature."

Morley patted him on the shoulder and left. York looked at his watch; it was noon. He turned on the television set for the local news and switched off the parlor lamps so that the room was almost dark. He stretched out on the sofa to watch TV, his bare feet hanging over the couch arm and his head buried deep in the cushion at the other end. In a matter of minutes he was asleep. The television tube cast a ghostly silver illumination over him, and the soft nattering of the announcer was almost drowned out by the sound of rain against the window.

* * * * *

As he watched Imai Hitsu harangue the crowd, Le Bombardier did not dwell at all on the morality of his impending crime. The death of other men was of no great concern to him, for he reasoned as a fatalist and cynic: if he were not the instrument of a man's death, there would be another sooner or later. A matter of a few more days or years of life were not, in his mind, grounds for profound consideration. And in his case, the end justified the means—the end being a million-dollar payment and the sense of a job done as neatly, efficiently, and perfectly as human fallibility allowed. To Le Bombardier, the essence of his work perhaps lay less in the monetary rewards than in his delight in his ability to function as much as possible like a machine, as a perfect extension of technology, without philosophical doubt, passion, or personal involvement.

Long ago he had come to realize that he felt the strongest when he felt the least. When he could remove from his mind, from his consciousness, every feeling but that of function, he was at his best. It had taken enormous self-control, an incredible strength of will to bring himself to this state, and Le Bombardier was proud of what he had become. He was a man who felt nothing—including moral and emotional pain. He was, he was happy to conclude, the perfect combination of businessman and technocrat, a truly modern man.

He reached inside his suit coat, then inside his shirt and fingered the small, round button-switch on the canvas cummerbund strapped around his waist. He gazed blankly at the audience as he pushed the button. There was a split-second delay. Imai Hitsu had just paused in his diatribe and the audience had just raised its obedient hands to applaud when a cloud of smoke swirled up from beneath the podium. It was followed instantly by a dull, thunder-like clap.

The plastique, secreted there by Le Bombardier an hour before the speech began, had detonated perfectly. The explosion roared outward and upward in a flash of light. Its force slammed against the abdomen, chest, and face of the stocky terrorist. It ripped open his torso, revealing a gaping view of his innards, and it turned his head to red jelly.

The body flew back ten feet. Imai Hitsu was dead instantly, though the blood-covered mass of flesh twitched and flopped before it became still. The explosion blew out the sides of the podium and knocked several men on the platform off their chairs. It showered slivers over the crowd. The smell of smoke and burned flesh was everywhere.

* * * * *

Chapter 6

Morley was concerned about York. There were times when the candidate had been so confused and disoriented by his surroundings that Morley had to shout briefings into his ear as if he were drilling instructions at a punchy boxer. But York had never produced the ultimate gaffe that Morley expected. He performed his role of hail-fellow-well-met, made his speeches, replied patiently to each question through endless repetitious interviews. In fact, York displayed such an aura of innate decency that even Morley, long a cynic about everything political, came to like him and eventually even to trust him, an attitude he had never expected to enjoy around any politician.

When he left York's suite, Morley went to the campaign staff headquarters next to a banquet room on the main floor of the hotel. The headquarters was equipped with several dozen phones, typewriters, and television sets to monitor network results. Morley sat at a phone, puffing fiercely on a cigarette as he talked with a politician in Cleveland. "You say it's one hell of a turnout? Damn! It seems to be happening everywhere."

He hung up. Something was emerging in this election that Morley had sensed but hadn't dared to believe. For the past month, he had noticed an intense and quizzical look on the faces of many people when they turned out to see York. Now he wondered if that meant that, even though the polls showed the President comfortably ahead, people were truly so dissatisfied that they wanted to vote against him and they had been examining York just that bit more closely in order to justify it.

For a moment Morley allowed himself to wonder how it would be if Gus York actually were elected President. He probably had the potential, Morley thought, but he would have to grow a lot. At first, Morley had seen York as a blank sheet of paper, a sheet on which he could sketch any face or write any message he wished. All that Morley had known of York when he was appointed campaign manager was that the man moved with the consummate grace of a natural athlete and that his wife was uncommonly good-looking. Handsome, graceful people made the political sell easier, but York's politics as well as his personality were a mystery to Morley. That he proved ultimately to be a basic middle-of-the-road Republican didn't matter greatly. The only campaign strategy worth considering involved nothing but counter-punching against the incumbent—attacking his record, his uncertain leadership, his blandness, his amazing lack of political acumen. It was simple. York had to be perceived as neutral, above the battle, while a spotty Presidential record was made the catalyst for voter reaction.

Of course, York himself had been sharply aware of his own naïveté, and ten minutes after he and Morley were introduced in Detroit, York said, "Sir, you are dealing with a political tadpole. You are the coach. I am the water boy on this team."

Morley had laughed and replied, "No one ever won a championship with a water boy. I may be the coach, but you have to be the star halfback, Governor."

Andrew Jackson Morley IV was a political professional. He had been born to the game. He grew up in Washington, in a mansion on Massachusetts Avenue that had been built by his great-grandfather who was Secretary of the Treasury in the Cabinet of Chester A. Arthur. Morley's paternal grandfather had been a Republican leader of the House who gave Woodrow Wilson fits over the League of Nations. His maternal grandfather was a lobbyist for and pal of John D. Rockefeller. Morley's father was a powerful, well-connected lawyer who handled much of the congressional lobbying for the sugar-refining industry.

As a boy, Morley had met many of the lions of American politics. At one time or another the entire Cabinet of Franklin Delano Roosevelt had been to a meal at his home, including Vice-Presidents John Nance Garner and Harry S Truman. Wendell Willkie was a close friend of his father, and so were Thomas E. Dewey, Robert A. Taft, Herbert Hoover, and Henry Wallace. Morley's godfather was Charles G. Dawes, who had been vice-president under Calvin Coolidge.

Morley attended Harvard and was a contemporary of Robert Kennedy. He then went to work for *The New York Times* as a Capitol Hill reporter. His connections were excellent, of course, and his perceptions and appreciation of the elephantine waltz of politics on the Hill were brilliant. But Morley possessed a strong thirst for whiskey (a legacy from both of his grandfathers and one great-grandfather). When he drank, he occasionally displayed a violent temper. He was married for a time to a charming and graceful woman, the daughter of a British ambassador to Washington in the 1930s, but Morley lost his temper too often and therefore lost his wife. He lost his job at the *Times*, too, after savage blow-ups with the bureau chief.

With an undamaged reputation for refined political instincts, he got a job with a congressional committee on the Hill, then moved to Republican Party headquarters, where, for a couple of dark months, he slogged through the public relations morass of Watergate. He quit when the committee refused to condemn Nixon soon enough for his liking. He then started a political consulting business and produced the surprise election of a Republican senator in Colorado in 1976 and a Republican governor in Florida in 1978. His occasional drinking bouts and his temper notwithstanding, Andrew Jackson Morley IV was a highly respected political professional, and when the Republican National Committee asked him to run the York campaign, Morley demanded—and got—$125,000 for his personal services for three months.

The ravages of his drinking and his insistence on habitually working twenty-hour days during a campaign showed in the ruddy network of veins in his face and the startling thinness of his body. His hands were bony and long and sometimes tremulous. He smoked feverishly and drank endless paper cups of coffee when he was not sipping paper cups of Jack Daniels.

The staff room was still relatively quiet this afternoon, with no more than ten workers present. When the election returns began to pour in in the evening, there would be more than a hundred, each receiving prearranged calls from specific key precincts around the country. This little command post could handle nowhere near the volume of material that the network computers would be digesting, but at least Morley would have readings of his own—narrower than the TV analyses, but more exact, he hoped. He had begged for a full computerized program to use during the campaign, but the national committee had refused to authorize the expenditure and Morley had to rely on his myriad contacts around the country—and his instincts.

In the lobby, Morley saw Appleton standing by the elevator bank. The Secret Service man was examining passing people sharply. Morley walked quickly to him and said, "Excuse me, sir, I am Jack the Ripper and I understand you were asking for me."

Appleton did not smile and did not reply. Morley could see himself reflected in the agent's dark glasses. He gestured toward the dozen heavily armed state troopers planted around the lobby. "Well, you've got plenty of help to scare away anyone bent on foul play. They have more guns than the National Guard."

"Those bozos worry me more than almost anything," Appleton muttered.

Morley nodded sympathetically. "They dress up like tin soldiers in a comic opera, but they all have the soul of Ghengis Khan."

"The whole place makes me nervous." Appleton gazed around the cavernous lobby, with its thirty-foot ceilings and its dusty potted palms. He looked up at the gigantic York-for-President posters, big as double beds, hanging from the ceiling. Appleton said grimly, "I was in China with Nixon in 1972, and everywhere they had those huge pictures of Mao. He was watching us all the time we were there. It made me nervous. Like I was an enemy from another planet. I get the same feeling from these pictures of York. That crowd of hillbillies this morning didn't do me any good, either."

"There's something sinister about mountain people if you don't happen to be one of them. Also something sinister about Chinese if you don't happen to be one of them," said Morley.

Appleton actually smiled, a small and fleeting upturn of the lips that Morley might have missed if he hadn't been very observant. He said, "I amuse you, Appleton. That seems quite an accomplishment." Morley saw another face appear next to his own in Appleton's glasses. It was the pale visage of the state police commissioner.

"Hiya, Mr. Morley. Hiya, Appleton," the commissioner drawled. "You all can both take off and rest up, fellas, if you want. We got things under control. Take a nap, Appleton." He winked. "Get laid."

Appleton's face took on an expression of such coldness that it seemed paralyzed. The Secret Service man said, "I'll take a raincheck on that. I want to keep as many of your men in view as I can."

The commissioner said, "We are also watching your men, suh."

The police commissioner spoke as if he were addressing a large audience. "We don't believe that the next President of the United States should be in jeopardy from anyone. We believe in guns as a protective measure. The next President of the United States is safe as a baby in a cradle in our hands."

Appleton snorted and Morley was about to speak when Morris appeared at Appleton's side. "Excuse me, could I have a word? Privately."

They moved off two steps. Morris spoke softly and handed Appleton an envelope. The address on it was scrawled in color crayon. Morley felt his scalp tingle and he moved to Appleton's side.

Appleton opened the envelope and quickly scanned the message, which was tightly written in several colors over the familiar cheap, lined tablet paper. A muscle in his jaw rippled, but his face was impassive when he looked up.

Morley asked anxiously, "Same as the others?"

"No."

He handed it to Morley. The campaign manager skimmed it. To him, the letter contained the same embittered and psychotic message of the others, racist obscenities and the threat of a terrible death—"today." Morley shook his head. "Jesus, what a lunatic." He looked up at Appleton. "What's not the same as the others?"

Appleton was grim. "He's got the exact number of York's suite this time, 2018 through 2020. He knows exactly where to find him."

"That wouldn't be so hard to find out. Most of the press know. TV is all over the place."

"It's not hard to find out. But it means this kook doesn't just have an insane hatred for some abstract authority figure. It means his mind is working well enough to plan something. It means he is really focused on killing York and is probably capable of making an attempt."

Morley watched Appleton's face, but the agent was imperturbable. "What are you going to do?"

The stubby legs of the state police commissioner were already churning across the lobby. He grabbed one trooper after another and pointed them toward the elevators. Appleton snorted. "That bastard. He's going to move the whole damn police department up to York's floor."

"Is that bad? That brute power and guns showing might discourage the guy."

"I know. But I don't trust those guys. Who's to say they won't get the wrong guy?" Appleton turned to Morris and said quietly, "Call Washington and see if we can get another dozen men in by tonight. I'll set up a room-by-room search to cover every window across the street. Then seal off the buildings."

Morley said, "What do you want me to do?"

"Keep York as close as possible to his room. Anyone who goes up the elevator to his floor will be double-checked here in the lobby. I think we'll be fine." He turned and hurried toward the elevator that was locked onto York's floor. It had already left, loaded with state troopers. Morley watched Appleton for a moment and saw again the flicker of the muscle in his jaw. Behind those inscrutable shades and that stony face, Appleton was a very nervous man.

Morley started to return to the staff room to make more phone calls, then decided on a detour to the cocktail lounge. His nerves were twanging, too, from the new threat. But he was also agitated and unsettled by the news he had received from his political sources around the country: it was now at least a possibility that by morning the color-crayon assassin might be stalking a real, live President-elect instead of a near-anonymous Border State governor facing certain defeat.

* * * * *

Le Bombardier had not been blown from his chair, but he fell to the floor as if in shock. A vast rumble of confusion rose from the audience. The men on the stage stood frozen in shock at first. Then some rushed to the smoking body of Imai. Some leaped off the stage and sprinted through the audience. Some ran to the sides of the stage, bellowing in fear that further explosions might follow.

Le Bombardier, as Steinbugler, pretended panic and dashed to an exit. In the street, he slowed and settled into a fast but casual walk. It was a full five minutes before he heard the first whooping of police cars and ambulances. By then, he was within a block of the bustling Daichi Holiday Inn. Unnoticed, he took the elevator and entered the room he had engaged two days earlier as the Dallas machinery salesman "Darryl

Michael Hagerty." He removed the clothing, wig, contact lenses, steel spectacles of "Steinbugler," and quickly applying his makeup, became "Hagerty" once more. He packed "Steinbugler's" items in the suitcase along with his own clothes and the electronic cummerbund, then went to the lobby and checked out, picking up the passport for "Hagerty" he had left earlier at the desk. He boarded the two-eighteen bullet train for Tokyo, and at five-fifteen P.M. he left the airport there for San Francisco aboard Pan American flight 901.

He felt very well, indeed. In all, including research and investigation of the habits of the dead Imai, the Kyoto assassination had taken six weeks to arrange. The Bishi Corporation had been prompt in its first payment—$500,000 in a Swiss bank account when he agreed to do the job, followed by another $250,000 a week before Le Bombardier was to kill Imai. Now, another $250,000 would be forthcoming. The job had been simple. It was, however, the best-paying piece of work of Le Bombardier's career.

* * * * *

Chapter 7

It was after six P.M. when York awoke. The room was lighted only by the glow of the television screen. The windows were black. York had not moved since noon, and his sleep had been so sound that the moment he opened his eyes he felt a peace and fulfillment so satisfying that he let out an involuntary groan of delight.

The television was showing a news program and York heard his own name: ". . . Augustus A. York, the Republican candidate. Polls are open everywhere. It is still raining in the South and East, snowing heavily in the Midwest and West. Yet the Associated Press reports a surprisingly large turnout, possibly as high as seventy-five percent of eligible voters. If that estimate should be correct, it will be unprecedented in the past quarter-century. . . ."

The election seemed utterly unreal. York realized that for the first time in months his sleep had been undisturbed by dreams of the campaign. Now it dawned on him that it was over, and a marvelous wave of euphoria lifted him. Looking at the television, he felt as detached from those reports of his own fate as if he were watching from a balloon drifting ever higher and farther away.

The newscaster went on: "Governor York voted this

morning in his hometown of Jezebel, Kentucky." The screen filled with a long shot of Amos Pollock's store looking forlorn in the rainy woods. Then York saw himself standing with Milly on the front porch. As he spoke, the camera moved in on him alone. He chopped his hand in the prescribed Kennedy style, and, sure enough, when he smiled, there was Will Rogers' wink.

He rose unhurriedly from the sofa. He turned the set off and watched as his image shrank to a tiny bright dot and disappeared into the black screen. He was happy. It signified the death of a personality he did not like—Gus York, presidential candidate.

He walked to the window and peered down into the darkened street. Rain pelted the pavement, which reflected the streetlights like a string of blurred pearls. York gazed absently at the roof of the building across the street. A movement there startled him. He focused his attention and realized that he was looking at a state trooper standing by a chimney. The man paced slowly the length of the building, then back. A rifle was slung across his back. He thought of calling Morley to ask him what the hell was going on, or of confronting that tight-faced Secret Service agent, Appleton. Then he decided that he would not bother. The mechanics of this campaign held no further interest for him. It was over. He was free.

A latch clicked and the bedroom door swung open. He saw Milly's silhouette. She wore only her slip, and the light behind her accentuated her figure through the thin material. She hesitated, unable to see anything in the dark parlor. York said, "Darling, I'm over here."

Milly spoke in a voice husky from sleep. "Oh, Gus, I feel so wonderful. I slept without a dream." She moved toward him, blind in the darkness, and stumbled in the tangle of television cables on the floor. York went to her and, with his arm around her bare shoulders, guided her to the sofa.

His palm cupped the smoothness of her shoulder as they moved and he hugged her to his side. Milly turned to him and put her arms around his neck. Her body eased against him as his hands moved across the naked skin of her back and down the curve of her hips. Milly hugged him hard and pressed her whole body tightly against his. At first, the embrace was one of relief and gratitude, two survivors of a wreck, lost from each other, and then found again. She moved against him. York moved his hands to hold her buttocks and pulled her closer. Her pelvis and thighs undulated against him almost imperceptibly. She kissed him, her tongue moistening his lips. As naturally as if it had never left him, the sensation of sexual arousal returned.

Milly said, "Oh, Gus, I love you," insinuating her pelvis tighter against him when she felt him respond. York bowed his head to kiss her neck. Then he stepped back and slowly lifted the hem of her slip up over her legs, her thighs, above the triangle of soft black hair below her belly, over her breasts, and over her head. He kissed her breasts and fondled the moist cleft in her pubic hair. She caressed him, undid his belt and trousers, delicately manipulating those articles of clothing, until he was naked from the waist down.

They lay on the couch and made love. She cried out and York did, too. Around them was the paraphernalia of mass communications—lights and cameras and microphones—but nothing was turned on and no one was tuned in, and the only evidence the world would have of these few moments would be a large wet patch left on a couch cushion by what was arguably the mightiest ejaculation ever produced on Election Day by a Republican candidate for President of the United

States. When they were finished, they lay together, silent and smiling in the afterglow of something that came very close, in York's mind, to being a certifiable resurrection from the dead.

At last he sighed, "Thank God." He paused. "No, thank *you*, darling."

Milly wrapped her arms tighter around his chest and snuggled her head against his neck. "Gus, you must have been so worried. You hardly ever talked about it."

"I know. I was—dammit—I was ashamed, Milly. And I was frightened because I was so helpless to do anything about it. My God, I've never felt that way before."

"It was the campaign. The fatigue, the tension—the whole thing was so humiliating. You couldn't help it. Neither could I."

He nodded. "That was the worst of it. *No* one could *do* anything. It was beyond my control, beyond my will." He caressed her thigh with his hand. "I hope it's gone. I hope it never comes back."

She moved her hand down his belly and gently, lovingly, began to caress him again. Soon he was hard and she kissed his chest and moved down to kiss his ribs, his belly. She raised her head for a moment and said, "I think it's just a matter of more tender, loving care, darling."

She lowered her head again. York felt like shouting for joy, but the love that Milly brought to him now was so intimate and so all-engulfing that he could only whisper, "Thank you, darling, thank you."

Two hours later the parlor was filled with TV technicians. A floor director, a headset clamped over his ears, ran final lighting and audio tests. The room was hooked up now, coast to coast. Down the hall, York and Milly entertained a crowd of politicians and their wives, mainly Kentucky congressmen and state party leaders. Milly watched her husband closely. He was flushed and ebullient, his eyes shining, and he looked more robust than he had for months. She, too, basked in euphoria. The lovemaking had been like sweet rain after a killing drought.

Andrew Morley moved to York's side, tapped his elbow, and spoke in his ear. Then he turned and nodded his head at Milly. "Time to talk to Walter." These would be the last hurrahs, a few television interviews with the network superstars. Then the lights would go out and the blessed oblivion of privacy would follow.

The CBS floor director spoke directions softly into his throat microphone as the Yorks entered. The CBS correspondent moved through the electronic paraphernalia on the floor to York's side, and the floor director said, "Governor, you sit on the couch. Mrs. York, too."

"Lights," said the floor director. The room was instantly ablaze, as if a bolt of lightning had struck and stayed. Every object and person was flattened and shadowless. On the TV screen, a commercial was playing. The floor director gave a countdown, and when he finished, the correspondent stood facing the camera as Cronkite introduced him. He said, "Thank you, Walter. Here in the suite with the Yorks we sense a long period of waiting ahead. As you said earlier, Walter, the polls have just closed on the East Coast. And though there are only the most scattered returns available, we know there has been an astonishing turnout despite the dismal weather." The correspondent sat in a chair and turned toward the Yorks. He said, "Good evening, Governor, Mrs. York."

York was perspiring heavily under the lights, but he displayed his wide smile and said, "Bob, good evening."

"One of the great turnouts in history may be taking place, Governor. You voted yourself this morning in little Jezebel, Kentucky. How did you spend the rest of this bleak day, sir?"

York's hand moved absently along the couch cushion and crossed the large wet patch. He started slightly. "Ah, Bob, I took a long nap and then—I simply enjoyed myself today as I haven't in a long time."

"And you, Mrs. York?"

Milly let out a husky laugh. "To tell the truth, I did exactly the same thing."

The correspondent turned toward the TV set and spoke as if Cronkite were in the room. "Walter, do you have a question?"

Cronkite said, "Governor, we know about this tremendous turnout. Usually that works against an incumbent candidate. Tell us, what do you think is going to happen?"

York said, "Certainly, a big number of voters should work in our favor. But we had to come from so far back, I just don't know if there's enough momentum to pull ahead. Like we used to say in Jezebel, you just can't beat a race horse with a mule unless you can get close enough to hit him on the head with a wagon axle, and I'm not sure we're close enough."

Cronkite chuckled. They spoke inconclusively for a few more moments. Then the correspondent signed off, promising more visits in the York suite as the evening went on.

The lights went off, bringing a twilight coolness to the room, and York sank back on the couch. His face glistened and his shirt collar was soggy with sweat. Morley tossed him a towel. The CBS man left the room. York rubbed his face and head vigorously, then took off his coat, vest, and shirt and toweled his bare torso dry. Morley looked at York's heavy chest, his ropy, muscled arms and shoulders. "You may be tired, but you look like you could still step in for the Bears, Gus."

York laughed heartily. "Andy, I may just decide to do that after this thing is over. I'd love to take a crack at some of those fancy-pants quarterbacks they got these days."

He put on a fresh shirt, then reached over to turn up the volume on the television. Cronkite was saying: ". . . only the barest scattering from New England, but some of the CBS-profile voting districts are showing surprising results. In Boston's tenth precinct, for example, a staunch Democratic bastion, York has come out trailing the President by less than fifteen percent of the vote. These are early returns, I remind you, and they may mean very little in the final analysis, but they are startling, indeed."

York turned down the sound and looked at Morley. "What's going on?" he asked. Milly frowned and turned to look at Morley, too. A flash of apprehension struck her; perhaps they were not entirely free, after all.

"I've been doing lots of phoning," said Morley. "Things are very strange. It looks like it might be really very close. Much closer than we ever anticipated."

York gazed at him, a distracted look in his eye. "I thought this'd be all over by nine-thirty. Have you got any real numbers, Andy?"

Morley picked up a yellow legal pad and moved next to York, scribbling as he spoke: "Bailey in Philadelphia and Tom King in Jersey are very optimistic, Gus. Their poll watchers say that spot-check interviews turned up an enormous amount of really vehement feeling against the President. More than we thought."

York spoke grimly. "Well, it sure as hell is not *pro*-York."

Morley glanced quickly at York, and frowned. "Jesus Christ, what do you expect? There hasn't been an incumbent ever beat by anything but an anti-incumbent turnout." He took a breath and went on writing figures. "I don't think I can bring myself to believe you're going to take New York; that's forty-five for him. But Texas looks good—twenty-five for you; New Jersey, forty-three, is strong; and Pennsylvania . . ."

As Milly listened, she felt an entirely unexpected emotion gripping her: bright red anger. It surprised her, but she could not contain it. She interrupted Morley with something between a shriek and a snarl. "*Andy!* Are you saying Gus *really* can *win!?* Are you trying to turn us into jibbering idiots! For God's *sake, let us alone!*"

Morley looked up, stunned by the ferocity in her voice. "Milly! What's the matter?!"

"All of a sudden you tell us that Gus might *win!* How can we adjust to that? What do you expect us to *do!?*"

"Adjust to it? Do? You've been running for President for three months, and it never occurred to either of you that a miracle might happen and Gus would win?"

"We haven't had enough time or peace of mind to think about anything but not fainting from fatigue in front of an audience," she said.

"I know, I know." Morley was soothing. "Look, I'm not saying we *will* win. I'm really only saying that it will probably be very damn close. A cliff-hanger—not the embarrassing defeat for you that everyone predicted."

The room door from the corridor opened and Eddie Hanson, the campaign press secretary, stepped in. "Governor, can you hold a little talk with the guys from *Time* and *Newsweek*, then sit for a couple of pictures for *Life?* Casual stuff. Shouldn't take ten, fifteen minutes."

York frowned. He finished buttoning his shirt and put on a necktie. "Okay, Ed. But I don't want it to take long. I want to talk with Andy, here."

York shrugged into his coat and left with Hanson. Morley looked warily at Milly. She felt tears stinging her eyes and blinked quickly. "I'm not going to cry, Andy." She paused, swallowed, then proceeded more calmly. "Everyone has gone out of their way to make us feel like born losers. We've been pushed around like wind-up toys. Gus is a proud man, and he's been reduced to a puppet. He . . ."

Morley interrupted. "Milly! Gus himself told me he didn't know a damn thing about running for President. He *wanted* to be told what to do."

"Yes, but he's been told what to do so much that he's forgotten his own personality."

Morley held up his hands in a calming gesture. "Milly, you two are exhausted. It all looks like a terrible nightmare right now. But it's not. Your entire perspective is warped by this exhaustion. It's temporary."

"I know. I'm better now than I was. If you'd told me this morning that Gus might be President, I'd have thrown myself out the window and taken you with me."

"Gus is a tough guy."

"No, he's not. He's big and graceful and he looks full of confidence. But that's all physical. That's the athlete part. Under it, he isn't sure of himself at all. He worries he'll do the wrong thing, show bad manners, embarrass himself. He's from a dirt road back in the woods, Andy. He never had enough to eat. He thinks people like you—Ivy Leaguers, silver-spoon people—are superior to the rest of the world, and especially to a hillbilly boy from Jezebel."

Morley was impatient. "Milly, dammit, you aren't giving him credit for anything. Sure, he came out of that godforsaken hollow, barefoot and barely able to read. But he not only became a football hero, he got to be Governor of Kentucky. That's almost as much as Abraham Lincoln did. You can't call a man like that a weakling."

"It isn't what you and *I* think of him—it's what he thinks of himself. There's a lot of mountain boy still in him. He is awed by money and by Harvard educations. He is awed by bankers with manicures, and Wall Street lawyers with yachts, and stockbrokers with Eastern accents! He's full of awe."

"If he's President, those people will line up at the White House gates to shine his shoes and sew on his shirt buttons."

"Of course. And Gus won't have the most remote idea how to react to that—or anything else about being President. His biggest limitation is that he isn't ruthless and he isn't cunning. He isn't deceitful and he isn't cold-blooded. To use power you have to be a mean, cynical son-of-a-bitch. Gus is not."

Morley sighed. "Yes. I know those things about him, Milly. I just think he can rise to the situation."

Milly turned to gaze at the dark, streaming windowpane. Her skin was the color of ivory, her hair such a deep brown it was almost black. There was no sign of gray. But she was in her forties, and tonight her eyes were dark and troubled and looked far older than that.

Morley was exasperated. "We can't turn around now. There's no resigning from a presidential campaign on the night it comes to a climax."

Her voice was very low. "No. We can't quit now. This is going to take some getting used to, Andy. I'll think about it in the morning. We won't know for sure until morning, will we?"

"Not if it's as close as I think it will be."

* * * * *

Chapter 8

Appleton prowled the lobby crowds. Perhaps two thousand people swarmed through the various banquet halls and public rooms of the hotel. It was a palpably Southern Republican gathering. An air of comfort bordering on smugness pervaded the throng. Appleton listened to their well-modulated murmuring. He saw no one remotely likely to have written threatening letters—or any letters—with a colored crayon. The atmosphere was laden with boredom rather than anticipation, giving the event the appearance of a well-heeled wake, another losing Republican election.

But shortly before nine P.M. John Chancellor was saying on NBC: ". . . even these early returns from the East, where the polls closed fifty minutes ago, seem to indicate that this election is going to be far closer than anyone has previously predicted."

There were desultory cheers from the crowd. Appleton heard someone say drily, "Yeah, one more state and he ties Alf Landon."

Appleton's own tension had receded. The search of adjoining buildings and subsequent sealing off of rooms that might have served as a sniper's nest made him feel easier. Another ten agents had arrived from Washington and they were posted around the hotel. York would remain in his suite until the time came for a concession speech. There would be no surprise appearances among the faithful, no strolls through the public rooms. Morley had given Appleton his word.

At nine-forty-five, CBS awarded Florida to York. Cronkite said, "Everywhere we are getting reports of the largest turnout in years . . ." People gathered in knots around the dozen large-screen television sets located throughout the hotel. A sense of excitement began to pervade the crowd.

Morley charged out of the staff office and said to Appleton, "Who'd have guessed it!" He rushed on to the cocktail lounge before Appleton could reply. Appleton kept moving through the throngs. About eleven, he noticed a tall, thin young man, really a boy in his teens. When Appleton first saw him, he was leaning against a lobby pillar, his arms folded loosely across the chest of his soiled raincoat. His face was speckled with pimples. He had tried to grow a mustache; a sparse, yellowish bristle lay across his lip. His shabby appearance made him stand out among the well-kept Republicans. His blond hair was tangled and wet, as if he had just come in from the rain. The boy had a distant, idle look in his eyes, as if he were drunk or mildly high on some drug. Appleton started to move casually toward him when an outbreak of applause and shouting erupted behind him. CBS had given the state of Maryland to Governor York. Appleton glanced instinctively in the direction of the noise. When he looked back, the boy was moving toward the front door. Appleton watched him go out into the rain.

By midnight the networks had been able to count no more than twenty states as definitely falling into either candidate's total of electoral votes. The crowd in the hotel was tense. People sat on every available chair or couch, and many were on the floor.

By two-thirty A.M., ABC had awarded fifteen states to the President, thirteen to York. The electoral vote total was 171 for the President, 149 for the governor, but there was still no clear trend, and twenty-two states hung in limbo, too close to call. The crowds were thinner and some people slept, amid a clutter of discarded pennants and shrinking balloons.

At five A.M., the lobby contained five hundred tenacious hangers-on. The TV commentators looked haggard and anxious. CBS had had to change half a dozen states from one candidate to the other. NBC had had endless troubles in the South, switching states as commentators apologized. John Chancellor said, "It's a bleak night for forecasters. If the original projections of pollsters had been correct, the President would have been comfortably re-elected and presumably sound asleep five hours ago. . . ."

Appleton went to his room and fell into delicious sleep for two hours, until he was yanked back to consciousness by his wake-up call. He turned on the television set. The sagging face of John Chancellor appeared, saying: ". . . to those of you who have been with us all night, my profound sympathies. To those of you just rising, you have my sympathies, too, for you have missed one of the most dramatic hairbreadth election nights—and mornings—in American history." He went on to say that the electoral count favored York by 11 votes. But there were still ten states with 70 electoral votes that NBC could not call for certain to give either candidate that total of 278 that he needed.

Appleton showered, shaved, and dressed. He felt surprisingly refreshed as he hurried down the corridor to York's suite. He almost laughed aloud when he saw the state troopers stationed there. They leaned against the walls like slowly deflating bright blue balloons, as sleepy as four-year-olds at an all-night costume party. Appleton's own men, Thomas, McCarthy, and Mikkelson, sat quietly. Appleton said to Thomas, "Is he still inside?"

The agent nodded. "Morley's been in and out, up and down all night. Room service was in and out a lot. York's been alone for an hour or so."

Appleton pointed at the agent's walkie-talkie. "When did you last check the other positions?"

"Twenty minutes ago. All quiet. The lobby is almost empty. Nothing across the street. Nothing out back. Nothing on the roof."

"You think he's going to win?" Mikkelson's voice was casual.

"Do you?"

"Possibly. Yes, possibly." Mikkelson paused. "I haven't seen much of him, but he seems to have some good moves. Might be a hell of a guy to work for."

"Better than Spiro?" Appleton's tone was acid.

"Different," said Mikkelson with a chuckle. "Definitely different."

* * * * *

Chapter 9

York sat in the faded easy chair watching the picture on the television. The sound was off. His cheeks were covered with a light, coppery stubble. His eyes were red-rimmed and his thoughts were confused, for he had not even dozed through the night and he had drunk a lot of whiskey. It was after eight o'clock, a cold and radiant morning. He had heard the rain stop at five A.M. and seen the first glow of dawn sometime after six. The changing weather, the clear sky following the foul night, the slow developments of the election made him feel as if he had passed many days in this hotel room.

He rose to open the window. Brisk, biting air poured in and he thought that he heard a band playing "My Old Kentucky Home." Could it be? He thought possibly the music was a figment of confusion and bourbon, but when he stuck his head out the window, he saw, twenty stories below, a gathering of several hundred people on the street, and, yes, a band, fully uniformed with brass instruments gleaming in the sun.

York leaned farther out the window. He heard a voice shouting over the music of the band: "Governor! Governor! Get back in! Shut the window!"

On the roof across the street, two rifle-bearing state troopers looked anxiously at him. Next to them, his hands cupped around his mouth, was the state police commissioner. He shouted again. "Get inside! Don't take no chances!"

Puzzled, York waved vaguely and closed the window. Again he wondered why the rooftops around him were of such intense interest to the police.

Morley rapped sharply at the door and entered without waiting for York to invite him. His face was more flushed than usual, his thinning hair tousled. He carried a stack of East Coast morning papers under one arm, a sheaf of scribbled yellow legal sheets in the other hand. He said, "All's well that ends well, Gus. We're within fourteen votes, and moving strong."

"I haven't been paying attention."

The phone jangled. "Oh, oh. I told them no calls unless it's *really* something *big*," Morley said. He picked up the phone, listened, then turned to York and cried, "Gus! We've got Oregon! We're within four votes!" He slammed down the receiver.

York was silent. As his impending victory drew closer, he found he had less and less reaction to it. No excitement, no joy, no relief, no fear. Only a pervasive perplexing sense of helplessness, a total lack of control.

"All we need is Utah or Hawaii." Morley spoke gently, as if he were explaining a very simple truth to a very simple man.

"I better tell Milly."

"Why not wait, Gus? She hasn't been in bed more than a couple of hours."

"She'd hate herself if she missed it, Andy."

The bedroom was dark, the shades drawn against the sunlit morning. He heard the faint chattering of the radio, and as he neared the bed, Milly turned and looked up at him. She spoke softly. "Congratulations, darling."

He grinned. "It's not certain. Haven't you slept at all?"

"It's too exciting, darling. It's like the last seconds of a football game."

"No, it's not. Not a bit."

"I know." She reached up her arms and York leaned over the bed to hug her. Then he lay down next to her and kissed her. He wanted to curl up against her long, supple body, bury his head in her breasts and stay there forever—or at least for this day.

Morley rapped sharply at the door. "Gus! Milly! We got Hawaii! CBS called it! You've won!"

York raised his head and looked at Milly in the gloom. Her eyes were wide and staring for a moment. Then she smiled. "I love you, Gus." He hugged her and buried his face in her bosom again. He felt the radiance of her skin, the protecting fullness of her breasts. She was Mother Earth, Minerva, Venus, all that was eternal in women's love. Then he noticed the pounding of Milly's heart. It was swift and frightened.

At noon the President conceded the election. He was gracious, tearful, and he promised cooperation in the transition between administrations. York, Milly, Morley, and Browning Dayton and his wife gathered in the suite to watch the speech on television. The vice-president-elect, a slim, handsome Californian, tanned and suave, had flown in from San Francisco on a Lear jet that morning when victory seemed likely.

Afterward, Dayton said to York, "We did it—Mr. President."

York said, "You brought in California, Brownie, no doubt about that."

Dayton ducked his head in gratitude. "And you brought in Kentucky, no doubt about that!"

Somehow he managed to say this without a trace of sarcasm, although his smile was noticeably tight. Victory for this Republican ticket had not been part of

Browning Dayton's plan. The 1984 presidential nomination had been his target. His scenario was obvious enough: the predictable defeat of the York–Dayton ticket in 1980 would have been blamed mainly on the inexperienced York, who would never be heard from again, while attractive, intelligent Browning Dayton cashed in on the national attention he received during the campaign. By 1984, he would be an almost inevitable choice to run for President.

Now, however, Browning Dayton would be consigned for four years to that most neglected backwater in American politics. John Nance Garner had once captured the essence and true significance of the vice-presidency when he said, "It's not worth a pitcher of warm spit." The significance of California's forty-five electoral votes in an election decided by three electoral votes could scarcely be exaggerated, which only added irony to the ignominy of Dayton's fate.

Morley sat at a desk putting the final touches with a blue pencil on York's acceptance speech. "Short and to the point," he said. He handed a single sheet of paper to York. The phone rang. He picked it up and listened. "We'll be down in ten minutes." He looked up at York. "Will that give you enough time? They say there's a hell of a crowd down there."

"Ten minutes, Andy. I'll take one look at what you've written and we're on our way."

Appleton entered the room. It was bedlam downstairs in the lobby. Crowds jammed the streets outside, perhaps 75,000 people. A school holiday had been proclaimed in Louisville, and many offices were closed to celebrate the first election of a Kentuckian as President since Abraham Lincoln in 1860. Appleton grabbed Morley's elbow. "Make it as quick downstairs as you can," he said.

Morley glanced at him sharply. "Well, Jesus, we have to give him a little time to enjoy this thing, Appleton. The man has just been elected President; he's not just going to scuttle in and out of his hole like some kind of rodent. We'll do it as fast as we can, but I'm not going to rush him."

Appleton turned away silently. The edge of pain in his stomach felt like an ulcer. His eyes were stinging. He thought he detected a faint ringing in his ears. He stood anxiously by the door leading to the corridor. He had rarely felt so nervous.

York looked up from the paragraph Morley had written. He said briskly, "Let's go!" To Appleton the words had the ring of a football coach in a locker room, and he wished this really was an occasion as mundane and devoid of danger as a football game.

He opened the door and walked ahead of York and his party. The corridor was mobbed. There were no fewer than ten state troopers, plus six of Appleton's Secret Service men. Many of York's staff people lined the walls, applauding when he appeared. Appleton stayed in front of York and Milly, while Mikkelson and Thomas moved along on each side, forming a horseshoe around them. They moved toward the secure elevator, which stood open and waiting. Appleton wanted to move quickly, but the corridor was dense with people and York kept stopping to shake hands with his staff.

Suddenly Appleton turned ice cold. Something was wrong. The door of a second elevator was sliding open down the hall beyond the crowd. The "Up" light above it was on, showing it had risen from below. No other cars were supposed to be able to stop at this floor.

Appleton pushed back against York. "Hold it!" he barked. The entourage bumped together, confused.

A tall, hatchet-faced man dressed in a gray work-man's shirt and trousers emerged briskly from the elevator. He had a belt with tools on his waist. His eyes were wide and burning, but he looked genuinely startled when Appleton moved toward him. He spoke rapidly in a high, tense voice. "It's okay. It's only a fuse." He gestured at his shirt pocket. Appleton saw his identification button and the small green pin, the correct code pin for the day, which had been issued to all hotel employees. The man stared at Appleton out of glittering eyes.

The Secret Service man began to reach out to detain the workman. Then he was stunned to glimpse a familiar face. Emerging from the elevator was the tall young man he had noticed in the lobby the night before. The boy craned his neck to see York. His eyes were fierce, his mouth twisted. Both hands were deep in the pockets of the soiled raincoat. He began to withdraw one hand and Appleton thought he saw a glint of metal.

Appleton sprang past the angular figure of the workman. He gripped the boy's arms, spun him, and clamped the boy's neck in a fierce grip with his forearm. The boy fought. They lurched back and then forward again. They fell. Appleton's forearm tightened sudden-ly and he felt something give in the boy's throat. As he landed on top of the boy, he heard a gurgling, strangled sound.

A woman shrieked, "A gun! Watch out, Governor!"

A barrage of shots thundered in the hallway, deafen-ing in the confined space. Appleton flung the limp body of the young man against the wall, then lunged back toward the Yorks.

Gunsmoke filled the corridor. It obscured his vision, choked his lungs. Someone screamed. Someone sobbed. A babble of voices rose in hysteria. Appleton saw York squirming on the floor with Mikkelson sprawled across him. Thomas held Milly York pinned against the wall. McCarthy had knocked Browning Dayton down.

Appleton saw the maintenance man lying on the floor. His body had been transformed into a long, shapeless mound. His gray work clothes were filled with bullet holes and glistened with blood. His head was scarlet pulp. A ghastly burst of brains was sprayed along the carpet for two feet beyond the body.

A woman writhed and shrieked beyond the work-man's body. Her left leg was a mass of blood. Five state troopers stood with .45's in their hands. The pistols still smoked. Appleton shouted to Mikkelson, "Get them in the room!"

He flung the door open, yanked Mikkelson up by the lapel, then dragged York to his feet and shoved him roughly into the room. "Get down on the floor!" he cried.

Appleton pulled Milly through the door. Her eyes blazed angrily and he saw her teeth bare as she snarled, "The bastards!"

Morley burst into the room, followed by the Day-tons. "Lie on the floor!" Appleton shouted. Everyone obeyed. He slammed the door viciously in the gray face of the state police commissioner, then addressed the Yorks, Morley, and the Daytons: "Stay here! Down behind the furniture! Don't get up until I see what the hell is going on! There may be more of them!"

He said to Mikkelson, "Get on the walkie-talkie. Tell everyone downstairs what's happened. Have them get some doctors up here. And ambulances! I think I broke the kid's larynx. And those apes shot at least one other woman. Jesus!"

Appleton flung open the door to return to the corridor. The commissioner was waiting. His lips quivered. "My boys done the right thing!" he shouted. "He had a pistol in one of them pliers' holders on his belt. He was right up on the governor! He had the gun out!" The commissioner pointed toward the bloody heap on the rug. "There it is." A small black pistol lay in the blood on the carpet.

"Leave it there," said Appleton. "Is there a doctor here yet?"

"My boys are givin' first aid to the other two we hit."

"Other *two?*" Appleton saw now that besides the woman whose leg was smashed, there was a young man lying on his back with a blood stain growing on the carpet beneath one shoulder. Appleton turned in rage on the commissioner. "A massacre! Jesus! It's just what I told you, you hillbilly moron!"

"Goddammit, we done the right thing! That man would've plugged the governor sure as hell if we hadn't shot him down."

Appleton looked at the body. It was as torn and blasted as if he had been blown up by a bomb. "You must have had all of your gorillas blazing away at once!"

He bent over the body and fished out a wallet, dripping blood, from the dead man's pants pocket and looked at the driver's license inside. "Walter Wertmuller. From Louisville." He turned the body over, not looking at the mess that had been the head. He examined the badge on the shirt. "He's the same one. He has the right button, too."

Appleton rose. He hated to ask the question. "What about the kid?"

"Dead," said a trooper. "Broken neck."

Appleton felt a stab of despair. "Who is he?"

."Allen Wertmuller—4789 Fourteenth Avenue," said the trooper, holding up a driver's license.

"A father-and-son team. Does he have a gun, too?"

The trooper took from the boy's pocket a small Smith & Wesson, Saturday Night Special. He also held up a crumpled envelope. It was addressed in a color-crayon scrawl to Governor Augustus York.

"We got our man . . . men," sighed Appleton. He took a deep breath, but he felt no relief. The moans of the two innocent victims grew louder.

Appleton returned to the suite. York was pacing the room, his face set in a dark frown, the question-mark crease deep between his eyes. Milly sat against the side of an armchair, glaring fiercely ahead. The wife of Browning Dayton sobbed quietly on the floor in a corner of the room. The vice-president-elect was conferring with Morley at the telephone. Everyone turned to Appleton when he entered.

"What can you tell us?" snapped Morley. He gestured with the phone. "Eddie Hanson is here. The press is going crazy. They know about the shots being fired, I've told them the governor and the senator are okay. Brief us—quick."

In spare, brittle sentences, Appleton recited the details of the assassination attempt, including the frightening buildup of the madmen's letters. When he was finished, Morley began to relay the story over the phone to the press secretary.

York had stopped pacing as Appleton spoke. His eyes were haggard and he said, "Those two had been stalking us for weeks?"

Appleton said, "Yes, sir. It's likely that they were. Two weeks, anyway."

"And you couldn't find out who they were? You couldn't do anything to stop them?"

"No, sir."

York gazed at him silently for a moment. Then he turned toward the sun-bright windows. "So we're at the mercy of all the craziest bastards in the country. They can kill us whenever they want to. We can't stop them, can we?"

York moved absently to the window and stood looking out. Appleton was alarmed. "Please, Governor, don't stand in front of the window. We think it's all over, but we can't be sure there aren't others, accomplices. A conspiracy."

Now Milly rose from the floor and confronted him with an angry gaze. "You aren't *sure* it's over?!"

"Not completely."

"How did you let it happen?! Why didn't you stop them *before* they got here? Why didn't you protect us!?"

Appleton adjusted his dark glasses. "We're lucky you weren't hurt, Mrs. York."

Milly's voice was quavering. "Aren't we ever going to be able to relax? To feel safe?"

"I don't know." Appleton couldn't think of anything else to say.

Browning Dayton suddenly rose from his seat. His voice crackled. "Are you the agent in charge? You ought to be doing something now! Get some more men in here! Show some power! Show some force! The next President of the United States shouldn't have to sit here holed up like a fugitive from justice."

Appleton kept his voice calm. "We have twenty agents here now, Senator."

Dayton's blue eyes were icy. "Let's order out the National Guard!" He turned to York. "Governor, you could do that. Let's show some muscle here!"

Appleton spoke as quietly as he could. "Senator, two

people were shot in the corridor because there was too much firepower around. I don't want to risk any more of that." He turned to Morley and said, "I don't want anyone to leave this room until I say so. I am in charge, and I won't allow it." Appleton didn't know if this show of authority would work or not. Officially, he was supposed to make all decisions in such an emergency, but he didn't know what he would do if they chose to ignore him.

Morley said to Dayton, "Appleton's right. We don't need the National Guard. There are enough state cops with guns around here to take the whole Viet Cong."

Dayton shook his head. "We should show force, frighten off anyone who ever thinks he can do something like this." He paused. "Has the press been allowed to see the bodies?"

Appleton said, "No."

"Get them up here! Let the world see what happens when someone takes a shot at the President! Let them see the blood, the bullet holes. Let them be thankful that Gus York is alive. Get Washington on the phone. Let's have a tough statement from the White House. Dammit! We have to look forceful in the middle of this chaos!"

Morley said, "Browning is right. I'll arrange to have a pool cameraman come up and a couple of people from the press." He went to the phone.

Appleton protested. "I don't think it's a good idea to have more people up here, sir. The situation is too touchy. We don't know enough yet."

York spoke sharply: "What's to be gained by showing all that blood and violence?"

Dayton said, "It's not a matter of what actually happens. It's the *impression* it makes. We have to appear *tough*. We're dealing in images here."

York said, "We've got these people dead. I don't know who they were. I don't know what they were doing. I don't think it's decent to drag them around in public by their heels."

"It's not a matter of decency, it's a matter of power!" said the vice-president-elect.

Morley slammed down the phone. "Okay. There'll be a pool of one TV camera, two photographers, and three reporters coming up. I'll run a press conference. Appleton, you be available to tell them what you know. Then we'll arrange a quick ceremony in here with the cameras already set up, and the governor can make his acceptance speech."

York shook his head. "Andy, are you sure this is the right thing? It just seems too damn cruel—to use two dead lunatics as part of a public relations act."

"Gus, you've trusted me in this campaign so far. Trust me now. It's the right thing," Morley said quietly.

"More packaging?"

Morley's face flushed crimson. He barked, "I don't like this damn campaign business any more than you do, Gus. Packaging isn't my business; politics is. We had to deal in some of it to get where we are—where *you* are now! *Mr. President!*" His voice sounded metallic as he spoke the unfamiliar title. "So don't start second-guessing me now."

York glared at him, then spoke more calmly. "Okay, Andy. A point well taken. But I'm tired of all this image-versus-reality crap. I'm damn mixed up as to exactly which is which."

Morley grinned tightly. "Governor, I hate to tell you, but that is exactly the point."

The pool TV cameraman, photographers, and reporters came to the blood-spattered corridor, interviewed Morley, Appleton, Mikkelson, the state police commissioner, and a couple of troopers. The gory details were duly transmitted around the world. It was shocking, sickening stuff, and television stations across the country dutifully forewarned parents that they might want to keep their children from looking at such scenes of violence and death.

An hour after the pool cameras and reporters left, York and Milly and the Daytons appeared before the cameras in the suite. York ran his tongue over dry lips and spoke quietly to perhaps 150,000,000 people: "I am saddened by the terrible thing that has happened here. It is a violent time we live in. But we must not hide in fear. I praise the Lord that we are alive, and I praise the quick action of the Secret Service and the troopers of the Kentucky State Police. This should be a moment of celebration, but it is not. It is a time of chaos and sorrow. We thank you for your votes in this election. We thank God for our lives. We, we . . . "

York choked and could not go on. Milly turned and pressed her head against his chest. Her face was stricken, her cheeks wet. York gazed bleakly into the TV lights for a moment. Then he said softly, "Please let us be alone. We are very tired." The lights went out, the cameras went dead, and the TV crew filed out of the room, silent as pallbearers.

* * * * *

Le Bombardier had decided he would work again only if there was a fortune—or a fascinating challenge—involved. As he relaxed during the long flight from Tokyo, he looked at his hands often. The fingers were long and narrow, slim as a woman's, but as he waggled them, the cords on the back of his hand danced with power. Possibly he would become serious again about the piano. He might return to Paris, that city of his childhood exile. Yes, perhaps he would return there, rich now and at leisure, once again become a serious pianist. It appealed to him.

At the San Francisco airport, Customs was lenient and he was into the terminal less than half an hour after the flight touched down. He took his bags to a men's room where there were individual dressing rooms. Inside, he removed "Hagerty's" wig, sideburns, and contact lenses. He stripped, showered, shaved, and took from his valise the navy turtleneck, corduroy jacket, jeans, and desert boots. Dressed in his own casual clothes, he packed "Hagerty's" in the suitcase, left the men's room, and went to a pay phone. He dialed a number. He said, "Darling? I'm back."

Half an hour later he parked his Porsche in front of a brick wall with a black iron gate on a small street on Nob Hill. He pushed a button in the wall twice and a buzzer sounded, opening the gate. He strode into the courtyard to a lovely red brick Victorian house. The door was opened by a young man. He was tanned; his blond hair was freshly washed. The two men looked at each other for a moment. Then Le Bombardier said in a low, admiring voice, "I missed you, darling." They embraced, and kissed, at first gently on the lips, then with eager tongues.

* * * * *

Chapter 10

Appleton awoke and saw it was still dark. This pleased him, for he had hours ahead to nestle in the warmth of the bed with Suzanne. He curled himself along her back and let the radiance of her skin work a gentle osmosis. Even in her sleep Suzanne comforted him, helping ease the despair that had gripped him since the election. Appleton kissed the nape of her neck and closed his eyes. She moved slightly and murmured, "Je t'aime."

Appleton felt sleep returning. Then the phone rang, raucous and threatening in the dark. He lunged for it and he heard a high-pitched man's voice: "You Appleton? In the Treasury Department?"

"Yes."

"This is Eddie at The Half Moon Bar on Fourteenth Street. We got a buddy of yours here, drunk out of his mind. He's broke a mirror and goosed the waitress until she won't come out of the can. He says you work together. You come get him in twenty minutes or we're callin' the cops."

"What's his name?"

"Morley. He can't walk, he can't talk, he can't see. Hurry up, or he's in the slammer for sure."

The Half Moon Bar was a seedy, cavernous place. When Appleton identified himself, the bartender pointed silently to Morley, who was seated in a booth near the back. His head was buried in his hands, his shoulders trembling. "He's half-passed out now. You owe for his drinks. He's flat. Eighteen-fifty."

Appleton paid and went to Morley. His tailored tweed suit was soiled and crumpled, the collar turned up over his bowed neck. His hair was matted, and when Appleton pulled him to a sitting position, he saw that Morley no longer had his glasses and that there was a bruise under his left eye and a cut on his lip. Dried blood was caked on his chin, and the buttons had been ripped off his shirt. And Morley stank like a skid-row flophouse.

"Come on," growled Appleton. He hauled Morley to his feet. Morley's legs were limp and unworkable, but he began mumbling and his eyes blinked open in a sickly red squint.

"Who's there?" he said. There was a note of alarm in his voice and he struggled to get his legs under him.

"Appleton."

"Thank God. Could've been a hell of a scandal, hell of a scandal. Poor ol' Gus York. Hell of a scandal. Be tragic. Love that ol' hillbilly."

Appleton put his arm around Morley's back and half-carried him toward the door. The toes of Morley's shoe tops dragged on the floor. They staggered to keep from falling. Appleton yelled to the bartender. "Some help!"

The two of them hauled Morley to Appleton's car and put him in the front seat. As they did, Morley chanted in a loud, singsong voice: "Harrison, Lincoln, Garfield, *MACK!* Harding, Roosevelt, Kennedy, *SMACK!*" He recited it like a child's nursery rhyme, emphasizing the rhyming words.

The bartender said, "He's been sayin' that same thing for hours. Half the time he's cryin', half the time gigglin'. He needs a doctor, buddy."

Appleton decided to drive Morley to the White House. It was one place where security was total: no hospital reports, no nosy orderlies. Morley was shuddering violently, his teeth chattering like a cupful of dice. When he could control his shivering, he chanted the rhyme again and again.

At the White House, Appleton drove Morley to the entrance nearest the Secret Service duty office. There were several bedrooms there, for the night-duty cadre. Bell, the agent at the desk, helped Appleton carry Morley to a bed, then hurried off to phone the physician who was always on duty. Morley lay shuddering on the bed, then suddenly sat bolt upright. "Who are you?!" he shouted.

"I'm Appleton, for Christ's sake! Lie down, you idiot!"

"Appleton! You know about the zeros. You know?" His face twisted and he began to sob. "The zeros! Oh, Jesus! The zeros are all over me. Oh god*damn* them!" He brushed at his arms desperately, then put his hands over his eyes. "Gus York is next! I love Gus York, that big hillbilly bastard, but Gus is next! That zero will get him!"

The doctor arrived and administered a shot. Morley shuddered and wept and babbled his rhyme of the Presidents' names for a few minutes. At last he relaxed and passed out. Appleton and the doctor undressed him.

"Is there going to be a lot of this?" the doctor asked warily.

"I don't know. He never did it once during the campaign. Drank a lot, but seemed to hold it all right."

The doctor wrinkled his nose. "He's really saturated."

Appleton nodded. "He works twenty hours a day. He's carried the full load of work ever since Election

Day. These transitions are strange. One bunch going out, the other coming in. Nobody's really in charge."

"Morley's the number-one guy, isn't he?"

"So far. York likes him. That should be enough."

"He'll be weak when he wakes up, but he should be okay. I'll stop in and see him in two, three hours. He'll be out till then."

Appleton looked at his watch: almost six A.M. Despite the temptation to return to Suzanne, he had to be here again at nine, so he decided to finish the night at the White House. He doubted he would sleep. Seeing Morley in this condition had shaken him. It seemed just another manifestation of the chaos which had dogged the York Presidency from the start. Everything seemed linked in a continuing chain of violence and misery.

A month had passed since the election, but Appleton still swallowed with involuntary anguish when he recalled the way the boy's neck had snapped beneath his forearm. York had sent him a handwritten note of gratitude for his part in saving the President-elect's life. Appleton had not only been cleared of any carelessness or wrongdoing, but he had been officially commended for his courage and quick reaction by Watson, chief of the Service.

But what if that young man had been an innocent high school student merely out to touch a celebrity? The question haunted him. Had Appleton known through some sixth sense that the boy was a killer? Or had he leaped on him—and *killed him with his bare hands*—without any glimmer of real evidence that the boy meant to kill York?

Appleton had tried to recall those instants precisely. But he could not remember if he had really seen a glint of gun metal. He suspected that he indeed had killed the boy without ever knowing that he was an assassin. He shuddered when he realized that his karate chop on the myopic supermarket clerk in Danbury might as easily have been fatal, too.

He was, for the time being, so unsure of his reflexes that he knew it would be difficult for him to perform his job well. He was like a boxer who killed a man with a punch and would, maybe forever, hold back a fraction of a second every time he swung and never again be the fighter he was before.

As he suspected, he could not sleep. He rose an hour after he lay down and went for a stroll in the cool morning air. He walked the length of the South Lawn and stood looking through the black steel bars of the fence toward Constitution Avenue. The street roared with rush-hour traffic. Hundreds of civil servants thronged the sidewalks. Appleton watched with a certain scorn; they were such bleak and faceless beings, the mice and moles of government bureaucracy. Yet, depressing as it was, they with their minuscule ambitions and petty occupations reflected the true size and soul of Washington far more than the power brokers, the diplomats, the statesmen who created history.

Appleton delighted in the fact that he had always operated in the rarefied atmosphere of the history makers, a place charged with the tension of great decision and graced with the luxury that goes with power. He reveled in the atmosphere of the Presidency. So antiseptic, yet so sybaritic, it was the closest an American could get to the opulence and insularity of a great king's court. Appleton believed himself to be a member of an elite palace guard, like Arthur's Knights, serving on the rim of history, privy to the greatest power the world had ever known. It was something he loved—when he let himself.

There was, he knew, an excellent chance that he would be placed in charge of York's security detail. It was enough that he had done his duty, reacted with courage in a moment of immense danger. The blood and chaos of Louisville were long gone, and so were the fatigue and fear that had so undermined him then. He would think of it no more.

At the duty desk, Bell said, "Morley's awake. He wants to see you. He doesn't seem to remember much of anything."

Morley was sitting on the side of his bed wearing a terry-cloth robe. He had showered and the smell of soap was strong and reassuring. He was wearing a pair of glasses from his office. He held a small mirror and studied the ruddy wreckage of his face. "A shave will help," he said. He rubbed the stubble, then held his hands palms down in front of him. Both trembled badly. "No blade this morning. Have you got an electric shaver?"

Appleton said, "You seem pretty used to this."

"I've had my share of binges." Morley paused. "I want to thank you for helping. It wasn't exactly the kind of thing that gets you decorated for valor, but I appreciate it."

"Is this, uh, going to happen a lot?"

"No. Absolutely not. The transition has been a bitch, that's all. Gus is still trying to get used to the size of the job. Dayton keeps trying to muscle in with his people. The Republican Committee, the big money—from Rockefellers to the Hunts—are trying to buy in on Cabinet jobs or ambassadorships. Everyone's pushing for someone. Besides that, the godawful scene in Louisville kept haunting me. I couldn't lie down to sleep without seeing that man's blown-up head. I just couldn't think of anything to do but get drunk."

"Every man to his own therapy." Appleton hesitated for a moment. "Do you remember that gibberish you were chanting?"

"Gibberish? I always get into poetry or something when I'm drunk, Appleton. One night, I'm told, it was 'The Love Song of J. Alfred Prufrock.' I get into lots of gibberish; all drunks do. I used to know a guy who, whenever he got truly loaded, would rattle off every winner of the Kentucky Derby from 1875 up to last year. Then he'd do them backward." Morley grinned, oddly pleased with these memories of binges past.

"No poetry, no horses last night. Your gibberish was something about a lot of Presidents, like Harrison and Lincoln and Garfield on up to Kennedy. What was that about? And then there were the zeros that were crawling all over your body."

"I know what it was—a pure alcoholic obsession. You've heard of that weird notion about Presidents elected in zero years?"

Appleton nodded. "They made a big thing of it when Kennedy was shot—how Presidents elected in zero years always die in office."

"Yes. I don't know why the hell it stuck with me. The damnedest things do. Once I recited paragraph after paragraph of the *Book of the Damned* by Charles Fort. Now, that is *really* weird." His voice turned deep and stentorian: "'*By progress we mean rape! Butter and beef and blood and a stone with strange inscriptions on it.*'" Morley shrugged. "I seem to store away bizarre matter that comes out when I'm drunk. I once recited the entire parking ordinance printed on a New York City parking ticket. Crazy, demented stuff."

"The zero thing fits that description."

"Right! Now I think I'll go shave and have some breakfast while I wait for the clean clothes I asked to have sent over. Please come to my office at noon. It's important."

Appleton was surprised. "Are you really feeling all right? If I drank what you drank, I'd be in a hospital for a week."

"How I feel is a sordid detail I'm going to ignore this morning. I have too much to do. With the help of a triple shot of vodka in this glass of orange juice, I will get through, on into a night of sound sleep. In the meantime, I have a full day to face."

Appleton left the bedroom and headed toward his desk. Morley was a volatile and fascinating man, possibly a political genius, although no one had yet given Andrew Morley as much credit for Augustus York's victory as they gave to the strange and oddly inept character that the former President had presented to the public. York's style and substance as President was not yet even slightly clear. Yet whatever it would be, Appleton guessed, Morley would be the key influence. Appleton thought back over some of the chief aides and confidants of Presidents he had known: Sherman Adams, Bobby Kennedy and Ted Sorenson, little Jack Valenti, Haldeman and Ehrlichman, Hamilton Jordan, Jody Powell. They were all different, but none seemed endowed with quite the capacity for hard work, erratic behavior, and unpredictable brilliance as Andrew Jackson Morley IV.

Appleton decided that he would likely find the presidential detail more interesting, more compelling than it had been for years—especially if he was promoted to chief of presidential security. Yes, he was looking forward to this job.

As he sat at his desk, Appleton could not help wondering about the zero-year phenomenon that had obsessed Morley in his drunkenness. It was something he had not thought of in many years—mainly because he had been convinced that it was such unadulterated nonsense when people brought it up following John Kennedy's death. Kennedy was, it was breathlessly reported back then, the seventh consecutive President elected in a year ending in zero to die or be murdered in office.

As a matter of curiosity, Appleton had looked up each one. He found that the string began after the election in 1840 of President William Henry Harrison. He was, at sixty-eight, the oldest man to be elected to the White House, and his life expectancy was thus severely limited, anyway. At any rate, he served the shortest term of office of all the zero-year Presidents. This was not entirely unconnected with the fact that his inaugural address was the longest ever given (about one hundred minutes) and that during the entire speech Harrison stood hatless and coatless in a cold rain on the Capitol steps. One month later, on April 4, 1841, he was dead of pneumonia.

Abraham Lincoln was first elected in 1860. He died on the morning of April 15, 1865, murdered by a gunshot wound in the chest delivered the night before by the political fanatic and actor John Wilkes Booth, from the stage of the Ford's Theater in Washington, D.C.

James Garfield was elected in 1880 and he died on September 19, 1881, after eighty sweltering days on his deathbed. The cause of Garfield's death was a foul combination of lead poisoning, bed sores, and internal infections resulting from an assassin's bullet lodged at the base of his spine. The assassin, Charles J. Guiteau, an outraged job-seeker who had been spurned by Garfield, stalked the President for more than a week before he found his chance to shoot him in Union

Station in Washington as Garfield prepared to board a train to attend commencement exercises at his alma mater, Williams College, in Williamstown, Massachusetts.

William McKinley won his second term in the election of 1900. Six months after his inauguration, he was dead, murdered by a demented anarchist named Leon Czolgosz, who shot him twice point-blank in the chest as the President reached out to shake Czolgosz's hand in a receiving line in Buffalo, New York.

Warding G. Harding was elected in 1920. He served without distinction except for several scandals, including the infamous Teapot Dome Scandal, which were perpetrated by various members of his administration. In the summer of 1923, Harding had embarked on a cross-country "voyage of understanding" which was intended to improve his fading reputation with the public. On August 2, 1923, Harding died in San Francisco of still uncertain causes. Some said it was pneumonia, others said an embolism, and still others claimed he died of a broken heart caused by the widespread disloyalty and corruption that had come to infect his administration.

Franklin Delano Roosevelt was elected to his third of four terms in 1940. He died on April 12, 1945, of a massive cerebral hemorrhage at his vacation home in Warm Springs, Georgia. He, of course, had been ill for some time.

Appleton had known too well the details surrounding the death of the last of the doomed zero-year Presidents. John F. Kennedy won election in 1960 at the age of forty-three. He was murdered on November 22, 1963, by Lee Harvey Oswald, who fired with astonishing accuracy through a lacework of tree branches from a sixth-floor window of the Dallas Book Depository Building. One bullet struck Kennedy in the neck and another in the brain as the presidential motorcade rolled past below. Kennedy was dead on arrival at Parkland Hospital less than half an hour later.

No sooner had Appleton run through his recollection of the seven dead Presidents than he decided to put the subject out of his mind—for good. The deaths were a matter of coincidence, a strange but scarcely supernatural set of facts that deserved no more thought than he had just given them. A jinx? A hex? Such was the suggestion after Jack Kennedy's murder. That was absurd. And, Appleton thought now, when he was made chief of security for President York, whatever problems he might have with the job, one of them would *never* be to concern himself over the specter of incipient supernatural forces working to bring down an eighth consecutive President elected in a zero year.

* * * * *

Chapter 11

Appleton had been sitting at his desk for some time when his intercom buzzed. He was wanted, immediately, in the office of Watson, the Secret Service director. They were old associates, though never warm friends. Watson was eight years older than Appleton, a veteran dating back to the Truman Administration. He was a steely, pragmatic bureaucrat, stern with his underlings but unfailingly jovial and obedient to his superiors. Appleton had barely sat down when Watson said brusquely, "This is going to come as a surprise to you. I want you to know before it drifts around as gossip— Mikkelson will be chief of the President's security detail. The President-elect likes him and was very impressed with his coolness when he threw himself in front of the assassin's gun. You, on the other hand, have not impressed Governor York. I'm worried about you, too, Appleton. I didn't like the way things went in Louisville. Too messy."

"You gave me a commendation." Appleton's voice was tight. His face tingled from the shock of Watson's words.

"You deserved it. You showed plenty of courage. But not much judgment. Too jumpy, too quick to see shadows. You're too jittery now to work around the President. Maybe, if you hadn't injured that woman in

Danbury, maybe if there hadn't been so much bloodshed in Louisville. It adds up to your being too skittish. Sorry."

When he could finally speak, Appleton's voice sounded to himself as if it were coming from another room. "What will I be doing?"

"You have close to ten years before normal retirement. I've looked up your records. You think you might want to retire early? That would be six years."

"Retire? I'm only forty-eight."

Watson shook his head briskly. "Reflexes go early in some men."

"I just needed a rest. Everything that went wrong in Louisville, in Danbury—all of it happened because I was too tired."

"No. I think it was more than that. Anyway, there's no appeal in this decision. It's up to the new President, who runs his security detail. He wants Mikkelson. Same thing happened to Youngblood when he jumped on Johnson the day we lost Kennedy."

Appleton said again, "What will I be doing?"

"Andrew Morley has a project for you. I know all about it. Something new." He peered over his glasses, his big head jutting forward, his jaw as bulldoggish as J. Edgar Hoover's ever was. "It's a job where your reflexes won't matter. I don't think you'll like it, though. Sorry. You're to see him at noon." He looked at his watch. "Exactly forty-five minutes."

When he finally entered Morley's office, Appleton had waited a half hour beyond the appointed time. He had sat on a hard chair along with an assortment of Republican power brokers—senators, party chairmen from different states, two well-known Washington lawyer-lobbyists, and a movie star who had appeared at a York campaign benefit. All were waiting to see Morley, who, at that point with hundreds of political appointments in his power, occupied the most influential office in Washington. Appleton had barely been able to sit still. His body felt rocked by shocks and jitters. But he had waited, outwardly unperturbed with only the flicker in his jaw revealing the tension and gloom that pervaded his being.

Morley looked amazingly relaxed and efficient. However, his hands trembled when he lighted a cigarette, and his face was so ruddy that it seemed to be lighted from within like a jack-o'-lantern. His words rolled out with his usual eastern-bred confidence: "You don't look it, but I'm sure you're devastated by the news about the security detail. There was nothing to be done. The governor was very moved by Mikkelson's actions. Anyway, this new project is terribly important. In a way, it's the premier security assignment for this Administration." Morley grinned in what was meant as an encouraging expression, but to Appleton it looked like a grimace of ridicule. Morley went on: "Of course, Watson doesn't know that yet. He thinks it's a phony little experimental thing I've dreamed up. York doesn't know about it, either. But, Appleton, when I finish explaining it to you, I think you will be terribly impressed that you have been picked for the job."

Appleton spoke glumly: "That sounds like a hard sell for a hell of a letdown."

Morley chuckled. "It does, doesn't it?" His face became serious. "But it's not. The job has to do with computerizing assassination profiles and danger ratios for the President."

"What? Listen, I know less about computers than I do about brain surgery."

Morley ignored him. "The idea behind it is to bring

presidential security into the twentieth century. You people walk around in shoes that don't squeak and you all dress like ad salesmen for *Life* magazine, but you are really nothing but a bunch of high-priced night watchmen at heart. Christ, Frank Sinatra probably has better security than the President does."

"Bullshit!" said Appleton angrily. "You just don't know enough about it. We don't spill our systems all over network TV, you know."

"I know it's better than it used to be. But you still leave too much to luck. You deal in percentages and probabilities."

"What else is there?"

"Nothing else. But this project of mine is designed to reduce the percentages and cut the probabilities that anyone will ever get a shot at the President. I want to reduce the mathematical chances of any attempt on the President's life to the smallest possible odds."

"How?"

"With a computer programmed to give us readouts on assassination potential against Gus York on any given day, in any given city, at practically any given minute. I've ordered an IBM 880, one of the most sophisticated computers for the reduction of probabilities. It's being installed in a basement suite in the Executive Office Building."

"You make computers sound like the greatest thing since religion."

"They're better! With enough data a computer can tell you just about anything within a tiny percentage of probability. If I'd had enough computer information during the campaign, we'd have known within a fraction of a decimal point what was happening on Election Day."

Appleton paused. "With this project of yours, would

we have known about the assassination attempt in Louisville?"

"Yes. But first let me tell you what the plan is. We're going to develop a huge load of input on every subversive, terrorist, and potentially threatening organization in the world—anyone who might be a threat, however remote, to the President's life. Terrorists, anarchists, Synanon freaks, Marxists, monarchists, Right-to-Lifers, radical students, American Nazis, Japanese Red Guard, the P.L.O., the I.R.A. You name it, any group that might offer a threat—however political, however paranoid, whatever the grounds. We'll have a name, a biography, a physical description on every single living individual who might pose a threat to the President."

"That's thousands of names."

"No. That's *hundreds* of thousands of names. It could get to be a million! I don't care. We want that data base to be enormous! If it includes the whole world—so be it." Morley lighted a cigarette. His fingers trembled but his voice was stronger as his enthusiasm increased. "The assassination profiles will be something like a fingerprint file that will give us insight into each one's psychological, political, and social makeup. Ultimately, we will grade them as to how much of a threat each might be to President York under certain specific conditions. Call it the Danger Ratio."

"On a *million* people?"

"It will take time, but once we've got the base data laid in, we simply add to it as each new set of kooks turns up. The initial source is obvious: you'll be plugged into every up-to-date police department in every city in the world. We'll be more intense in the States. Every sheriff's office and village constable will be asked for names and brief psycho-biographies on certain types of criminals or trouble-makers or members of potentially dangerous organizations. As an example, we would have had your man, the dead janitor in Louisville, included in our data—and we would have cut him right out of the hotel staff during the time that York was there."

"Why would we have known about him with this when we didn't turn him up in our security checks of employees?"

"He was a member of the Ku Klux Klan a few years ago."

"That doesn't make him an assassin."

"Those letters were written by a hyper-racist. And you didn't tie that in with the fact that he had also been picked up on suspicion of writing threatening letters to several city officials in 1972. And again in 1976. No proof, no conviction, but it's on the record. Without the computer to put it together in a neat, quick package and send up a red flag, you didn't make the connections about this guy. But they were there!"

"We're human." He sighed.

"That's exactly the point. The computer is infinitely better than the human mind when it comes to probabilities. It takes the probabilities in a million situations—a million *times* a million situations!—and it comes up with lists of possible and probable conditions. We are trying to deal in the smallest possible odds that someone we don't know will try to knock off Gus York under conditions we haven't anticipated."

Appleton's voice was wooden. "We cannot screen him off from every crazy in the world. The problem is infinite."

"I know that! Jesus! All I've been talking about is *averages!* Trying to cut the probabilities! No one said you can create a perfect vacuum around the man. The problem *is* infinite. But percentages are *finite!* Odds are *finite!* We are talking about finite realities, Appleton, about improving—mathematically and measurably—the odds that Gus York will *not* be assassinated in office! That's not so mysterious, is it?"

Appleton decided he would say no more. The effort was too great, and Morley's onrushing explanation could not be stopped, anyway.

"We need enormous input, a huge data base. You will have access to anything you want from the C.I.A., F.B.I., all Defense intelligence systems. Interpol and Scotland Yard and the intelligence agencies of NATO. The K.G.B. will come through for us, too."

Appleton looked up, surprised. "The Russians?"

"Sure. They don't want the balance of power threatened by assassination, either, so they'll help, up to a point. If we'd had this thing in 1963, with a tie-in from Moscow, I think their reading on Lee Harvey Oswald would have been better than our own. We'd have had him under surveillance—or at least kept him away from working that day at a place right on the President's route. The big point politically, Appleton, is that eventually we'll make this whole operation available to every country in the world. Knowing these bastards and what they're like and what they're up to—it's a great advantage in dealing with them."

Morley paused, then spoke more calmly: "This thing has to be kept absolutely current. The whereabouts of potential assassins in areas where York will be traveling has to be freshly updated and correlated almost to the minute. If York gives a speech about abortion, then goes to Detroit the next day, we check the Right-to-Life types for high-risk mental cases who might be specially angered. We make sure where they are during

York's trip there." His voice was hard. "That's not so damn far out, is it, Appleton?"

Appleton remained silent. So did Morley now. He glared steadily at Appleton; his blue eyes barely blinked. At last the Secret Service man was forced to reply: "No, it isn't so far out." Indeed, as he listened, Appleton was beginning to see the logic of it all.

"Thanks." Morley's voice rasped with sarcasm. "Now, for the rest of it. I also want to cross-program in psychological and political data covering the principals in every assassination and every assassination *attempt* in the world over the last 35 years. I want the guy who tried to kill Sukarno and the guy who used the knife in the Japanese Diet. I want data on the Algerians who tried to blow up de Gaulle and the generals who tried to kill Hitler. I want stuff on Sirhan Sirhan and James Earl Ray, and on the two women who tried to get Ford in San Francisco. . . ."

Appleton gasped. "Why? What will it prove?"

"I don't know—that's the point. There might be some patterns, some scraps of information, some consistent aberration or relationships that aren't clear until you get them all hooked up together in the computer. There could be patterns of some kind. Who knows what? We may find that eight percent of all assassinations in the twentieth century were done by bombs, that five percent were done by women with red hair when the population of the world shows only three percent of the women have red hair. That's an aberration—that's not average. It might help in our planning."

"It might not help at all."

"True! But we will be alerted, forewarned, if there are some patterns in that material. I am not leaving anything to chance when it comes to protecting Gus York from bloody-minded freaks like that lunatic in Louisville. *Everything* is to be done, Appleton, to keep that from happening again. *Everything!*"

Morley's eyes had turned cold, the blue in them all the icier for the ruddy flush of his face. He pulled a bottle of Jack Daniels from his desk and poured some into a paper cup. "Want some?" Appleton shook his head. Morley took a swallow, then cleared his throat. "There is one other thing I want in this program. That is the 'zero factor.' By that I mean I want every scrap of detail that can be dug up about the conditions and situations that prevailed during the deaths of each of the last seven Presidents elected in a year ending in zero."

Appleton started. "What?!"

Morley's grim expression did not change. He glanced at his watch. "I've got half the power in Republican politics waiting out there for me. I've got to fly out to Hilton Head tonight to York's transition headquarters. I'm not screwing around with this stuff to give you a cheap rush. And I'm not going to sit here *selling* you on it. Just listen to what I'm saying, because you will be expected to know it—and to *do* it—when I'm finished. What was similar about Roosevelt's death and Garfield's? Time of day? Position of the stars? What had preceded the deaths?"

Morley paused, his eyebrows shot up, and his eyes were wide and innocent behind his spectacles. He said crisply, "Frankly, I can't believe this myself. As I told you this morning, I think the zero phenomenon is one hundred percent coincidental, disconnected, random. But I don't *know* that. I do not *absolutely know it!* If it were by some wild quirk a real curse—whatever that may mean—then it's obviously beyond our means to do anything about. But I certainly don't believe it is. And I just want to see if anything comes out of it—*anything at all!*"

Appleton spoke cautiously. "Some of it makes sense. The assassination profiles program is something we probably should have had years ago."

Morley ducked his head in a mock bow of gratitude. Appleton continued: "But some of it is pure black magic."

"Not necessarily. We won't know what it is until we get it all together, mixed, and programmed for probabilities and variables. We don't know for sure."

Resignedly, Appleton said, "But I don't know anything about computers. How can I run a program like this?"

"You have been brought in from the cold, my friend. You are possibly lucky to have a job at all. I don't care if you think you *can* do it or not! You *will* do it!" Morely's voice rose angrily. He caught himself, took a deep breath and another short sip of whiskey. "Okay. I'm tired, hung over, and sick of all this," he said more softly. "That's the program. You've heard it. Will you do it?"

"Will I? I have to, don't I?"

"Yes. You do."

Appleton rose from the chair. He felt stiff and weary and confused. He turned silently toward the door, refusing to say another word to Morley. But Morley's voice crackled at his back: "Your new office is 1017-B in the Executive Office Building. Down in the basement. The crews from IBM are setting up the computer. You have a staff assigned, including one of the best computer programmers from the Pentagon." Appleton remained at the door, his back turned. Morley's voice softened a bit. "You'll get used to it, Appleton."

Outside Morley's office, Appleton hesitated. He saw, waiting impatiently, the assembled members of the Republican power bloc. They glared as if he were to blame for their long wait. Appleton wanted nothing more than to return to where this dismal day had begun—snug and warm next to Suzanne's warm body. But it was only three in the afternoon and she would not return from her job in the press and V.I.P. reception office at the French embassy for two hours. Consequently, he turned and headed toward office 1017-B in the E.O.B. He thought he might as well see what oblivion looked like.

* * * * *

Chapter 12

York lay in a chaise longue on the patio of his condominium at Hilton Head. The Atlantic breeze was fresh and salty. It ruffled his coppery hair. The soft flow of the wind across his bare chest reminded him vaguely of the feel of Milly's hands on his skin. He grinned at this new feeling of contentment. At first, he and Milly had been like a pair of plane crash survivors, numbed by the enormity of the horror they had experienced. Now, more than a month later, their sanity was somewhat recovered and their natural vitality had renewed itself.

Milly came out onto the porch, her shoulders brown and shining in the sun, her white smile cutting like a bright light across her tanned face. "Darling, let's take the bikes for a long ride this afternoon. A picnic and . . . "—she dropped her voice to a husky imitation of Mae West—" . . . we'll go swimming in the nude somewhere out on the banks."

York grinned. Milly was as vivacious now as when he had first met her. The night before she had sat at a piano in the main bar and, to the delight of York and three dozen members of his transition staff, sang "Stormy Weather," "Smoke Gets in Your Eyes," "Mood Indigo"—a whole repertory of the dated dance-band standards that had been her specialty.

York knew her songs were far richer in nostalgia than in musicality, yet God knows her face was as radiant, her eyes as alive with romance now as almost twenty years before.

"I can't go anywhere," York answered with a grimace. "I have meetings with fat cats and polecats, tomcats and every kind of Republican bird and beast you can name. Don't tempt me, darling. I've never played hooky with a naked woman, but I suspect it would beat the hell out of bullhead fishing, which is what I did when I really played hooky."

"You can't postpone them? Just skip out for two hours?"

He shook his head. "I have to take hold of this now, Milly. Andy's been in Washington three weeks now while we've been resting and recovering. He'll be back tonight with a whole raft of ideas. Hell, love, we have to put together a whole government by seven weeks from now."

"We've needed every second we had to recover. Especially from Louisville."

"I know it," he said.

"Those first days here, I couldn't look anywhere—not on the beach, not in a corner of the bedroom, not *anywhere*—without seeing that man's blown-up body. And the dreams . . . You yelled or screamed or got up and walked somewhere every night the first two weeks."

"It's an old habit from boyhood. I used to walk in my sleep all the time. Woke up more nights than I can count in a dead-white moonlit clearing in the woods. Always talking to my dead granddaddy or my dead friend Orville Wallace, who was run over by a freight train. My mama used to say that bad dreams were good because they released your craziness, cleansed the mind of black thoughts that would drive you insane otherwise."

"We've come a long way this month," Milly sighed. "Even the idea of living in the White House is beginning to seem natural."

York raised his eyebrows. "Milly, I must confess I am beginning to like this situation. You can't believe the service you get when you're President. You can't believe the bowing and scraping. Everybody walking quiet and talking quiet. 'Yes, sir; no, sir.' Makes me nervous, Milly, but I *am* learning to like it."

"What makes me nervous is that I feel so *watched*."

York sighed. "Privacy is not a privilege of the mighty, my darling. Power, prosperity, mighty perquisites go with this job." He laughed. "So we give up swimming naked for a chance to run the world for a few years. Not a bad trade, is it?" Milly did not answer.

The machinery of transition to the York Administration had begun to grind slowly the week after the election. Morley and a dozen assistants held the first of hundreds of meetings in Washington to assemble and sort through recommendations for people able, willing, or deserving of appointment in the new Administration. Now that York's vacation was over, the scene would shift from Washington to the beach resort of Hilton Head, where the so-called Transition White House would be located. Already fifty staff men and women had moved into the bungalows and condominiums of the resort. Conference rooms and offices were equipped, and a York Administration switchboard with a hundred phones had been installed. A temporary TV studio and a dozen mobile TV control-room vans had been imported. A huge press room with facilities for two hundred was ready. A helicopter landing pad had been built. Even a special post office had been created to handle the tons of York Administration mail. Couriers flew in via Lear jets four times a day bringing briefings from the White House to keep York up to the minute on decisions and events in Washington.

Inexorably, the gargantuan machinery of the Presidency was pressing tighter around Gus York. Ultimately, it would surround him and isolate him from all other forms of life. He did not fully comprehend that yet, but the transformation of the resort into a gleaming presidential command post, manned with armies of executives and technicians, and hooked up with communications to the world, did give him his first realistic insight into exactly how vast—indeed, how *super-human*—were the powers of the Presidency.

His meeting that morning was with half a dozen Republican power brokers, an informal steering committee of advisors that party headquarters had created to advise York during the transition. Included were the House and Senate minority leaders, plus a small, glittering collection of businessmen, lawyers and various mover-shakers with money, influence and/or power to burn, plus Vice President-elect Browning Dayton, plus a tremendously fat, rich, silky smooth Texan named Len Buhler, who had become the national party chairman replacing the distraught and vituperous Peg Ironwood.

The group gathered on a sun-splashed veranda. Breakfast was over and as the coffee cups were refilled, York said, "Where do we start? The Cabinet? Might as well. Secretary of State? I'm here to listen to what you have to say."

Dayton cleared his throat. He was tanned, and he wore a tennis sweater, sneakers, and white pants. He looked ten years younger than he was. "Governor, we all have our ideas about the Cabinet. But there's something to discuss first, something a little closer to the White House."

"Okay."

"The administrative staff is the question. Governor, who do you propose to be your chief of staff?"

Before York could reply, Buhler, the party chairman, spoke in a growling drawl: "The question is: Who will replace Morley? Chief of White House staff is more important to this transition process and to your Administration than any Cabinet job. I have some suggestions, and I know the others here do, too."

York was stunned. "Replace Andy Morley? What the hell does *that* mean?"

"Exactly that, Governor," said Buhler. His obesity added a surprising authority to his words. "Replace Andy Morley."

A congressman from Indiana spoke up in a tranquil, ministerial voice: "He's not the kind of man that job demands, Governor. He's a drinking man. You know that. He's got a bad record for holding jobs. There's a real question whether he has the, uh, moral size to hold that job."

A California lawyer spoke in a flat, commanding bark: "Washington hasn't been your bailiwick, Governor. Spending all your time in Kentucky, you might not realize that the chief of staff position is more demanding, more important than any in your administration."

York held up one large hand. "Hold it! Goddammit! I may not be an insider, but I am surely aware that that job is as important as any I ever fill in my life. And I have never—not once—considered the possibility that Andy Morley would *not* have the job." He was a bit breathless from surprise at this early conflict.

The group was still, an electric tension running through them. This was a power play of great magnitude, York realized.

A New York City broker was the only one in a full suit and vest and tie at the breezy resort, and he spoke with a clipped inflection reminiscent of Morley's own speech: "Andrew Morley is a brilliant media consultant. He has a first-rate analytical mind for domestic politics. He is well connected in the party—or at least he was. But Andrew Morley is a drunk and a volatile personality. Among his friends in the Republican establishment and among those people who knew him in school, as I did, he is not considered reliable."

"Then why did you appoint him to run my campaign?" asked York.

There was a tick of hesitation. Then Len Buhler drawled, "Because no one thought there was a chance you'd win, Governor. We threw Andy in because he'd done well in a couple of other campaigns. But I tell you, he would not have been the campaign manager if there had been any other candidate with a glimmer of hope."

York spoke carefully. "But now that this bedraggled and godforsaken campaign produced a victory—and a Republican President—I am telling you that Andy Morley is the man for that job as long as I am the man for my job." He looked at the faces around him, stiffened in disapproval, and he was, for an instant, intimidated. But he continued loudly: "I will not consider any other man to be the quarterback of my team."

The New York broker said sarcastically, "Come now, Governor, this is no football game where you talk of quarterbacks and touchdowns and goal-line stands. You will control a good part of this earth, Governor, and a good part of the fearsome technology of destruction and war that has been developed on this planet in this century. Don't utilize football slang in that context. It sounds like Jerry Ford."

The California lawyer added, "Morley cannot produce the kind of cooperation from businessmen that you will need."

A senator from Illinois said, "That's true on the Hill, too, Governor. Morley is not well thought of. You can't stand fast, refusing to compromise at all, you know. The point is along the lines of what the late Sam Rayburn said to young freshman Congressman Lyndon Johnson: 'Son, to get along, you got to go along.' There is a mutuality, shall I say, Governor, that is involved in all things that ever get done in Washington."

York was angry. "I am not going to succumb either to blackmail or to sugar-tit promises. Andy Morley is my chief of staff. He is an intelligent and honorable man, and dammit, I have been known to take a drink myself. There will be no more said about it."

A glassy silence fell over the group. Despite the firmness of his stand, York felt uneasy. These were slick, confident people. They represented the core of national political power. They were the root source and soul of American government as it really operated. No decisions were made without the acquiescence of these people, without their influence, their advice, their money. They could make him, and they could certainly break him. He would have to do his best to keep conflict at a minimum, and that would not be difficult in picking the rest of his Administration; he felt about no other man and no other job as strongly as he felt about having Andrew Morley as his number-one aide.

"Let's get on to the next subject," York said.

Len Buhler spoke as if there had been no argument: "The oil people have submitted one list and the construction crowd has come in with another for suggested Cabinet and sub-Cabinet appointees," He turned his bulging eyes on York. "These, of course, are just suggestions."

As the weeks of December slipped past, the suggestions for Cabinet posts became appointments. York did not resist—or particularly resent—the pressure of various special-interest groups. He was woefully ill supplied with powerful friends or associates in business and politics outside Kentucky. He did not push for a heavy contingent of Kentuckians—nor did he want to: the lesson of the last Administration had been well learned. Using Andy Morley's advice and experience as his best touchstone with the realities of the game, York watched as his Administration took on size and life. The process was, as always, a machine-like fitting of people to positions, weighing a man's intellect, judgment, and natural ability to perform a job against his political clout, his contributions, the party debts he may have accrued over the years. As Morley had said to York early in the game: "You are finding parts for an engine. It is a great big political engine, and that means that efficiency isn't *necessarily* the main object of every part. There are a hundred reasons for picking these parts. Some of them aren't too pretty. But, then, who ever heard of a pretty engine?"

York grimaced, then grinned. "I'm learning, Andy,

I'm learning. I just wish sometimes that 'practicality' and 'payoff' didn't mean the same thing so damn often."

* * * * *

Chapter 13

As he looked at himself in the full-length mirror, York felt a rush of triumph. He wore the traditional black frockcoat and gray striped trousers of formal morning dress. A top hat was tilted forward to his bushy eyebrows. The inauguration would begin in an hour. He was delighted with his appearance. Just the right stuffy look of dignity, plus a sense of continuity in that this was the same Victorian apparel worn by Taft and McKinley, Teddy Roosevelt, Franklin Roosevelt, Woodrow Wilson, John Kennedy. . . .

His valet brushed York's shoulders. A small, graying, energetic man, George had been at this job since the years of Harry Truman and had developed an easy familiarity with his charges. He said, "Governor, I want you to know that these very shoulders laid low many of my favorite members of the Redskins in many a game. Now that I see them up close, I can see why."

York grinned. "So now, in revenge, you have me all dressed up so I look like a nightclub tap dancer, right, George?"

"No, sir. You look exactly like a President," said the little man as he stepped back to look up at York's monumental figure. "Exactly."

"Well, don't either of us forget that under this fancy thread there is nothing but the body of an aging

Chicago Bear, aching and whining from all those licks it took."

"Not too many Presidents took licks like that, Governor," said George.

A soft tap sounded at the door. Milly entered and for a second York was truly stunned by her appearance. Her gown was ivory silk and her only jewelry was a gold locket that had hung on the watch chain of York's grandfather. He took a breath. "You look like a bride," he said in an awed voice.

She did an exaggerated curtsy, then moved toward him, seeming almost to float. The door clicked softly as George slipped out. York embraced her and she kissed him, leaving a lipstick smear on his mouth. She leaned back in his embrace and began to dab at it with her fingers, but he held her closer. She put her arms around his neck and playfully pushed against him, the pulse and warmth of their bodies exciting them both.

She stood on tiptoes and tightened against his hardness. She whispered, "What would the chief justice say if he knew about that?"

York held her tighter and then he chuckled. "Seems a little out of place in these fancy pants, doesn't it?"

She burst into husky laughter and stepped back. "Darling, the nation would be delighted to know it is going to be led by a President with such healthy drives!"

York laughed. "Healthy drives! Damn right! And I'm going to *stay* that way! I am not going to let them bamboozle me, take away my pride and take away my *self*. I've made a decision: I'm going to be the Kentucky mountain man that I am. Milly, goddammit, I'm even going to put my hands in my pockets when I feel like it. In public. When I'm making speeches. Whenever I damn well feel like it! I'm going to be myself."

Milly embraced him again. "I thought you might come around to that."

His eyes beamed as he strode excitedly about the room. "Hell, *yes*, Milly! Yes, *ma'am!* I might get up at midnight to go 'coon hunting on the South Lawn. I might just decide to rassle one of those barbered-up stuffed shirts from the Republican Committee at the next Sunday school picnic. I might stock the fountains with bullheads. I might go *barefoot,* for God's sake, to the Cabinet meetings. I don't *know* what all I'm going to do, Milly, but it's all going to be me!"

An hour later he stood high on the steps of the Capitol. A biting wind swirled in gusts. It ruffled his hair and brought tears to his eyes. The chief justice read the oath of office and York's cheeks gleamed wet as he repeated it. When he turned to kiss Milly, she dabbed at the tears with the fingers of her gloved hand, and they laughed.

A crowd of perhaps twenty thousand spilled below him like a carpet spread down the Capitol steps and out along the streets and on into the park across from the Capitol. Their breath steamed white in the frosty sunshine and their faces gleamed. When York finished his brief address, the crowd thundered approval, and he felt a surge of exhilaration. He raised his arms to the sky, hands opened and palms upward. The tears that streamed down his cheeks now were no longer caused by the wind. A marine band played the march hymn, "Hail to the Chief." He was the fortieth President of the United States. He felt he would live forever.

* * * * *

Le Bombardier and his lover lazily watched the televised inauguration of President York from their San

Francisco home. They made sardonic remarks at the rustic bigness of the man, snickered at the seemingly endless documentary profiles of his Horatio Alger-like rise out of backwoods poverty to the White House. Le Bombardier had no ideological interest in politics, nor did he have more than the slightest passing interest in the rumpled former football player. For, of course, he had no idea at that moment that their lives would ever cross.

Indeed, it would have been hard to imagine two lives less obviously destined to intertwine. The single most formative event in the early years of this cosmopolitan killer was the Russian Revolution, and he had not even been born. The revolution had forced his father and mother to flee Russia in 1919, leaving their vast coal mines in Shakty in the steppes to the Bolsheviks. They settled in Paris, in an anxious and neurotic community of exiles. Born in 1924, Le Bombardier grew up in a wildly warped environment. His father, a handsome and gentle man, could find no suitable work to support his family in the luxury they required. Thus, he began a life-long series of vaguely explained "voyages" with rich and often older women. Le Bombardier's mother, a frail, wide-eyed woman, spent most of her time in Paris sipping vodka and weeping in a darkened parlor. It was a bleak and demented home, but thanks to the persistent labors of his father, Le Bombardier was able to attend schools in Italy, Spain, and Germany. He became fluent in the languages of these countries, and he also spoke French, English, and his family's native Russian. He was considered a prodigy at the piano, and for a time he was taken out of school, tutored, and forced to practice the piano twelve hours a day. Eventually, he rebelled against this regime, and by the time he was in his teens he had also become a splendid horseman, a good cricket batsman, and an excellent soccer goalie. His early education included other broader forms of learning; when he was fourteen he was seduced by a regal and exquisite Russian duchess in her seventies. She told him that she had also been a patron of his father and that the young boy was, in her opinion, a far more accomplished lover than his father had ever pretended to be. At sixteen, his uncle seduced him in the compartment of a train traveling between Paris and Nice.

All this, plus the harsh, cynical atmosphere of Europe in the late 1930s, understandably made him suspicious of everything and everyone. At that time, too, politics were so volatile that expedience seemed the only way to survive; passion and commitment to causes or to people seemed foolish and even dangerous. To espouse a deeply felt conviction, to speak one's opinions freely, even to love someone absolutely—these things were neither practical nor possible.

In 1941 his father died. Le Bombardier was later told he had passed away in the arms of a rich and syphilitic young Austrian count. It was likely true; the last money to arrive at the darkened apartment in Paris was in Austrian shillings. A year later, his mother slashed her wrists with the glass shards of a vodka bottle. Le Bombardier was then sent to England by his uncle, where he spent the remaining war years. The uncle visited him periodically and demanded that they become lovers or he would send no money and Le Bombardier would be left penniless and alone.

Thus, before he was twenty, Le Bombardier was keenly aware that there was nothing in the world he could trust except his own cold calculations—and the colder, the better. Like his father, he became a gigolo for a time, and in the 1950s his photograph was often seen on the society pages of Europe's newspapers in the company of rich women, some beautiful, some old, some lame and disfigured.

At one point, one of his patrons became obsessed with the idea of murdering her husband, a well-known corporation president and playboy. Le Bombardier was fascinated by the challenge, and ultimately, after weeks of analysis and investigation, produced such a masterly and meticulous plan for killing the man that the murder has ever since stood as one of the most popular unsolved crimes in the world.

Le Bombardier found this a powerfully satisfying experience. Eventually, he performed this same service for two other women and a man he consorted with. It was only a short step to offering his talents to a wider international market where motives for murdering were more impersonal, more businesslike—and more profitable. He was able to establish connections and an underground network that allowed potential customers to communicate with him. His reputation for precision workmanship was beyond dispute. So—ironically enough—was his reputation for integrity. He had once taken $250,000 from an American oil company representative in advance payment for the negotiated assassination of a Greek owner of a mammoth fleet of oil tankers. The man had threatened to bar American shipments from his vessels, as well as from some 50 percent of the other tankers' fleets in the world unless he was paid several million dollars. The extortion scheme did not particularly offend Le Bombardier, nor did he feel any moral compunction to help keep the American economy afloat by killing this man. Nevertheless, the man died of a heart attack two days before Le Bombardier was prepared to murder him, and within a week, the American oil company received a money order for $175,000—repayment of all the advance except for Le Bombardier's expenses and fee for "preliminary procedures."

Le Bombardier always succeeded when he performed, but, more important to the businessmen and politicians he dealt with, he always kept his bargains. Thus, he had arrived at the pinnacle of his profession, such as it was. But as he watched the grand figure of Gus York stand at the pinnacle of his own career, on the steps of the United States Capitol, this gusty, bright day in January, 1981, he felt nothing about the man or the occasion. On this day, Le Bombardier was consumed by his own deep sense of luxury and comfort in his opulent home. He still soared from the intense satisfaction of his success in Kyoto and from the euphoric realization that he might never have to work again. Now he felt a rising tide of desire and he turned to the lovely young man next to him on the sofa and said, "Darling, I need you to love me. Now."

* * * * *

Chapter 14

Appleton gazed bleakly through his dark glasses at Norman Brandeis. He was a short, thin, sallow man with beady black eyes. Brandeis was Appleton's chief computer analyst—a genius, Morley had said, at the arcane business of wiring computer circuitry to produce formulas of logic better than any human mind could ever imagine. Morley had entitled Appleton's project Computerized Intelligence on Personnel Hazard and Environmental Risk, so it would have the acronym CIPHER—"In honor of the zero factor." Of Brandeis, Morley had said, "They tell me he's brilliant. He's so good that I had to threaten to demote a four-star general before they would cut him loose."

Appleton found Brandeis less impressive. He was one of the most banal human beings he had ever encountered. At times he seemed to be the symbol and the epitome of the civil servant. Brandeis brought his lunch in a crumpled, brown bag each day, and in the apparent assumption that Appleton laid awake each night wondering what was in it, Brandeis began each morning with a brisk recital of his lunch menu: "Pimento and cheese loaf on pumpernickel bread, two pieces of celery, black olives, a couple of Lorna Doones, hot coffee." Brandeis was also compulsive in his fascination with the lunches of other people. He questioned each secretary and assistant programmer about the contents of their lunch bags every day. He had been plainly disappointed when he found that Appleton never brought his lunch and, instead, ate at the White House mess.

Brandeis complained frequently about the brevity of the official civil service lunch hour, which was not an hour at all, but only forty-five minutes. He told Appleton, "Human beings in the twentieth century have advanced to the point where lunch is a ritual. It is a measure of prestige and significance how long a man can take for lunch. Forty-five minutes is the lunch hour of a laborer, not an executive." He would say these things as he bit ritualistically into his egg salad sandwiches and his Hydrox cookies, taken from his inevitable brown bag.

As Appleton listened day after day to Brandeis on lunch, he could not help but recall some of the sumptuous meals he had enjoyed during various trips with various Presidents: truffles in Paris, Salzburger pastries in Vienna, Peking duck in China. He decided that the sybaritic aspects of the Secret Service were something he had not appreciated sufficiently.

And neither, he decided, had he been sufficiently appreciative of the taste of clothing among his former colleagues. They dressed in the muted-suit-and-black-shoe wardrobe of bankers and attorneys the world over, boring attire with scarcely a spot of plumage or color to lighten the propriety of it all. By contrast, Brandeis dressed like a circus clown. He mixed plaids and checks and stripes in his polyester double-knit wardrobe of leisure suits and three-piece interchangeable "outfits" so that Appleton thought at first it was his idea of a joke. But, of course, it was not, for Brandeis had no sense of humor.

All in all, Appleton felt imprisoned by routine and suffocated by ordinariness. Each morning, Brandeis and the CIPHER staff discussed the TV programs they had seen the night before, reliving again the antics of Laverne, Shirley, Mindy, Mork, Fonzie—names that Appleton was only vaguely familiar with. An enervating sense of melancholy gripped him when he heard these conversations, but Appleton maintained his usual stiffness.

The banality of Brandeis notwithstanding, programming for CIPHER had progressed smoothly. Morley pressed constantly for finished readouts, but Brandeis told Appleton that he doubted it would be usable until late in February. Mikkelson had been told of the project and visited Appleton a week after York's inauguration. He could not entirely disguise his supercilious attitude toward Appleton, but he tried to be congenial.

Rather than reveal his own frustration, Appleton was abrupt and businesslike with Mikkelson.

A gray-haired woman, a secretary with a perennial whine in her voice, approached Appleton's desk while Mikkelson was still in the room. "Sir, excuse me, but the requisition forms we have for software circuitry are all wrong, all wrong."

"Yes?"

"They are all TD-190's, Mr. Appleton."

He waited for her to go on, but she plainly felt the situation was self-explanatory. "I don't know what that means," said Appleton.

"They're Treasury Department forms." The self-pitying whine went on. "We need White House forms—EO-1782's."

Appleton sighed. "So order the right ones."

"I need your signature."

He signed the piece of paper she put on his desk. When she left, he looked up to see that Mikkelson was not troubling to conceal a smirk. Appleton refused to speak, and Mikkelson finally said, "Better get those forms right, old man. Morley is getting mighty impatient." At the door, he turned and said archly, "And I'd like to see some results, too."

Appleton swallowed his irritation and turned back to CIPHER. Enormous amounts of data were arriving. A special Telex network had been arranged with hundreds of police departments and intelligence agencies around the world. Profile after profile poured in defining people who might someday conceivably wish to kill a President. The range of personalities, types, and motives was mind-boggling and terrifying. Profiles ranged from muttering old anarchists to the bright young fanatics of Italy's Red Brigade. There were former American Communist Party members, survivors of the Baader-Meinhoff gang in West Germany, the American Nazi Party, the once-fierce Black Panthers, the long disbanded Students for a Democratic Society, The John Birch Society, the Jewish Defense League. There was a smattering of profiles on the few pathetic remaining members of the People's Temple of Jim Jones and a huge list of the wild-eyed patriots of Free Cuba groups in Miami. If there was a loud-mouthed lunatic in Cincinnati known for raving on street corners, there was also the secretive and efficient terrorist corps of the Japanese Red Guard, trained to kill for politics.

The data grew daily. By mid-February there were almost 300,000 names on file, with that many more on the way. Everywhere, the response from law enforcement or intelligence agencies had been superb, including the Soviets, who weighed in with background on certain defectors and dissidents inside and outside the Soviet Union. Brandeis worked out codes and keys for organizing the data in the computer. He keyed them to psychological definition, physical appearance, political orientation, and modus operandi if they were functioning terrorists or trained killers.

Appleton plowed through every scrap of raw data himself and sent hundreds of requests for clarification of fuzzy details or incomplete descriptions. As the material increased and more was classified and computerized, Appleton realized with a sense of almost explosive revelation that if this data had been available in 1963, this infernal machine would definitely have coughed up the name of Lee Harvey Oswald and the fact that he worked at a building on John Kennedy's motorcade route. They definitely would have had Oswald under surveilance and Kennedy's murder would *not* have happened. . . .

Appleton also checked to see if CIPHER might have worked in regard to the assassins of the other three Presidents. Again, it was impressive; CIPHER would almost certainly have warned about Lincoln's killer, John Wilkes Booth, for he was notorious for the fanaticism of his politics of slavery. He definitely would not have been allowed into Ford's Theater. William McKinley was murdered by the well-known anarchist Leon Czolgosz, and he could not have gotten within point-blank pistol range of the President if CIPHER had existed. The murder of James Garfield probably could not have been stopped. Charles Guiteau was an ostensibly respectable man who had flown into a rage because Garfield did not appoint him to the civil service job he wanted. Though he stalked the President for days before he killed him, Guiteau's background offered no reason for programming his name into the computer.

As Morley had said, lessening the odds for assassination, however little, would make it all worthwhile. Cutting three out of four was miraculous. Appleton's admiration for Morley rose considerably.

The data on past assassinations and attempts seemed less useful than the current profiles, although the historical trivia was fascinating to Appleton. Incidents ranged from the shooting of Archduke Francis Ferdinand in Sarajevo in 1914 to the murder of Huey Long on the Capitol steps in Baton Rouge in 1935, from the unsolved assassination of Malcolm X in 1963 to the murder of Mayor Cermak in Chicago in 1933 (a bullet probably intended for Franklin Delano Roosevelt). The attempts on Hitler's life were in the data along with the murders of Mahatma Gandhi, Martin Luther King, Robert F. Kennedy, labor leader Joseph Yablonski, Dominican dictator Rafael Trujillo. Again, Brandeis and his assistants patiently categorized the data and fed it into the computer in order to produce a comprehensible composite pattern of twentieth-century assassinations—weapons used, places, times of day, political motivations, psychological insights. . . .

Along with historical information, every police and intelligence agency involved in CIPHER had been asked to report immediately any new assassinations or attempts, complete with as much detail as possible. One of the first responses came from the prefect of police in Kyoto. Prodded by the Japanese intelligence agency which had been most enthusiastic about CIPHER, Kyoto began to transmit details on the assassination of the Labor agitator Imai Hitsu. There were no clues as to the identity of the killer. The authorities had ascertained, however, that plastique had been used to kill Imai and that the explosion had likely been triggered by a remote-control device in the vicinity.

After grilling members of the Red Independence Party, it was ascertained that a mysterious German named "Steinbugler" had been on the stage with Imai and that this man had disappeared immediately after the explosion.

The description of "Steinbugler" was vague: six feet, two inches tall, stooped, steel-rimmed spectacles, a brushed-back graying pompadour, sharp features, with many pockmarks, about fifty or sixty years old. The Kyoto police found that no one named "Steinbugler" had been registered at any hotel or ryokan in the city. They found a black imitation leather suitcase in an alley with some clothes made in East Germany, but nothing further to identify them as "Steinbugler's". They checked the ticket lists of airlines flying out of Japan, but of course there was no "Steinbugler" on any of them. The trail went cold.

This data arrived for CIPHER in January, but it was a month before Brandeis completed a proper program that could set up a correlation of assassinations over the past ten years. Now the Kyoto killing suddenly took on new significance. It was CIPHER working at its best. The computer produced the information that the modus operandi of the Kyoto murder—plastique exploded by a remote-control device while the victim was in an exposed public place—had occurred in no less than seven other assassinations since 1975. The victims included an Arab oil sheikh, a pearl merchant in Hong Kong, an army general in Bogota, two Italian industrialists, a German scientist thought to be a traitor, and a French cabinet minister. In each case the form of the murders was identical, and in four of the killings a tall man with sharp features and pockmarks like "Stein-bugler"—though differing in many other physical characteristics—had been noticed in the vicinity at the time of the murder.

Once CIPHER detected these coincidences, Appleton sent a query for more details to Interpol and to each city where the killings had occurred. This produced a message from Interpol which indicated that because the two Italian and the French murders had all occurred in a period of eighteen months, Interpol detectives had initially considered the possibility that they were done by one man. They had applied the code name "Le Bombardier" to his file. However, when he did not appear again, to their knowledge, the idea and name were forgotten.

Appleton revived it. The knowledge that there was a Le Bombardier, an expert in plastique explosives who seemed capable of striking anywhere in the world in a variety of guises, could be of enormous value. Because of the vast difference in the types of victims, it was obvious that Le Bombardier was not a political fanatic, but a professional assassin. Appleton was now terribly impressed with CIPHER.

If it could produce Le Bombardier, there was no telling what other wonders it might work.

* * * * *

Chapter 15

Milly sat on a sofa in the Princess Room waiting for York to arrive for lunch. Sun streamed through the arched windows; the soft yellow walls and woodwork caught the light and held it until every surface, even the air, seemed infused with sunshine. Milly loved this radiant room with its muted decor and exquisite antiques.

It was the environment of royalty—at least in these years of the imperial Presidency, it was what passed for American royalty. Thus, it was as alien to Milly York as it would have been to any other American, save that rare handful bred to old money. Milly's world had had little money, old or new. Her Slavic parents were in their forties when she was born. Her father, a tall and sinewy man, was a laborer in the steel mills of Pittsburgh. Her mother, thin and dour, was compulsively neat, slaving in her home as if cleanliness were her only possible redemption in this mortal world. Both died within ten months of each other when Milly [*]—her name was Woiscosky then—was nine. The year was 1944, and she was bundled off to live with her father's older sister in a town in downstate Indiana. Aunt Sofia was charming, superstitious, and a flirt. She was as funny and girlish as Milly's parents had been somber and aged. Aunt Sofia's husband, a flamboyant traveling

155

salesman, had died years before of a heart attack in a hotel bed with a whore in Newport, Kentucky. Aunt Sofia had shrugged at this sordid circumstance and buried him without bitterness. She then went blithely on to live her life, which included a few traveling salesmen of her own. By the time Milly moved in, Sofia was in her fifties and had finished her career as a source of free love for salesmen. She subsisted by giving piano lessons on a square-shouldered upright piano in the parlor. The day Milly arrived, she barely had time to drop her suitcase and drink a glass of milk before Aunt Sofia sat her down to practice scales.

If Aunt Sofia's romantic life had come to an end in physical ways, it never flagged in her mind or her dreams. She was a radio soap opera fanatic and scheduled her piano lessons so she was free to listen daily to the episodes of "Helen Trent," "Portia Faces Life," and her favorite, "Our Gal Sunday."

Each day when Sofia's piano lessons were finished, she would regale Milly with an ad-lib recapitulation of each program, far funnier and far steamier than the one on the radio. Milly listened, round-eyed and entranced.

Milly was fourteen when Aunt Sofia suggested that she become a singer. It was 1949 and Sofia was convinced that since there was a critical shortage of English lords in soap-opera Indiana, Milly's next best path to wealth and fame lay in the big bands. Milly had a sweet, clear voice. She first sang and played the piano with a high school swing band. When she was seventeen, she graduated from high school and went on the road with Buddy Koopmans' Engineers of Swing. They traveled the Midwest for a year, playing one-night stands. She called herself Milly Waters, and night after night she sang "Little Brown Jug" and "That's My Desire" in school gymnasiums filled with brush-cut

boys in broad-shouldered suits and flushed girls en-
snared in their first wired uplift bras. She was called a
"thrush" by Buddy Koopmans, a "warbler" when she
joined Cy Bieterman and his Kings of Swing, a
"chanteuse" when she sang with Jack Karos and his
Sultans of Swing.

In those days Milly learned to fend off advances from
every kind of man—Rotarians and fuzz-cheeked boys,
thirty-second-degree Masons, state legislators, pot-
blind saxophone players, boozed-up bartenders. She
lost her virginity at eighteen to a young blue-eyed
trumpet player she thought she loved. But when he left
to go East, she turned to a tall, gentle trombonist for a
while until he went West. From time to time she had
short affairs with musicians she liked, and for one brief
period in 1954 she was married to Jack Karos, the
leader of the Sultans of Swing. That marriage found-
ered after six months because of Karos' drinking, and
though it was a dark and occasionally violent time,
Milly was remarkably unaffected by it all. In 1956,
when she was twenty-one, Milly joined the band of Bob
Venturi, a middle-aged, soft-spoken clarinetist. His
band, the Venturi Kings, had a permanent house job
in the Satin Room of the Blackwell Hotel in Chicago.

Escape from the grind of one-night gigs was heaven-
ly, and, partly out of gratitude and partly out of
fondness, Milly moved into Bob Venturi's apartment in
Chicago. It was a low-key love affair, more affectionate
than passionate. They worked 'til dawn, ate Chinese
food at an all-night restaurant on Rush Street, then
slept all day. Milly never cooked or cared about the
appearance of the apartment, which was bland and
shabby to begin with, and she was content to let a
once-weekly maid simply neaten up the place.

She never thought of herself as being particularly

liberated in those days, but she was. She worked at what she liked to do. She lived with a man she liked but did not particularly want to tie herself to for life. She reacted to housework and the accouterments of homemaking as nuisances to be avoided rather than the keystones of life.

Not a great deal had been reported about Milly during the campaign, but now that she had become the First Lady, practically every woman's magazine and TV show did profiles about her, emphasizing her years as a band singer. Milly had scarcely considered what her background might mean in terms of being a President's wife. But now she had a vague, uncomfortable feeling that the American public would have preferred her to be more like the spick-and-span house cleaners and washday wizards they saw on television commercials. That she was out of a mold so unusual for women of her generation seemed to make the nation a little nervous. She wasn't at all sure herself what category she might fit, and at this point six weeks into her husband's Presidency, she was a little nervous, too.

Milly looked at the table set for lunch. The wine goblets were from Dolly Madison's crystal set, the bone-china plates had been first used by Zachary Taylor, the silverware had been selected by Mrs. Theodore Roosevelt. She felt she was an exhibit in a museum display, ensconced in luxury, yet no more at home in it than if she had set up housekeeping in the rotunda of the Capitol. None of it was hers—and none of it was *her*. Milly wondered what she could do to keep for herself a way of life that was her own—go back to playing the piano in a cocktail bar? She burst out with involuntary laughter at the idea—the First Lady of the land a cocktail pianist? She laughed again.

The door opened and she looked up as York entered the room with Morley and Eddie Hanson, the press secretary. Their voices were tense and low and they were all frowning.

Morley said, "The time to hit Tip with it is at breakfast tomorrow, Mr. President. If you bring it up then—before the tax program has been released to the public—he is going to be more receptive. He can do some fiddling and find a way to push for the public works cuts. In fact, he won't have any choice."

York's voice was edged, metallic, a tone that made Milly nervous. "I just don't see that that follows, Andy. Why does he not have any choice?"

"Mr. President, he can't afford to be out on a limb with their tax-cut proposals at the same time he's pushing those heavy pork-barrel public works projects."

York shrugged. "Okay. If you say so. I don't understand why it's that simple, but maybe it is. I'll tell him at breakfast."

Eddie Hanson said, "Mr. President, the press briefing is at three. We should have something for them on the threat of the Cruise missile strike."

York frowned. "I still don't know what the hell to do about it if they strike."

Morley said, "I talked to Mills at Treasury and Slaughter at Defense, Mr. President. They think we should crack down right now. Send troops in to do the work if they strike. Slaughter says we have to show the Russians our defense programs are so important to us that we'll do anything to keep the arsenal viable."

"Even using federal troops as scabs?"

"Yes. It's not exactly pretty, but we're dealing in the national defense. We have to *look* convincing."

York looked at Hanson. "Give them something vague about high-level meetings, Eddie. I want to think about it a little longer."

Hanson said, "Maybe I could hold off the briefing a couple of hours. That might be better than coming in empty on it."

"Okay, do that. Now, I'd like to have a private lunch—alone—with my wife."

Hanson looked at Milly as if he had not noticed her before. "Afternoon, Mrs. York." Then he said to the President, "The network guys tape their last pieces around six, sir. It would be good to have something on the strike for them for tonight's shows."

Morley and Hanson left, and the door closed with a light click. Milly looked closely at York. The lines on his forehead were deeply engraved. He saw her studying him and grinned. That surprising radiant visage blended with the sunny aura of the room. He kissed her and sat down as she rang a small silver bell to summon a butler and maid with lunch.

"I feel like the Queen of Sheba," she said. "What time did you start working this morning, darling? It wasn't light when you got up."

"It was four, maybe. I didn't look. I keep waking up and playing things over in my head. There's so much to digest. Christ, the reading—I never read as much in a whole year of law school, Milly, as I get now in a week." He chuckled. "And I never was much for fast reading—always moved my lips. Hell, I even catch myself moving my lips when I read those godawful nuclear codes for annihilating the planet." He shook his head and laughed deeply.

Milly felt a surge of pleasure as he relaxed. The servants brought a salade Niçoise, French bread, and a light crisp Chablis that Milly's secretary had ordered for them. The servants left and Milly whispered, "I feel like Cinderella. All this is going to disappear and I'll wind up with nothing but a scrub bucket."

"It's pleasant, isn't it?" He sipped the wine. "Yes, I like the surroundings, but I'm not sure I like some of the people around the neighborhood."

"Why?"

"I signed the appointment this morning to make Bob Gellatin ambassador to India." He grimaced.

"That sleazy old newspaper publisher with the cheap platinum-blonde wife?"

"That's the pair."

"India! My God, Gus, that wife of his is going to kick the first beggar she sees."

"Gellatin wants the job. It was promised to him. He arranged for a lot of money to come into the campaign. A million, I guess."

"A million? There's a limit on how much he could contribute, isn't there?"

York put a forkful of salad in his mouth and chewed slowly. "Yes, there's a limit. He arranged it through a bunch of fronts with his papers and some other companies he owns. Also, he gave us lots of positive coverage during the campaign. The Committee took care of it all and Len Buhler made the promise to him. I just have to deliver it, that's all."

Milly put her hand over his. "They're not really your obligations, Gus."

"They might as well be. When someone on the committee makes a deal like that, it's as if I did it myself. I can't renege on it."

"You can't do what you think is right?"

York frowned. "There's a problem with that—I'm not sure I *know* what's right. I'm not sure I have the reflexes, the political intuition. I don't know how

Washington works. I don't know the big establishment boys, the money people."

"You've got plenty of advice."

"God, yes! I get advice from everyone. Jerry Ford keeps calling. Kissinger . . . every damn corporation president in the country gives me advice. Even that bastard Nixon writes me notes."

"Gus, you just have to learn to trust your own instincts."

"Milly, that's what I'm trying to tell you—I don't *have* any instincts! The economy is terrible. The energy crunch is here. The space program has to be totally dismantled or given a huge appropriation to keep it going. The trade balance with Japan . . . Milly, all these things are serious problems, desperate problems—and I don't have any real instinctive idea what to do about *any* of them."

She felt a small surge of alarm as she watched him speak. His eyes had widened at the enormity of what he was saying and he had for a moment the look of a small, helpless boy. Her voice was a soothing purr, husky and maternal. "Gus, darling, you mustn't do this to yourself. You mustn't expect yourself to be so perfect. You have to give yourself time. Instincts aren't always something you are born with. Sometimes you have to learn them."

"I made up my mind after the election that I wouldn't be their trick pony anymore. I was going to be myself." He looked at her and his eyes were sad. "Now I'm beginning to wonder exactly who the hell I'd be if I *could* be my own man."

She caressed his cheek. "Darling, we are just two plain people. *People!* Not saints, or angels, or tin gods. We're a man and a woman. We can't be more than that just because you ended up being President." She paused. He said nothing. She said, "I love you." She took his hand.

He smiled. "I love you, too. Don't worry, I'll find my way." They finished lunch. Then he kissed her and left the room.

Milly suddenly felt chilled. The sunlight seemed dense and threatening, and she longed for the concealment of darkness. She tasted the Chablis. It suddenly seemed sour.

A polite, light knock sounded at the door, and Bitsy Rogerson, Milly's personal secretary, a former debutante and Vassar honors student, entered. She hesitated at the door, her eyebrows raised to question whether Milly was ready to see her. Milly looked up glumly. "Come in, Bitsy." She was carrying a notebook bound in white Moroccan leather. She opened it and, in a tightly reined voice, read Milly her schedule for that afternoon: a picture session with the cerebral palsy poster child at two-forty-five, followed at three by a meeting with visiting mayors, and at five by an interview with Barbara Walters of ABC-TV news. That had to conclude by six because at eight there was a state dinner for five hundred guests in honor of the prime minister of Italy and his wife.

Milly sighed. "Thank you, Bitsy. You keep my life filled with such interesting things."

Bitsy Rogerson had no sense of humor. "Thank you, Mrs. York," she said, and went on eagerly. "Did you enjoy your lunch? Salade Niçoise is always a lovely meal. And the Chablis should have been just the right touch."

"It was." Milly waved her away. "I'll be down in ten minutes." She wanted another few moments, even a few seconds, of freedom. The kind of afternoon she faced aroused in Milly the same sense of helpless rebellion she had felt toward the gray, crawling hours she had faced as a child in school. When Gus was governor of Kentucky they had managed to reduce the socializing to an event or two each week. Now there was no relief. She was the White House hostess, a symbol of a nation that imagined itself full of gracious women who stood firm behind their courageous men— *always* smiling, *always* witty, *always* eager to shake a hand, kiss a cheek, pass a platter of hors d'oeuvres. Sixteen hours a day, the charade would go on, maybe more. Milly's dislike went beyond the loss of so much time in empty social gestures. She also was beginning to feel the withering effect of constant exposure to people who seemed, more and more, to be scrutinizing her with an odd ferocity, as if probing to find blemishes on her skin, gray in her hair.

None of it was personal; none of it was done because she was the individual she was. No, the hostility, the scrutiny simply came with the franchise of being First Lady in a country that liked to devour its celebrities and demean its leaders for real or imagined imperfections.

Milly sipped once more at the wine. The sourness made her wince. Four years of this life was almost beyond her imagination. And *eight* years? She gulped down the remaining half-glass of Chablis in one swig, as if to dispel that distasteful possibility.

* * * * *

Chapter 16

A week later, on the morning of March 9, Norman Brandeis arrived at the CIPHER suite and announced that his lunch consisted of meat loaf on rye bread with mayonnaise, a bag of Frye's potato chips, celery sticks, a package of Twinkies, and a Thermos of lemonade. Then he sipped his morning coffee and discussed with two secretaries and an assistant computer programmer the bizarre vicissitudes and good fun they had witnessed on television the night before while watching "M*A*S*H," "Mork and Mindy," and a Milton Berle special.

Only after these matters were dispensed with did Brandeis enter Appleton's office and tell him that CIPHER was, insofar as he could see, ready to function.

"You mean it is finished?" asked Appleton.

"I have done everything," said Brandeis. "A computer program is like raising a child, however. You can never be absolutely sure that it will turn out the precise way you had in mind."

"But we can give a demonstration? Today?"

"As Mork said to Mindy last night, 'Hotcha billy-billy.'"

"What?"

" 'Hotcha billy-billy' means 'You're darn tootin'' on the planet Ork."

Appleton blinked behind his dark glasses. He spoke sharply: "Goddammit! What does it mean on the planet Earth?"

"It means 'yes.'" Brandeis was easily awed by a show of authority.

Appleton summoned Morley, Watson, and Mikkelson for the demonstration. When they arrived, Morley gazed at the computer. "What do we do—hit it with a bottle of champagne or give it a loyalty oath?" he cracked.

Appleton was tense, and Brandeis was the color of chalk, jittery as a new father in the presence of such high-powered people. Appleton told the gathering, "We can pick a random situation and show you the specific readings on individual security risks and logistical probabilities affecting the President's safety."

Morely said, "Why be random? The President is going to Cleveland and Detroit next week. That should be a good test."

Brandeis had dressed especially clownishly for the occasion in a yellow-and-green-striped shirt, a black-and-pink-dotted tie, and a rust-colored plaid suit. He stepped stiffly to the console of the computer, not unlike a very nervous pianist approaching his keyboard. His bright eyes blinked anxiously and his voice trembled. "What time of day will the President be in Cleveland, sir? In Detroit? Which streets will the motorcade follow?"

He asked a series of questions, then punched the data into the computer. The computer hummed for a minute or so, then spewed forth a roll of paper that contained a list of about a hundred names and addresses.

Morley gasped. "Good God! That many people want to kill the President in Detroit?"

Brandeis' button-eyes blinked rapidly and his pale lips moved woodenly: "You will notice they are graded, Mr. Morley, sir. There is a risk factor in these lists, and the names are run in order of their potential risk to the President—including those who live or work near the motorcade routes."

"And?"

Appleton spoke up. "On the highest risks, we can order surveillance or a police check or a phony arrest or maybe just an interview. We can lock them up or just scare them by letting them know they have attracted official interest."

Morley studied the list. "It's complicated. But it does cut down those percentages—a lot."

Watson said, "This thing would've produced Oswald, wouldn't it?"

Appleton nodded and told them what he had learned about other presidential assassins. Morley whistled. "Three out of four. Great!"

Brandeis droned on: "We have also programmed a daily or weekly 'climate of life' in cities the President will visit. For one thing, it gives us a reading on what we call the 'agitation factor.' That means current events or incidents or controversial issues that have arisen and might exaggerate passions against the President."

Morley said, "You mean like Proposition 13 in California in '78?"

Appleton shook his head. "More subtle than that. For example, the police shot and killed a boy in Detroit the other day. They thought he was holding a knife on an old man. Actually, the old man had tried to molest the boy. People are angry about the incident. It increases the instability of certain types of people in our profiles. In Cleveland, there have been a series of fires, probably arson. That also excites some people differently."

Morley said, "Agitation factor, eh?"

Brandeis went on. "Also incuded in the 'climate of life' data are certain statistics—crime, for example, unemployment, patterns of violence in political activities over the years, causes of death. We have data on the religious preferences, population ratios of race, of blue-collar workers, of senior citizens and teen-agers."

Morley said softly, "Agitation factor, climate-of-life factor—what about the zero factor?"

Brandeis said in the same wooden voice, "It is part of the probabilities in the program. It changes slightly all of the figures for this President. Of course, any other President—until the one elected in the year 2000—will have his program written without a zero factor."

Morley snapped. "By the election in 2000, there will *be* no zero factor! That's why we have this goddamn machine in the first place."

Brandeis turned whiter. He ducked his head obsequiously. "Of course, sir. Sorry, I'm sorry."

Watson said to Morley, "Does the President know CIPHER is finished?"

Morley paused a beat, then said, "No. I've seen no reason to bother him with this kind of detail."

This sounded logical enough. York had been immersed in problems since his inauguration—the critical trade imbalance with Japan had suddenly raised all sorts of fire in Congress and York had been trying to head off a move to create a whole new restrictive system of tariffs against Japan. There were also renewed and increasing threats of the wildcat strike at a major Cruise missile plant in California, a strike that could spread to other defense factories.

Mikkelson said, "Let's get down to work for the trips next week. We have hotel staff lists, routes and all. Let's start cross-checking."

Brandeis looked at his watch. "It's twelve. I have my forty-five minutes for lunch now." He looked about, his bright button-eyes glistening. "Meat loaf on rye, celery sticks, potato chips, Twinkies, and lemonade." He paused to allow for comments, but there were none, so he left the room.

The gathering stood in silence until Morley asked, "Why did he say that?"

"His lunch," said Appleton with a sigh. "He likes to recite his lunch."

Morley paused. "And does he always dress like that?"

Appleton nodded.

Morley grinned and threw out his hands expansively. "See!? I told you the little bastard was a genius." He rushed away to his office in the White House, his pants legs flapping. Appleton, Mikkelson, and Watson turned to prime CIPHER for its first job of protecting President York.

Promptly forty-five minutes later, Brandeis returned to join them and he expressed interest, even excitement, over the fact that they had just ordered ham sandwiches on pumpernickel and coffee from the White House kitchen.

* * * * *

Chapter 17

The President's trips to Cleveland and Detroit went off without complication. The Secret Service was pleased by the cooperation police offered in corraling the few people deemed serious threats to York's life. Security had been particularly tight in Detroit when York spoke before a convention of Teamsters, ordinarily a hostile audience for a Republican. The political risks were far greater than the physical ones in that appearance.

An invitation for York to speak to the Teamsters had been received at the White House a month earlier. Morley had almost decided to turn it down without mentioning it to the President, but when he happened to bring it up casually, York reacted with immediate enthusiasm. "Yes! I accept. That is exactly where I want to make a speech."

"Mr. President, they will be rough on you. Inflation, wage controls, big steel trying to raise its prices while the companies don't want to give a nickel more to labor. The Cruise missile strike question. It's a hot spot."

York was adamant. "Andy, it's a place to begin *my* idea of what this Administration is all about. I don't want anyone to write the speech except you. And me, of course."

In Detroit, York faced the stony faces of five

thousand Teamsters. They grudgingly gave him a light breeze of applause when he appeared, then sat on their hands, daring him to melt their dislike. But York stood there coolly, an imposing giant, his face ornamented with the scars of football games like the medals on a war hero. He talked easily, his drawl comfortable and genuine.

He spoke briefly of the harshness of his boyhood. He spoke of the ache he felt now, realizing that fifty years after the Great Depression, the U.S. still had several million people living at that same desperate level of subsistence. He spoke with sympathy for the plight of the blue-collar man. The crowd applauded sporadically, weakly.

Then York swung into his conclusion. "This," he cried, "is a Republican Administration, proud of Republican principles, pleased with Republican ways! But, I am here to tell you, that this is not an Administration that is slavish to the past. Yes, we have our roots. But I consider my roots to run deeper into the poor bald mountains of Appalachia than ever they have been in the philosophy of the Republican Party.

"Before I was a Republican I was a man, a common man. And that is where my allegiance lies: to you, to the common man! Not to the institutional or the vested interest! Not to the banks! Not to the corporations! Not to the unions! Not to the Republican Party! My allegiance is to the common man and his struggle to endure!"

The crowd broke into crackling applause. The excitement was building. York went on, speaking more gently now. "My daddy believed in a wrathful God, in ghosts, in the healing effects of whiskey. He never did know how to read much. But he had the stuff of courage and endurance. He was poor; he was hungry.

He died young. He was, in the eyes of the wealthy and the powerful, a failure. But he was the salt of the earth, and it is to men like my daddy, common men—men like you—that I pledge my allegiance."

Now the crowd thundered its approval. Some men rose to their feet. York held up one hand and shouted, "This is an Administration of common men! Not big government! Not big business! Not big politics! Not big money! We stand for *you!* We stand in common cause! Together!"

Five thousand Teamsters leaped up, shouting and whistling. York raised his hands high, palms open toward the ceiling, his smile dazzling. It was an hour of unmitigated triumph, and he rode high on a wave of elation.

Three days later, the threatened wildcat strike occurred at the Cruise missile plant in California. York summoned to the White House the leader of the recalcitrant union and the chairman of the board of the conglomerate that owned the plant. The President would allow no lower-echelon executives to substitute or attend. He told the two men that the only alternative to their settling the strike—immediately, within hours—was to call out troops to take over the striking workers. "You will both be out the money involved," he said, "because we will freeze all funds as long as the troops are working. And, I'm telling you, once they are in the plant, I intend to keep them there for a good long time. Months."

The board chairman was an exquisitely groomed old man who had been in the Nixon Cabinet for a time. The union president was a paunchy ex-plumber who had moved into the rocket-builders' union as a matter of pure expedience. They hated each other on sight, but they had no choice about whether they would attend or not. They met for three hours alone in an anteroom of the Oval Office and settled the strike.

York announced the agreement at a press conference. The two of them stood on each side of him glaring angrily at the TV cameras. "I'd like to introduce you to a pair of common men," said the President, "who have arrived at a common cause: peace between themselves and a newly solid foundation under the defenses of this nation."

The common-man theme, though it was scarcely new, struck a chord. That it was Franklin Roosevelt's originally seemed to make it all the more popular. York's open renunciation of vested interests was received warmly by editorial writers who spoke of "new Republicanism" and a "rebirth of reality."

Through the spring and summer, York took the reins of the Presidency with a certainty that impressed everyone. He met with the Russian premier in Vienna in May and they began the third round of SALT talks with a promise that both countries would consider the total outlawing of nuclear weapons. In June, he steered through Congress an Administration bill that appropriated more than ten billion dollars for the installation of solar-heating systems in schools and public buildings in many sections of the country. He continued to emphasize his concern for the "common man" and, thus, he continued through the summer to irritate the entire right wing and much of the middle ground in the Republican Party.

When Morley expressed concern over this in early August, York said, "This time they'll just have to follow me instead of me following them. Dammit,

Andy, I'm doing what *I* think is right, and I won't be steered off. And, along that line, what is the latest on Cuba?"

Morley said, "There are only a few minor points to be ironed out, Mr. President—exactly what the wording of the trade agreement will be, a little more horse-trading about who we should send down there as ambassador."

"Okay. When will the official ceremonies take place?"

"By the first of September, if we want."

"Great. I've been thinking about it. Where should we sign the stuff? Somewhere neutral, like Bermuda or Guadeloupe?"

Morley grinned. "There is only one place for it to happen: in Havana. You go to Havana."

York looked up, delighted. "Perfect. Damn! The old political merchandiser does it again."

Morley shrugged. "Nixon goes to Peking to open China. York goes to Havana to open Cuba."

York frowned. "I'm not sure I want to be paired with that guy even when it comes to making history."

"Don't worry, you won't be."

York went to Cuba on the second weekend in September and met Fidel Castro in an atmosphere of celebration and euphoria. Flags crackled in the Havana wind and the streets were bright with flowers and bunting. York radiated vitality. Milly charmed Castro. He turned into a huge fawning boy, grinning around his cigar, almost blushing through his beard, when Milly put on an impromptu concert one night, playing the piano and singing love songs of the 1940s as if they had all been written especially for her and Fidel Castro.

Television covered the three-day visit in detail. It was, commentators and politicians agreed, one of the finest hours for the York Administration.

* * * * *

One week after the President's triumph in Havana, a telephone rang in the cramped, shabby law office of one Edward Soong on the edge of San Francisco's Chinatown. Soong heard a voice with a faintly Latin inflection: "I have been trying to contact Bill Brody. Is he out of the country?"

Soong straightened up in his chair and replied carefully. "No, Bill Brody is on vacation in Baja."

The voice said, "Please have him call Alfredo." He gave a number in Miami.

Soong hung up, wrote the phone number on a piece of paper, and sealed it in an envelope which he addressed to Bill Brody. He left immediately for the Wells Fargo Bank branch on Fillmore Street, opened safe deposit box number 3476, and dropped in the envelope. The box was otherwise empty.

At a pay phone Soong dialed a number. He let the instrument ring twice, cut it off, dialed again, let it ring twice, hung up, then dialed once more and listened. Someone lifted the receiver at the other end and Soong said slowly, "Bill Brody. Bill Brody." The receiver clicked, and Soong returned to his office, knowing that the following day he could return to safe deposit box number 3476 and find an envelope addressed to him. It would be stuffed with ten one-hundred-dollar bills.

An hour after Soong's call, Le Bombardier took the envelope from the box and called the number in Miami. Le Bombardier would fly to New York, take a room at the Carlyle Hotel, and wait to be contacted. Le

Bombardier hurried to his apartment, packed, and told his lover he would be gone a month or more. His lover wept a little.

Le Bombardier took a morning plane to New York and arrived in the late afternoon. He checked into the Carlyle, then spent the evening in the Carlyle Room sipping champagne, eating oysters and listening to Bobby Short at the piano.

The next day his room phone rang and a man's voice said, "Meet me in Bemelman's Bar at eight o'clock tonight. I will be wearing a blue blazer and a plain yellow necktie. My name is Juan Cardozo. How will I know you?"

"I will know you."

At eight Le Bombardier entered the bar. Marian McPartland was playing light jazz on the piano in the darkened room. Le Bombardier was dressed in a tailored pin stripe suit, white shirt, and tie. He wore a small gray mustache and round, horn-rimmed spectacles. His hair was tinted gray and the contact lenses in his eyes were a light brown. He sat next to Cardozo at the bar, ordered a Scotch, then said to the man, "I am Bill Brody."

Cardozo turned. Le Bombardier saw that he had a thin aristocratic face and that his clothes were very expensive. Cardozo nodded and they shook hands solemnly as they moved to a table in a darkened corner. The music of McPartland floated around them. Cardozo explained in a low voice that he represented a group of rich businessmen in Miami, all exiled Cubans, all men of great wealth whose fortunes had been accumulated in the years since they had been forced out of Cuba by Fidel Castro. "We are angry men, passionate men," said Cardozo. "We have nourished our hatred for the Red Dog of Cuba for all these years. Now it is more fierce than ever. He has been made legitimate, exalted by your United States President. This outlaw can now operate as a respected world citizen, selling the sugar he stole from our families. He is free to do as he wishes because of President York's stupid action. We want revenge."

Le Bombardier said, "You want me to kill Castro?"

Cardozo hesitated. His pale face was deadly serious in the dim light. "No. We want you to assassinate the President of the United States."

"York?"

"He is the one who caused this. Castro, dead, would only be a hero, immortalized, perhaps revered more in death than he possibly could be in life. No, it's York who is the assassin of freedom and justice in Cuba. York signed the papers that make the Red Dog legitimate. York must die."

"You sound fanatical," said Le Bombardier.

"We are men of strong feeling. To allow a criminal like Castro to thrive, to prosper, to attract admiration—this is to annihilate Cuba as surely as if you dropped a nuclear bomb."

Le Bombardier said, "I am uninterested in politics. I was an exile of sorts myself. I accept whatever political coloring happens to be necessary to survive. I have no feeling at all toward these things that upset you."

"That, of course, is why we have come to you. We need a man without emotions. We would jeopardize the plan because of the very fanaticism that leads us to want it done."

"The price?"

"Ten million."

Le Bombardier raised his eyebrows. "Ten million dollars? My God!"

Cardozo smiled thinly. "The price is the measure of our fanaticism."

"You must guarantee it by putting half into an account in Switzerland before I start."

"Of course."

"The rest when the President is dead."

"Agreed. We knew what your conditions were. We are offering you ten million because we knew it was probably far more than you have been paid. Money is no problem. We have plenty. We could not risk the possibility that the best on earth might refuse us because of a few dollars."

Le Bombardier held up his hand. "I haven't accepted yet. Not absolutely. I must do research on the man York. I know nothing about him."

"Of course."

"Give me a week." They parted after shaking hands again.

Le Bombardier dealt in abstractions when it came to his victims. Each represented a puzzle to be solved through logic and technology. The murder in Kyoto had been easy; the man was not a chief of state and only had one dull-minded bodyguard. Others had been more difficult. The French politicians had been surrounded by government bodyguards, and the Italian industrialists had had as many as a dozen guards around them. Le Bombardier's approach to each assassination was to analyze methodically each detail of his victim's habits and regular movements until he discovered some flaw that would allow him an opening—and plenty of time to prepare.

The solution to the murder of Augustus York would be difficult. Few men in the world were as carefully protected as a United States President. Yet, if he could master this assassination, Le Bombardier knew that it would contain an element far beyond the money he collected and the cold pride he felt in his own mechanistic perfection—he would be writing history. First, the devastating immediate effect of a presidential murder would affect the panorama of current events— and thus alter the contemporary history of the world. But given the zero-year phenomenon, Le Bombardier would also create waves of fear extending beyond the immediate shock of York's death. In the year 2000, the election would be fraught with more nightmarish potential than any in history. The zero factor, having brought down eight consecutive Presidents, would be a very real force in politics. No matter how scientifically sophisticated the world had become by then, there would be no choice but to respect the forces of the supernatural, of ancient superstition and occult practices in selecting the man who would presumably still be the most powerful individual on earth.

Le Bombardier found this all delicious to contemplate. To produce a clear and measurable impact on history appealed to him more than it might to other men. For it was history on the rampage, violent and uncontrolled, that had produced his own bizarre and rootless childhood, and the subsequent perverse and violent ways of his adult life.

To people who knew him socially, outside his professional milieu, Le Bombardier's way of life was so vague and changeable that no one was surprised if he suddenly appeared after long absences. This was the case in New York City after his meeting with Cardozo the Cuban when he went to visit a lovely woman painter, a famous name from the 1950s pantheon of abstract expressionism. She welcomed him at her apartment with a warm embrace and said, "I shouldn't ask where you've been or why you haven't seen me in eight years, darling. But *where* have you been? And *why* haven't you seen me in eight years?!"

"I have been in San Francisco, and I haven't seen you because you are in New York."

"San Francisco? You can tolerate that pretentious little backwater?"

"It is empty, but it is beautiful."

"And have you a lover, too? Also empty and beautiful?"

"Of course."

"Is she spoiled and demanding, a fierce little kitten of a woman?"

Le Bombardier smiled. "All of those things. Almost."

They had late supper at the Russian Tea Room, then returned to her apartment on Fifth Avenue and sipped brandy overlooking the Metropolitan Museum of Art and Central Park ten floors below.

The lovely painter said, "Do you still like Wagner?"

"Wagner is always a favorite."

She leaned over and kissed him, her tongue gently rubbing his lips. They went to her bedroom, where she turned on a tape of Wagner's *Rings* and they made love until morning.

After breakfast in her sunroom, Le Bombardier returned to the Carlyle, where he changed into casual clothes—a turtleneck, tweed jacket, gray slacks. At noon, he entered the New York Public Library and ordered microfilms of *Time* and *Newsweek* and *The New York Times* covering the 300-odd days since Augustus York had been elected President. He read swiftly, making notes about each day's activities, searching for details in every phrase of every story. He read with particular interest reports about the assassination attempt in Louisville, noting every detail of information concerning the security defenses around the President. It took Le Bombardier five days to complete his study.

From the Carlyle, he telephoned Cardozo. "I will do it."

"Excellent. When?"

"I don't know. It could be several months."

"Months? Oh, come now."

"Yes, months. Perhaps a year. I cannot hurry this. You must be patient."

"My partners will want to know something more. A year! We are not spending ten million dollars to wait for you to do something in a year!"

Le Bombardier quietly hung up the phone. When it rang a moment later, he said, "I am not negotiating this, Cardozo. How I do it and when I do it must be solely my decision. If there is any disagreement with this, any at *all,* then there will be no assassination."

Cardozo spoke meekly. "The money is already in your Swiss account. We knew you would never turn it down."

Le Bombardier smiled. "Good. Absolute trust. That is what I require."

"We know that."

"Thank you," said Le Bombardier. "We shall not speak or see each other again."

He hung up and settled down to study the life and times of Augustus York. To kill a President without the passion, the madness—and the purest blind luck—that most assassins brought to such an undertaking was a monumental task. Technology, logic, and intricate, precise calculation were all that he had going for him, and Le Bombardier knew that the odds against his succeeding were great. But he had never felt more prepared to accept a challenge—or more delighted with one.

* * * * *

Chapter 18

York was scheduled to visit New York City in October to participate in the Columbus Day parade up Fifth Avenue. Milly decided to stay in Washington. "I need one more parade and public appearance like I need a case of smallpox," she said.

A week before the trip, the CIPHER crew culled out the highest-risk security cases from New York City lists in the computer. The Secret Service was as at ease with the situation in New York as anywhere, for the police there were expert in the practice of celebrity security. They had protected every kind of superstar from a pope to the Beatles.

The computer produced an even fifty names of men and women potentially very dangerous to the President. The general atmosphere in the city was negative toward York for a number of reasons—not the least of which was that he had refused to sign a bill allowing the hugely expensive Westway to be built.

However, the high-risk assassin profiles that CIPHER spewed forth were connected with more volatile issues. A number of men in the fanatical Puerto Rican group, FALN, seemed extremely dangerous, but the New York police had long ago infiltrated the group so thoroughly that movements of the most suspicious members were easily followed. A few black radicals who once had connections with the Black Muslims and had for years been suspected as the murderers of Malcolm X were brought in for routine shakedowns that would keep them off the streets during York's visit.

When the New York police teletyped a report detailing their action on each of the fifty suspects, Watson said to Appleton, "This thing really looks like it is worth the money. It improves our percentages enormously."

Appleton said, "Yes, but it's still just percentages. It's not perfect."

"Any edge is worth it," said Watson.

The presidential party landed at La Guardia Airport and was whisked into Manhattan along Grand Central Parkway and over the Triboro Bridge. Three full lanes were blocked off for the motorcade. Once across the East River it sped down the F.D.R. Drive to Forty-fifth Street, then rolled across blocked intersections to Park Avenue and the Waldorf-Astoria Hotel. It was just after noon. York was scheduled to confer briefly at the Waldorf with the mayor of New York, then to move on to Fifth Avenue and the parade.

The mayor, a lanky, thin man with a pleasant face that concealed a bad temper and an evil tongue, was waiting in the President's suite. No one had expected a particularly warm reception; the mayor had issued the day before a scathing statement denouncing York's refusal to sign an appropriation for the Westway. Still, no one was prepared for either the swiftness or the savagery of the mayor's assault. "When you reject New York City, Mr. President, you reject the intellectual and esthetic soul of this country," he snapped, after the initial, formal greetings.

"Reject?" said a surprised York. "I didn't reject

anything except one high-priced road that will probably do more harm than good."

The mayor's eyes narrowed. "This city is all this country has going for it. A body dies without a brain. New York City is the brain of this country. It is the only class act we have." The mayor fairly hissed, "Maybe if we had a winning football team, Mr. President, *you* could understand the merits of this city."

"You get yourself a winning football team, Mr. Mayor, and we'll talk again!" York drew himself to his full height and gazed down on the man. "You get yourself a civilized mayor with some manners and we can *really* talk again!"

The mayor looked up at the President's angry face. "You make Jerry Ford look like Socrates!" He turned and left the suite; his flustered aides scrambled out behind him.

York took a deep breath. "Jesus! That man is a fanatic."

Morley and Eddie Hanson were stunned. Morley said, "He's crazy! But it's mostly all crazy politics, Mr. President. He's got to run for office again this fall. Making you the *bête noire* and the Westway the Holy Grail is one way to establish his character."

York said, "It's also one way to establish a broken jaw."

An hour later, York and the mayor rode in separate limousines to the parade reviewing stand. When they arrived, the Secret Service moved snugly in around York. With police surrounding him, the mayor pushed through the excited crowd. People began to applaud the President, whistling and shouting, "Gus! Hey, Gus!"

At the steps to the reviewing stand, the mayor began to climb the stairs, then hesitated. As angry as he was, he knew it would be a breach of protocol if he mounted ahead of the President. As he stopped, York's Secret Service men bumped into the policemen in front of them, and the procession jammed up. At that moment a young man, his hair greasy and disheveled, his eyes burning, shouldered violently into the Secret Service agent at York's left. The agent fell.

"Liar!" the young man screamed. He raised his hand and swung a long gleaming butcher's knife at York's neck. The President threw up his arm to protect himself, and the blade sliced like a razor through the cloth of his coat and split the flesh of his forearm.

His arm was an instant fountain of blood. York looked at the wound in shock. Mikkelson grabbed his shoulders and spun him away from the assailant. Two Secret Service men and a policeman wrestled with the attacker until one of them managed to drop him with a blow to the back of the neck.

When the scuffling was over, Mikkelson swiftly ripped open the President's coat sleeve and shirt so his arm was bare to the shoulder. The slash was six inches long and had severed an artery. Mikkelson quickly found a pressure point that stopped the spurting, and a policeman brought out compresses from a first-aid kit to stanch the bleeding.

Cameramen and photographers recorded the entire scene from the stand above York. Mikkelson bellowed, "Get the limousine in here!"

Agents and police violently shoved people aside as the limousine rolled through the crowd toward the President. York's face was a ghastly ashen-white. Blood was splashed across his shirt and dripped off his fingers. He leaned against Mikkelson, who had also been sprayed with blood. They climbed into the car. A squad car siren shrieked as it pulled out in front. The two vehicles sped down Fifth Avenue directly into the oncoming parade. Bands, majorettes, Boy Scouts scattered as the cars raced through them on the way to St. Clare's Hospital.

The attacker proved indeed to be insane. He revived in the hospital emergency room and began ranting incoherently, thick-tongued and incomprehensible, as if he were drunk.

He was a schizophrenic mental patient who had escaped from a hospital in Westchester County two days before. As his ravings became more coherent, it was clear that he had no idea who President Augustus York was or that he was the man he had attacked. The young lunatic had been under the misapprehension that his victim was a psychiatrist whom he had come to blame for his misfortunes.

Later Mikkelson called Watson in Washington. "The President's okay, but it took thirty stitches, including a couple in the artery. He's weak, but he's up. We'll fly back down there tonight."

"How'd that crazy get so close?"

"I have no idea. He must have had that knife under his jacket. I don't know."

"The computer missed him."

"There's no way we could have dug out a nutball like that. He didn't even know who he was trying to kill."

"Is the President really all right?"

Mikkelson paused. "Physically, yes. Emotionally, I don't know. He's edgy as hell."

"You can't blame him. This is twice in seven months that someone's tried to kill him. It's enough to make a stone statue twitch."

York sat disconsolately in his suite at the Waldorf. The pain in his arm was intense despite the pills he had taken; the black sling was restrictive. He had grown accustomed to pain and physical discomfort in his days as a football player, but this wound had been inflicted under such savage conditions that he was weakened by the shock. His hand trembled as he sipped a glass of whiskey. Eddie Hanson, the press secretary, said, "I've briefed them, Mr. President. They know the details on the injury and whatever we know about the assailant. They . . . uh, they've heard also about the . . . uh, spat you had with the mayor. They're wondering about that."

York said glumly, "If they want a quote about the mayor, tell them that for all I know, the son-of-a-bitch arranged for that loony bastard to kill me."

Hanson hesitated. "The only thing, sir, is that they got some quotes from the mayor's men before the knife attack happened. They just wanted to check them out."

"I have no comment on any of it. Eddie, I just barely sneaked out of this with my life."

York swallowed more whiskey, but it did no good. His voice trembled. "The bastard. The bastard. The son-of-a-bitching bastard."

Morley came to him quickly. "Mr. President, rest now. We'll be going to LaGuardia at seven to go home. It's rush-hour traffic and the police don't want to get snarled in that. Take a nap; a couple of hours should help a little."

York stood up and staggered slightly, then, walked to the bedroom with Morley supporting him. Every movement sent a throb of pain up the arm. York clenched his teeth as he lay down. Morley softly closed the door. The room was dark, the shades drawn against the mild October afternoon. York could hear the sounds of New York traffic twenty floors below.

He had been weak before he lay down, but suddenly

now his body was shaking. The pain was bright and constant in his arm. He closed his eyes but behind his lids he could see nothing but the twisted face of the madman, his mouth forming the word "Liar!"

York opened his eyes wide and stared at the ceiling. His mind filled with shouts, with siren whoops, with babbles of fear and alarm that had arisen around him as he lay bleeding on the sidewalk. He visualized Mikkelson with his chest spattered and his face splotched with York's own blood.

York squeezed his eyes closed again and tried to calm his jittering body, but he was seized by a numbing sense of dread. Twice in less than a year he had been the target of total strangers out to murder him. If two had already tried, how may hundreds—*thousands*—more lunatics and fanatics were out there gnashing their teeth in uncontrollable hatred of *him?* He shuddered. It was a realization as frightening as any nightmare he had suffered as a boy. And it was real—and irrevocable. Someone was stalking him. Someone would always be stalking him as long as he was President. . . .

As he lay in the darkened room, the street noises below became menacing. To him, they contained the sound of hordes of assassins marshaling their forces to kill him. Then the room itself became threatening, full of shadows, dark corners, closed closet doors. He sensed the forms of several men near him, heard their breathing, the shuffle of their feet. He lay stiff, immobile on the bed, drenched with sweat, his eyes squeezed shut, his arm throbbing with each beat of his heart.

At last he forced himself to open his eyes, then to rise to his feet. He stumbled to the window and pulled open the drapes. The lemon light of an October afternoon filled the room. York looked out on the gleaming glass buildings of Park Avenue. He looked up at the clean sky. He breathed deeply, then returned to the bed, still feeling weak. At last he dozed. He dreamed now of Milly. She smiled and spoke loving words to him, but her face was streaming blood. It dripped from her chin, her earlobes, the tip of her nose. Occasionally York whispered, and once or twice he shouted during this cruel hour of sleep. At seven, Morley roused him and they drove swiftly to the airport and boarded *Air Force One* for the short flight to Washington.

* * * * *

Le Bombardier had read about York's visit to New York in the newspapers two days before it was to occur. He was not, at that point, even close to being ready to make the attempt on York's life. He had for a moment considered the possibility of doing it right then. However, a small story in *The New York Times,* outlining the number of police and Secret Service men that would be used to protect York had persuaded Le Bombardier that caution was in order. It would be foolish to risk ten million dollars, to say nothing of his own flawless reputation, just to do something that was momentarily convenient. He had put it out of his mind. Yet, he had made it a point to be among the spectators at LaGuardia Airport when *Air Force One* landed. He watched as the presidential party was escorted through the terminal to a fleet of waiting limousines with seemingly countless motorcycles, squad cars, and policemen in attendance. He hailed a taxi and followed the motorcade into the city, scribbling notes on each detail of security he had observed.

Le Bombardier had watched the bloody assassination attempt from his chosen vantage point less than ten yards from the place where York was attacked. He had been mentally recording the details of the security around the President when the young assailant leaped out of the crowd. Le Bombardier had watched with intense concentration as the knife flashed and York's blood spurted bright as rubies in the sunlight. So focused and detached was his mind that even as the would-be murder weapon descended, Le Bombardier was not only recording the moves of each security agent and policeman, but calculating exactly how close that gleaming knife had come to ruining Le Bombardier's ten-million-dollar payoff. It was very, very close, and Le Bombardier chuckled at the irony inherent in the fact that a fool—indeed a madman—using the crudest of weapons could come so near to accomplishing in a few crazed seconds the same deed that he in his marvelous precision and technological expertise would take months to engineer.

Once again, he ruminated about the disadvantage of being a sane and dispassionate technician instead of a lunatic when it came to the antic work of assassination.

* * * * *

Chapter 19

The assassination attempt produced an orgy of reporting. Network news departments produced mini-documentaries and instant specials the night of the attack. TV cameramen had caught every detail of the lunatic's attack, each lurch of alarm in the security force. They showed the swift, reflexive life-saving move of the President's arm, the first bright geysers of blood, the clubbing down of the madman, the immediate and efficient efforts at first aid. They had caught all this in brilliant color lighted by sunshine with the sound of band music in the background.

The still photographs were almost as stunning. *Time, Newsweek,* and *Life* all prepared cover stories with page after page of color pictures. Newspapers played the story as if it were a national disaster with massive black headlines and full-page photo layouts. Reporters went off on peripheral themes and offbeat approaches to the phenomenon of assassination. Some dealt extensively with the psychology of it all; others wrote long historical pieces; some reported in depth on security practices around the President, past and present.

The New York *Post* first brought up the zero phenomenon. Three days after the attack on York, the *Post* splashed a typically tasteless headline on page one:

ZERO CURSE
DOOMS YORK
PRESIDENCY?

The *Post* reported in detail the coincidence of the deaths of the zero-year Presidents, stretching the material into a week-long series that dealt with the lives and deaths of each of the seven. The *Post* managed to make all of the deaths seem somehow interconnected, and though the stories were sensationalized beyond credibility, the possibility that something supernatural and very sinister loomed over the Administration of Augustus York suddenly seemed quite real.

The idea of a "zero curse" caught the imagination of others in the media. All the networks did a documentary on the phenomenon. *The New York Times Week in Review* produced a turgid essay on the powers of the supernatural in major events in world history. William Safire of the *Times* took it seriously, tying it in with strange episodes that occurred in the Nixon years, but James Reston discounted it as if he were God. *Time* produced a rather pretentious essay on the significance of curses and superstitions in the history of mankind, summing up by proclaiming that man had always been the product of his superstition and that the difference between superstition and religion was one of only slight degree.

York was oddly affected by the introduction of the zero curse. It confused him and troubled him in ways he did not understand. He said irritably to Morley, "What the hell am I supposed to do now—pretend I was elected in 1981?"

Morley said, "We ignore it, Mr. President. It's all hype for the media. Those hyenas will do anything to hype a rating or sell a paper. There is nothing to it, and there is nothing we should do about it."

The uproar died away quickly, fading into oblivion as hundreds of other media-nourished fads had done in the past. The American attention span was brief.

York recovered quickly from the wound in his arm, and in three weeks, except for a slight throb where the artery had been cut and stitched together, he suffered no more pain. Milly was still concerned about the state of his mind. At times, he seemed distant and vague; on other occasions he was cheerful, even buoyant.

One day, a month after the New York attempt, he was uncommonly quiet during their regular lunch tête-à-tête, and she asked him what was troubling him. He simply shook his head, saying nothing.

"You haven't been sleeping much, darling. I hear you tossing and muttering all night. Are your dreams bad?"

He took a sip of wine and looked up at her. "Milly, I don't want to talk about it even to you. It shames me that I have let it get to me."

"What do you mean?"

He paused, then spoke in a low voice: "I can't get that zero-curse thing out of my mind. It haunts me. I manage to forget about it for a while, let it drop, do my work, sleep soundly for a week, for days. But then it comes back and I lie awake haunting myself with it. I even worry about it in broad daylight."

This was the first time he had mentioned it to her, and Milly was alarmed. "Gus! That's just a crazy coincidence! It's impossible that it has anything to do with you!"

"I know that. In my mind, my conscious, logical, rational mind, Milly, I *know* that very well. But there's some kind of mean mountain demon sitting way down in the back of my brain. It keeps ticking off little warnings about that zero thing, about all the people who want to kill me." He looked up at her; his eyes were as bleak and clouded as if he were feeling physical pain. "I've gotten this feeling that maybe I *am* cursed."

Milly rose and embraced him as he sat in his chair. "Cursed? Darling, you've been one of the most blessed men I know. You have nothing to be afraid of. Life isn't jinxes and curses. It just happens the way it happens."

York wrapped his arms around her waist and turned her so she sat facing him on his lap. He smiled and put his hand against her cheek, gently leaning forward to kiss her. "I love you," he said. They embraced again.

A butler entered briskly with a tray of pastries. He saw the President and his wife entwined like a pair of honeymooners. The golden light of the room infused the scene with such tenderness that the butler paused for a moment and gawked in wonder. It filled him with such pleasure that he quickly tiptoed back to the service room to tell the other servants what he had seen, but he was chortling so that he could barely speak.

But after York returned to the Oval Office, Milly was frightened. She knew he was a sensitive man of odd moods. When she had first met him, almost twenty years before, he had been the Hillbilly Gladiator, a handsome, laughing giant of a man with the dazzling smile and impish humor of a boy. He was near the end of his playing career, but he still had the rollicking enthusiasm of a college sophomore.

York and Milly had met when he and two teammates brought their dates to the Satin Room. Bob Venturi invited the players to the stage, introduced them, then suggested that each might like a token dance with Milly in the spotlight. The other two guffawed embarrassedly and turned down the offer, but Gus took Milly in his arms and they performed a sweeping, graceful waltz around the empty dance floor. The customers and the band rose to their feet in applause. Gus asked if he might call her, and she said yes. She and Venturi had separated four months before, a civilized parting in which both admitted that their love affair had simply faded out.

She and Gus dated for six months, eventually made exuberant love every day, then were married in a boisterous wedding that was rampant with Chicago Bears. She was pregnant in two months, and the baby, Augustus Alvin York, Jr.—Gussie, they called him— was born in the spring of 1963. They were both ecstatic. York got his law degree on the baby's two-month birthday. He had debated retiring from the Bears for a year or more. He was, after all, thirty-six years old. But whenever the prospect of no longer playing football came up, he turned somber and silent. The intensity of his depression surprised her, frightened her. In the summer of 1963 he resolved the question of retirement by going back to training camp, driving himself into splendid condition, and playing a glorious season in which he beat out one of the brightest young prospects in the game. York caught ten touchdown passes, an old man beating back age for one more year.

By the next season, he had started working in a law firm in Paducah. He and Milly bought a house there. The idea of entering politics had been suggested to Gus York by a senior partner in his firm. After all, he was a celebrated name in Kentucky—why not cash in? But that June he was restless as a migratory animal and he began again the ritual of conditioning himself to play—jogging, weightlifting, calisthenics. Then he twisted an ankle doing a wind-sprint. He limped home in pain, a look of shock on his face. That night he sipped whiskey with Milly as a soft summer dusk folded down over the house. After a long silence, he said, "It's over, darling. I'm too slow, too soft, too old." He held his glass up in a silent salute of farewell. "I resign."

She went to him and hugged him. "Will you really do it?"

He smiled sadly. "I ache everywhere. My ankle feels like it is full of hot needles. It's over."

It wasn't quite. Gus was black and moody for a couple of weeks. Milly knew she had been naïve to expect that this man could simply cast away a life he had been immersed in for more than twenty years. Football had given him emotional highs, intense passions, and keen satisfactions that no person could fathom who had not committed himself to the game as Gus York had.

One sunny July afternoon as they sat on the bank of the river behind their home, Gus said, "I keep feeling half-dead, numb. My body seems all used up, like a mummy in a coffin."

"Is it that bad?"

"The odd thing is that I *feel* I'm the same as when I was in college. I don't even *look* that different. But I can't move the same way. It's like I've been invaded by some demon or ghost."

"Gus, good God, you're thirty-seven years old—that's why you can't run like you used to. You're mortal. It's just nature moving on."

"Maybe. But I feel like something's gotten into me, something cold, something dead." He gazed bleakly at the slow-moving brown waters of the river.

Milly said, "Gus, it's your imagination." But he did not reply.

It was his imagination, of course, and by the beginning of the professional football season in late September, he was reconciled to retirement. It was 1964 and he got involved briefly with the Republican campaign in Kentucky, the benighted run of Barry Goldwater against Lyndon Johnson. York did not like the fanaticism that infected the Goldwater wing of the party. However, he made campaign speeches for the slightly more moderate state Republican ticket, which also went down to defeat.

The joy of fatherhood was constant with York. The baby, Gussie, was a roly-poly jovial child whom York tossed around like a delightful toy, laughing and whooping while the baby gurgled and chirped. The two of them were like an absurdly outlandish Mutt and Jeff, one truly a giant, the other a burbling doll, frolicking in unconfined fun.

It was the next summer, on a hot, still afternoon in August, 1965, that Milly left Gussie with a baby-sitter. About three P.M. the sitter noticed the child was not sleeping in his crib. She began a search which, as time went on, became more frenzied. At three-thirty she called York at his office and he rushed home. Milly returned at four-thirty, and Gussie was still missing. By then, there were policemen and firemen everywhere. Dozens of men prowled the banks of the river. At five o'clock, a small flotilla of motorboats was making circles on the water as they dragged the bottom. At six, the body of the child was retrieved with grappling hooks.

The funeral was a hysterical affair. York's sobs were deep and broken. Milly, faint with grief, shrieked periodically. Despair lay over her like tons of cold stones. At the grave, she swayed, her knees buckling, and nearly pitched into the hole when the tiny white coffin was lowered into the earth.

Mad, black days followed, now all but unrememberable to Milly. She did recall a conversation in which York said, "I might have saved him. I had a premonition something bad was going to happen. Two nights before I dreamed that I saw Gussie and he was sleeping on the lawn, and when I tried to go to him—I wanted to kiss him—I couldn't get there. Some kind of barrier was there, invisible, all around him. I couldn't get through whatever it was. I should have known, Milly, that Gussie . . ." He began to sob and could not finish the sentence. He did not mention the dream again.

Three weeks after the funeral, York disappeared. He left Milly a note that said only, "Don't worry. I'm in Chicago." She had not been concerned. Her grief was too consuming to allow room for any other feeling. When he returned three days later he looked more stricken than even at the time of Gussie's death. He was unshaven, his eyes rimmed in crimson. He told Milly what he had done.

"I wanted to talk to Gussie, just once more. I wanted to hear him laugh just once more. I went to an old lady on Rush Street, a spiritualist, the sign downstairs said. I wanted her to bring back Gussie." His eyes were bleak and hopeless. "Once when I was a boy, an old woman, a gypsy, traveling through Jezebel, gave a séance at our house. We asked her to bring Grandma York back to see us. Grandma had died a month before. We sat around a kerosene lamp and we all stared at the flame and, pretty soon, Grandma was there in the room. She was whispering, though you could hardly understand anything. I could smell the way she used to smell. Lavender water. She was really there.

"I went to this old woman in Chicago, Milly. I was drunk, I think, but it didn't matter. I would have gone, anyway. She fixed up a séance for me. She told me Gussie was in the room. There was the sound of a baby's voice, gurgling and laughing. It wasn't Gussie. He wasn't there. I went back twice more. The same thing. I drank a lot after the third time. I started walking the streets. I walked all over Chicago during that night. And all of a sudden there was Gussie with me, Milly. He was in my arms, solid and chubby as ever, laughing at me. And he stayed there for hours while I stumbled all over town with him. We were talking to each other, laughing. I had Gussie back then."

Milly could scarcely bring herself to answer. "Gus . . . Gus . . . no, you didn't. He's dead."

Gus wept. "I know it," he sobbed. "I know it."

Time mended this madness and healed their grief. They did not speak again of Gus' experience in Chicago. But Milly wondered now if her husband might be turning again to some long-buried need to believe in the spirit world and the supernatural.

Three soft taps sounded at the door and Bitsy Rogerson entered with her white leather notebook. The afternoon schedule for the First Lady, she said, included greeting top executives of the Girl Scouts of America, taking tea with several opera stars who would sing at dinner that night, exchanging a recipe with three famous French chefs who were touring America, and cutting a birthday cake with the oldest member of the Daughters of the American Revolution.

* * * * *

Chapter 20

York knew that his idea was bizarre, even laughable, but there was a logic to it that could not be denied. After the episode in New York, Morley explained in detail about CIPHER, hoping to ease York's understandably heightened anxiety over assassination. Such a system of predicting would-be assailants, then screening them off, was a perfectly sound method of security precaution. York had been pleased.

His new idea had come to him in the throes of insomnia and pain after the New York attack, and it had stuck with him now for more than a month. Yet he was reluctant to bring it up, even to Morley, because he knew that any rational, practical man would be, first, skeptical of the whole concept, and, second, deeply concerned about the President's emotional condition. The idea was that strange.

Still, York felt that he had no choice but to bring it up. He summoned Morley to the Oval Office and spoke bluntly: "Andy, I don't sleep much anymore since New York. I have an obsession, I guess you'd call it, with the thought of assassination. First, I want the security detail beefed up—a lot. Second, I want to ask you whether you think CIPHER is doing everything it should be doing."

"No problem on more Secret Service. We'll even double it for a while if it makes you feel better. As for CIPHER, there was no way we would have found that fellow in New York. You just can't screen out every off-the-wall lunatic. You'd have to have a crystal ball to know he was going to strike."

York took the opening and plunged ahead. "Okay. That is what I'm talking about, Andy—a computerized crystal ball."

"What do you mean?"

"When I was a boy in Jezebel, we used to have people coming through—people with 'powers,' we'd call them. Faith-healers and gypsies, fortune-tellers, spiritualists, clairvoyants, strange folks blessed with insights and understandings that ordinary men never had. They used to attract crowds, and people believed in their powers. I did, I know."

York paused and tried to gauge Morley's reaction. Morley's blue eyes were wide behind his spectacles, but he said nothing.

"Bear with me, Andy. It may have been superstition or blind faith, or maybe the things they did were real. I saw a man heal an old lady who hadn't walked without a crutch for forty years. I saw a little girl handle a barrelful of poisonous snakes. I saw my grandmother returned for a few minutes from the dead. I was a child then, Andy. I believed those things. And . . . and I believe some of them now, I think."

Morley took a quick breath, as if he wanted to speak, but York held up a hand. "No. Let me get it all out. Then you can talk. What I want is for you to add another element to CIPHER. I want you to put in data from people who think they can tell the future . . . who think they can tell *my* future. Now, don't argue. Just answer yes or no if that is possible."

Morley gasped. "Yes or no? You're talking about programming bats and black cats into a computer, Mr. President. Yes or no? My God, it seems to me that the answer lies in the question—it should never have been asked, Mr. President."

"Okay. But I've asked it, and I want an answer. Not only that—I want the answer to be *yes!*"

Morley stared hard at the President. "I don't think it's possible."

"You are the man who thought more computerized information could have given us an accurate reading on the election. That is a forecast, isn't it?"

"Yes, but it's based on statistics. Hard, tangible statistics—past voting patterns, demographic changes, vital records. It isn't based on some old witch poring over a boiling caldron of bats' wings and newts' eyes."

"We will make our own statistics, our own patterns. We will ask a hundred, a thousand, a *hundred thousand* psychics or clairvoyants or futurists—whatever—to predict what will happen to me. We will build a base of data about it that will, eventually, begin to make sense. With enough information, we can keep refining the patterns, building on the right guesses until we have a few of these forecasters who will be right. Why not?"

"My God, you're talking about computerizing black magic!"

"Something like that. I'm frightened of the future, Andy. I want to know all I can about it."

Morley frowned. "Mr. President, before we go on with this subject, let me speak very candidly. This fear of yours is a reaction to the New York City incident—specifically. It is not a permanent condition. I think it is also exaggerated by the fact that you still feel uncomfortable in the White House. This job is a matter of conditioning. Lyndon Johnson knew more about the

White House and Washington power than anybody who ever got to be President, but even he couldn't quite keep it all together. Given the complexities, there is no way that any mortal, ordinary man can completely comprehend it in the first year—or less—of his Administration. Being President is, by definition, traumatic. You're still traumatized by it, Mr. President."

York nodded. "It's one hell of an adjustment. But knowing that doesn't lessen my anxiety. Call it a trauma, call it an obsession, call it a neurosis. I want CIPHER programmed to tell me what's going to happen."

Morley tried another tack. "Mr. President, if this ever gets into the papers, they'll call you certifiable. Spending tax money to build a computer base of Tarot card-readers and star-gazers. Can you imagine?"

"It will not get out of the White House. And, from now on, I don't want to hear *if* it can be done—I want to hear *how* it can be done."

Morley paused. His voice was suddenly businesslike and efficient: "Okay. There has been research done in parapsychology by the C.I.A. and the defense intelligence agencies. They used clairvoyants and precognitive types to locate Soviet missile bases, hidden installations. I don't know how much of it worked. Duke University has been involved in this sort of thing for decades. There are others—some guys at Berkeley and around Palo Alto. I just don't think any of the experiments have been consistently successful, Mr. President. It's all probabilities, concepts—nothing of real substance."

"You can program CIPHER to use some of this material?"

"Yes, we can try it. No one knows what will come out of it."

"I know that, Andy. I just want the *possibility* set up, something that *might* work."

"Okay. But I'd like to make one condition for you, Gus. I'll get this going in CIPHER, but you must promise to have a full checkup—physically, emotionally, psychologically, everything. Is that a deal?"

"It's a deal."

"You might just need a tranquilizer of some kind, Mr. President. Something to take the edge off this pressure."

York shook his head vigorously. "No drugs, no pills. I never even let them put analgesic balm on my sprains back at the Bears."

"Well, just so we get the doctor involved."

"I will. And I want that computer programmed with as much of this psychic stuff as you can get together."

"It's a deal." Morley left and York felt suddenly relieved of some great burden. He turned his swivel chair to the French windows that looked out on the rose garden.

The day was radiant, a morning of such clarity that it seemed reflected from a mirror. York watched as a gardener dug at the roots of a rose bush. The man's concentration was total; his face exhibited a oneness with his work that appeared religious. His gloves were dirty with soil, his shirt damp across his back. Suddenly, he sensed that he was being watched and turned in York's direction. The President smiled and waved. The gardener waved back with a dirty glove. York found himself envying the man, the ordinariness of his occupation, the simplicity of his task, and the beauty of the flowers he produced.

* * * * *

Chapter 21

That afternoon, Morley took a drink, then another, before he went to Appleton to tell him about the President's orders for CIPHER. When he had finished speaking, Appleton said nothing.

"You have no opinion at all about this?"

Appleton spoke slowly. "Yes, I have an opinion. My opinion is that either everyone around this place is crazy, or *I* am crazy." He paused, then went on quickly. "Also, you smell like eighty-six-proof octane. I'm wondering if your mind has lapsed again like it did that night last fall. I find this whole thing is totally demeaning."

Morley felt anger rising. "I don't have to answer to you about drinking or anything else, Appleton. But I do have to answer to the President about the CIPHER program. You'll do as he asks, of course."

"Of course." The dark glasses seemed more opaque than usual to Morley. Appleton's tension showed only in the bitter line of his lips and the rigid set of his shoulders. His impenetrable self-control irked Morley. "And you say it is demeaning? You ought to be grateful you got this job. And you think maybe everyone around this place is crazy, eh?"

Appleton interrupted. "You gave me an order. Why don't you let me do it? Cool off. Sober up."

Morley's temper snapped. He pointed a long, trembling finger at Appleton. "Don't tell me to sober up, you glass-eyed robot! You gumshoe bodyguards all think you're some kind of supermen! You're nothing but a bunch of constipated night watchmen! You call *this* job demeaning, Appleton? Your whole life has been demeaning!"

Appleton started to leave his chair, but Morley pushed him back. The Secret Service man clenched his fists, began to rise again, then sank back, resigned to letting Morley continue his diatribe.

Morley's voice had an edge of meanness. "So you call this demeaning? You—the stupid, willing asshole who spent his life standing between the President and some lunatic's bullets. What a job for assholes! To die for a cheap politician! You weren't putting your life on the line for saints and messiahs! Not even for statesmen. Think about those guys! Eisenhower! Stupid as that smile of his. Mean, narrow, *stupid!* Kennedy! Your hero! And you end up playing pimp and beard for all his cheap shack-ups. You call *this* job demeaning?! And Johnson! The meanest vulgarian to come down the pike, holding meetings while he takes a crap! A liar, a crook, a deceitful, warped man. You were willing to die for Lyndon Johnson—and you call *this* demeaning?! And Nixon! What the hell kind of a life is that to get killed for? A cheap, paranoid crook, the most dishonest man ever to sit in the White House. Ford! God, Ford! Bozo the Clown, covered with bumps from stumbling, a certified cretin. Die for Ford? Appleton! You asshole! Look at the last guy here! Sweetmouth Sunday school teacher. 'I'll never lie to you.' And he turns into the most expedient President in years, a clumsy hypocrite. Die for a born-again peanut farmer? Hell, yes, Appleton!"

Appleton had not moved. Suddenly Morley reached forward and snatched off his glasses. The Secret Service man blinked. His eyes were haggard, bright with anger and pain. Clearly the attack had drawn blood. Satisfied, Morley lowered his voice: "Demeaning? Appleton, your life for the past twenty years has been demeaning." Morley handed the dark glasses back to him. "And the trouble is, you *know* it. You've hated your job—and you've hated yourself."

Morley watched as Appleton glared at him. The Secret Service man put on his glasses again.

"I want the program started today," Morley said crisply.

Appleton remained silent.

Morley returned to his office and poured himself another drink. The confrontation with Appleton left him feeling hollow and dissatisfied. It was cruel and unjust and, of course, the Secret Service man was right: York's demand for a computer program to tell the future was an insult to any man's intelligence.

* * * * *

Le Bombardier took the Eastern shuttle from New York to Washington on November 13. He had stayed in New York more than a month, keeping his suite at the Carlyle and continuing his liaison with the lovely painter. He had worked at a leisurely pace, spending many hours at the meticulous business of forging a full set of credentials and papers. He was now Albert Sauvart, a middle-aged journalist from the south of France assigned as a stringer in Washington for several French papers. He wore a slightly shiny and imperfectly cut blue blazer, gray checked trousers in similar condition, scuffed black shoes, a slightly soiled white shirt with a striped necktie. Around his middle was strapped a padded cummerbund to make him look paunchy. He assumed a somewhat duckfooted walk. His hair was dyed almost black and glossed with hair oil. He slicked it back from a part in the middle, and his sideburns were snipped at the ear tops. A small black mustache, meant to be natty, merely gave him a meek appearance. Steel-rimmed spectacles framed his eyes. His cheeks were powdered with talcum and he trailed the scent of heavily perfumed shaving lotion. He carried a large old Gladstone valise and an old leather briefcase, bulky and strapped. These, as well as the Albert Sauvart wardrobe, had been found after a week of patient touring of pawnshops in New York.

In the briefcase was the French passport of Albert Sauvart, 51, born in Aix-en-Provence, plus working papers for a visa in the United States, several letters of introduction to the French embassy from the various papers in Nice, Cap d'Antibes, and Marseille that he was supposedly working for.

In Washington, Le Bombardier took a taxi directly to the French embassy on Massachusetts Avenue and presented himself at the desk which received immigrating Frenchmen. He explained to the clerk that he planned to stay in the capital for several months, eventually filing a letter from America each week or so to his string of papers. He showed his passport, his working papers, the letters from his editors. Le Bombardier's normal French was impeccable Parisian, but he was careful to use the slightly blurred inflections of the south of France.

There was no hitch in his documents or his appearance, and the clerk said, "Let me introduce you to Mam'selle Debernard. She is assistant chief of protocol and press relations, and perhaps she can help you, too."

Suzanne Debernard shook his hand briefly, but warmly, and said, "Monsieur Sauvart, you will be needing press credentials. We can give you general temporary passes to the Congress and to the White House for briefings and the like. But if you wish access to the Pentagon or other agencies that are deemed sensitive, we shall have to pursue an extensive security check."

Le Bombardier ducked his head almost obsequiously, but his smile was sly. "*Non*, my dear Miss Debernard. It is not military secrets that I am after, only to capture the essence of American government in print. I shall be quite happy with the most superficial credentials."

Suzanne smiled and said, "Superficial credentials it will be."

Le Bombardier said, "I am a slow writer and a slow learner. I doubt that I shall be able to find any worthwhile observations for many weeks. For now, I suspect press credentials for the Congress and the White House will suffice."

"We shall look forward to your stories, Monsieur Sauvart," replied Suzanne.

But Le Bombardier did not want to be considered with any affection or special interest by these people who might interfere with his work by becoming friends. He arched an eyebrow and addressed Suzanne. "Ah, Mam'selle, the French restaurants in Washington—is their fare edible?"

"Some are all right."

"You could give me a list? Perhaps you might accompany me, a poor provincial Frenchman, to a few?" He dropped his head and leered at her bosom.

"Perhaps we can start tonight?" His smile was slightly wolfish as he reached out to touch her shoulder.

Suzanne drew away. "I think not."

Le Bombardier wanted no one to mistake his behavior as being anything but gauche. Openly scrutinizing her behind, he said to the departing Suzanne, "Ah, warm friendships are forged in foreign lands among strangers with a common country. We shall meet again? We shall be warm?"

When Suzanne turned to glare, Le Bombardier continued to leer at her. Satisfied, he left the embassy. Next he rented a room on L Street from the classified section of the *Post*. From there he went to the White House to try out his temporary press pass. At the guard's gate a phone call to the French embassy verified his identity, and he entered the executive mansion.

In the White House press section, Le Bombardier spoke heavily accented English. A clerk showed him the bins and boxes where daily press releases, official statements, and briefing transcripts were distributed. He was also shown the location of a typewriter and the Telex to file his stories back to France. His steel-rimmed spectacles, badly cut clothing, and oiled hair marked him immediately as a foreigner, and an unimpressive one at that. However, his ilk was common at the White House. Foreign correspondents and communications media people from all over the world frequently toured the White House and were constantly slipping in and out of the press offices. They went virtually unnoticed.

* * * * *

Chapter 22

The Crystal Ball program of CIPHER had been predictably complex to organize. For five weeks, into early December, Appleton and his staff had worked to accumulate information. He had no faith at all that Crystal Ball would produce anything useful. But as Morley had told him, there were others in government besides the President interested in the investigation of psychic powers, and this impressed him.

Appleton found that the C.I.A. had indeed begun an intricate series of secret experiments in psychokinetics and had recruited a small army of psychics, clairvoyants, and precognitive types. The C.I.A. men told Appleton that, so far, they had developed little of practical use from this program, although some aspects looked promising. For one thing, they had been trying to detect missile dispersal in the Soviet Union through the mental images of clairvoyants. There had actually been a surprising number of cases in which intelligence sources inside Russia verified the missile location visions of the seers. The trouble with this particular program, the C.I.A. men said, was that they could only act with certainty on the clairvoyant's information after they had it verified through some other intelligence source. They could not depend on it as the sole source of information. "But even though we can't trust it completely, it does give vaguely useful guidance," said one C.I.A. man.

"I guess that's what we're after, too," Appleton said, "vaguely useful guidance."

The F.B.I. had several clairvoyants and psychics as paid consultants, he learned. Duke University had a long, ongoing program, as did the University of California at Berkeley, U.C.L.A., and the Institute of Parapsychology in New York City. Appleton tapped these sources for dependable people who might provide insights into the future of the President. Ultimately, he developed a list of some fifteen hundred people as widely scattered over the United States as they were scattered through the various branches of the occult: astrologists, psychics, card-readers, numerologists, clairvoyants, psephologists—the variety was immense.

The cover story for the operation, invented by Morley, was brilliant for its simplicity as well as its credibility. The fifteen hundred participants were told that they were participating in a nationwide experiment in conjunction with a series of television documentaries to be produced sometime in the next two or three years. Predictions about the life of President York over two years offered a viable test of their ability to tell the future because his existence was so public and, therefore, the predictions could be accurately correlated with actual events. Morley even sent TV crews to film some of the participants to make the ruse more believable.

Each of the selected readers of York's future was to transmit daily his or her insights, intuitions, stargazings, whatever, collect via a Telex number in Chicago, where the ostensible headquarters for the TV production was located. This was merely a blind receiving station, and the material was passed on directly to CIPHER in the Executive Office Building.

Participants were instructed to file their predictions by using a series of codes that categorized the material into specific subjects—such as health, safety, travel, emotional condition, and such. The codes could then be fed into the computer in these prearranged categories.

Early in December, Brandeis entered Appleton's office. He wore an outfit that was blinding in its mixture of colors and patterns, not far from the lurid costumes worn by vaudeville comedians. Yet Brandeis' expression was that of a mortician. The contrast brought an involuntary snort of laughter to Appleton's lips. "What's on your mind?" he asked.

Brandeis replied in a thin voice, "The Crystal Ball program is ready."

"Why do you look so sad, then?"

"I'm not sure it will work. Whoever said you could turn fortune-telling into statistics?"

"God knows I didn't say you could."

Brandeis frowned. "Well, we tried, but for the first time in my life, I really doubt what the computer can do. It may never tell the future. Why should it?"

"The only reason I can think of is that the President says it has to."

"Even Presidents can't make a computer do what the human mind can't do."

"You mean, tell the future?"

"Yes. But we have enough data in CIPHER now to make comparisons, to select some of the most probably accurate sources, to begin to weigh the different reports. What we need now is a pattern for the future to see which predictions deviate most and which least."

"That figures."

"We will use random days. Pick a day, then check back and see how the readouts were, which of the sources was closest. We'll be able to measure their consistency—if there *is* any consistency. We need to set up a series of best possible probabilities. Then we can begin to average out the others against that. It's going to take a couple more months to shake down right."

"The damn thing might really tell the future?"

"Not likely. It is possible if we can correlate and grade our sources accurately enough that it will give us something once in a while. But I doubt we will be able to depend on it." Brandeis turned to leave, then looked back at Appleton, his eyes gleaming. "I have a banana, cream cheese and walnut sandwich on pumpernickel, and lemonade for lunch today. There is no way I could have predicted that last week." After a meaningful pause, he left.

Appleton closed his eyes for a moment and let his mind focus entirely on himself. He had been accustomed to assuming for years that he was a consummate cool customer, the ultimate non-neurotic. No more. Morley had been right: the Presidency, that impersonal institution, had been Appleton's major source of self-esteem. He had depended on its size to make him big, and its power to make him strong. His ego fed from the Presidency. He measured his moral stature against it. His exalted opinion of himself as an elite man grew from it—and from almost nothing else. Yet, what had the Presidency *really* done for him? Made him a gumshoe and a beard, bulletproofing for cheap politicians. It had demeaned him, made him small. Nothing had brought this home to him with such impact as this ludicrous assignment of trying to make a computer into a crystal ball.

His support through these dark days was Suzanne Debernard. Fittingly, they had first met during his other darkest period, that bleak and hysterical weekend after Kennedy's assassination. Appleton had been thirty-one, a gaunt and haunted young man with scorched eyes that revealed his trauma over the President's murder as well as the anguish of his cracking marriage. Suzanne, then in her early twenties, was a secretary at the French embassy. She was assigned to act as translator between the Secret Service and the security guards who accompanied President de Gaulle to John Kennedy's funeral. She had been drawn to the melancholy young agent. They met for a drink the week after the funeral and spoke of many things—but not the assassination. By the first of the year 1964, Appleton and Suzanne were seeing each other two or three times a week when he was not in Texas or traveling with the peripatetic President Johnson. Finally, in the spring of that year over dinner at her apartment, he brought himself to speak about his crushing sense of loss and guilt over the murder of John Kennedy.

"I feel it was my fault," he confessed miserably.

"How could it be? You were in no position to know about the killer."

"But if we had gone over that route and seen . . ."

She patted his hand. "You are only men."

He talked then for the first time about the true depth of pain he had felt over Kennedy's death, about the torrent of tears that he waited for but which never broke. She leaned over and kissed him. They slept together that night, and for two years they were lovers. Then Suzanne was sent back to Paris, then to the French embassy in London, then to the embassy in

Tokyo. In 1977 she returned to Washington as an assistant chief of protocol and press at the embassy. In the intervening years, they had seen each other a dozen times, no more, mostly when Appleton accompanied presidential visits to places where she happened to be working. The exchanged a few letters. Both had other lovers in the interim. When they first met after her return to Washington, they kissed as friends, intending only a brief brush of lips. But they held the kiss and then they embraced. Suzanne wept and Appleton blinked rapidly behind his dark glasses. Soon after that they moved into the apartment in Georgetown and they had lived together since.

Lately, they had spoken often of his distaste for his job. The night after Brandeis' pessimistic report, he asked Suzanne, "What the hell could I do besides the Secret Service?"

She smiled. "You are a wonderful lover. You could become a gigolo."

"I could also become a night watchman. Morley would appreciate that."

"Please don't be so dark about this. It is only a job, only your work."

Appleton had not been able to tell her the specifics of CIPHER because it was highly classified. What she knew was that he had been relegated to working with a computer and that his closest colleague was a clownish genius named Brandeis.

"Has the computer taught you anything you could use?" she asked.

"Only to sit and listen to Brandeis describe his lunch. I wouldn't want to be anywhere near one of those things."

"Will you be changed from that assignment?"

"I doubt it. And I doubt very much that I can convince myself I should go back to the security detail. Morley was right about that, you know."

"Maybe he is too smart about things. If he must get drunk to say what he believes, he is perhaps a weak man."

"He's not weak, not Morley." Appleton paused. "I wish I could tell you everything this job involves. It's lots stranger than you know."

"You mustn't mention anything that can get you into trouble."

"I won't. I can't."

"See? You are loyal to your work, after all."

"Not loyal. I'm as programmed as the damn computer."

She sighed. "This last year has been so hurtful for you. You have been so humiliated. Can't you leave?"

"I guess I'd like to. But I don't know *how* to. I don't know what else I can do. It's a job that doesn't lead to anything, really. Some kind of protection detail for a corporation president? Bodyguard for a millionaire's kids? Christ, everything it points to is worse than the job is now."

Suzanne frowned. She embraced him, holding his head against her breasts, bending to kiss his ear. "You are much, much more than your work. A job is a very small part of you, of any man. You are a vital, physical man who has been disappointed in one small part of his life. You have much more to do, to give, to be. You are my love, my lover . . ."

Appleton hugged her. He wanted to immerse himself in her love, to escape from this emptiness, this ultimate disappointment in finding weakness where he had always assumed strength. He felt helpless, but now he kissed Suzanne's neck and she murmured soft French words which he did not understand. She tightened her arms around him and her lips were moist and soft. Her tongue moved slowly over his lips and he felt himself drawn out of the darkness of his mood, toward the consuming passion of their lovemaking.

She whispered, "Let's go to bed. I want to love you. I want you to feel me love you."

They did not turn on a light in the bedroom. They undressed quickly and in bed they clung together. He caressed her breasts, her hips, the downy mound, and she hugged him, pulling him onto her, into her. Appleton felt only the love she had for him. He felt protected by it, lost in it. Outside their bedroom window a streetlight danced violently in the December wind and the shadows of tree limbs whipped back and forth across the pane. They made love for a long time. Appleton felt fulfilled, renewed, at ease with himself when they had finished. But, of course, in the morning when he returned to his office, he discovered again that even Suzanne's love could not permanently block out CIPHER or Brandeis' lunch or President York's insistence on doing the impossible.

* * * * *

For several days Le Bombardier returned to the White House and asked questions of the press staff and correspondents. He was polite, bowing his head and taking notes in a fussy handwriting. He began with circumspect queries about York's popularity: Do the people like him? Why? He was given the latest polls by the White House press staff—forty-nine percent approve of his job in office; thirty-one percent disapprove; the rest don't know. White House correspondents were more acerbic.

"He is a very common, folksy man and he appeals to

them because he is obviously genuine, obviously honest—none of that television plastic we've had for so long," commented a friendly reporter from the *Washington Star*. "But York himself doesn't seem completely sure of himself. His instincts are probably good, very liberal for a Republican, but he doesn't trust them."

A fellow from the *Boston Globe* stated, "He is doing some things without checking with the established party men first. This will get him into trouble. He might have the maverick reflexes of a Harry Truman, a very ordinary man capable of very big things, but so far he's unsure."

These observations were not of interest to Le Bombardier, but he listened in order to get other facts he was looking for:

Does he travel often? Less than he used to.

Does he schedule these trips far in advance? Rarely. More likely he springs them on the public a day or two before he goes.

Why is that? No reason, really. He was very nervous after a couple of assassination attempts; that's probably it. But it's natural.

Does he attend diplomatic receptions in Washington? Not often.

Has he been ill? Not that anyone knows. He seems healthy, though he often looks tired, and these days he is sometimes very jittery at press conferences.

Le Bombardier spent the first week at the White House press rooms, insinuating himself where he could. The man from the *Washington Star* liked to drink, and Le Bombardier accompanied him to bars on two different evenings. The second night he stole the *Star* reporter's wallet. He found a Washington Press Club card, as well as a permanent White House press card and a V.I.P. pass to the congressional press galleries. These Le Bombardier put in the lining of his sagging Gladstone bag. If he needed them, it would be an easy job to forge them in the name of Albert Sauvart.

He attended press briefings twice daily at the White House and also went to a press conference where President York himself appeared for a fifteen-minute period. The President spoke about a number of difficult subjects and seemed quite comfortable with all of them. He flared up once when a reporter asked him if he had yet firmed up plans for a trip to Los Angeles in early December. "Nothing has been said about that trip. It is not scheduled, and it is not 'firmed up' in any way. It's two weeks off. Why should we be making plans for it already?"

The reporter was taken aback by York's ire. "Security precautions. Just getting the place cleared for you," he said lamely.

York spoke harshly. "Security is no problem. There is no trip planned."

Later Le Bombardier heard snatches of discussion among reporters who recalled that the Los Angeles trip had been in the works for more than a week and there was no reason they knew why York should be touchy about it. Le Bombardier now realized that solving this particular assassination puzzle would be more difficult than he had thought.

The density of the protective screen around York was impressive. Even inside the White House, in the corridors he was able to observe, there seemed to be a Secret Service agent or a marine guard stationed every few yards, which surprised him. He had realized beforehand that he had never stalked a man so well protected as the President of the United States, but he had not imagined quite such an impenetrable army of security men.

Another major problem was York's apparent obsession with keeping his trips a secret until the last possible moment. This gave Le Bombardier no chance to plan or prepare a specific site, an element which was essential. Somehow the assassin had to learn far in advance about an appearance where York would be vulnerable to attack. The planning had to be perfect. There would be no hit-or-miss attempt, no long-range firing from towers or through trees (Le Bombardier was an abominable shot with firearms, anyway, and actually a bit frightened of them). Patiently, he waited for the flaw to appear in the armor around President York.

It was not easy for Le Bombardier to put up with delay. He disliked the apartment he rented; it was infested with roaches, and uncomfortable and drafty in the raw weather which clamped down on Washington in late autumn. Everything was alien to the mild climate and lavish dwellings he had become accustomed to in San Francisco. To relieve his anxiety, Le Bombardier frequently visited the National Gallery of Art, admiring the work of the Old Masters. While not the Louvre, it helped his frame of mind to stand before the familiar dark warmth and clarity of a Rembrandt or the exquisite detail of a Vermeer. He also attended concerts of the National Symphony Orchestra, a shockingly unpolished ensemble, he thought. And in his room he played tapes of Wagner hour after hour. But nothing could make him forget the horrible banality of his environment.

Early in December, he arranged an interview with a State Department press attaché through the French embassy, as much to maintain his cover as a working journalist as to discover anything useful. The interview lasted three mind-numbing hours. It ranged with deadly throughness over every foreign policy subject from the Common Market to NATO arsenals, and only once did there arise any helpful information. The attaché, a thin, gray man of overweaning self-importance, told Le Bombardier that York was considering a visit to London or Paris in the winter: perhaps in late January or early February. The trip was not certain; it had not been written into his calendar yet, but a few preliminary moves had begun.

When Le Bombardier left the office, he realized that the European trip offered him the best opportunity he had found so far for killing the President. It would at least give him a few weeks to make the preparations. At the French embassy, he learned from an underling that the trip was actually far closer to reality than the cautious man at State had indicated. The tentative dates were set: February 3 to February 5 in London; February 6 to February 8 in Paris. The logistics were still somewhat uncertain, but York would stay at the U.S. embassy in both cities. Le Bombardier thought he might have found the first sign of the flaw he so badly needed.

* * * * *

Chapter 23

Browning Dayton waited in the anteroom of the Oval Office. He was not a happy man. He was worried about the drift of the York Administration, worried because of its effect on the country, on the Republican Party, and mainly on himself. He had never been a true Republican conservative. Many of the old-fashioned principles of the party offended him. His stance had been moderate, occasionally even liberal. He had found it eminently practical to be on the side of the angels—such as civil rights—whenever he could. Like most politicians, he was a decent man when he could afford it, and he liked to take positions that gratified him morally if they didn't cost too much politically.

Thus, he spoke out in the 1970s against phone tapping, mail surveillance, and the use of the Internal Revenue Service to intimidate the "political enemies" that the Nixon Administration found almost everywhere. Though he was only a second-term congressman from northern California during the Watergate scandal, Browning Dayton had been among the first in his party to call for the resignation of Nixon's top staff men and had been among the first to condemn the President himself.

Dayton had taken a risk, but he had felt right about what he was doing. More importantly, he was convinced that anything Richard Nixon did to retaliate would be so clumsily handled that he would do no serious harm. He gained valuable political mileage by being on the anti-Nixon bandwagon early.

Of course, there was no such scandal brewing in the York Administration. But Dayton had been endlessly alert for a situation that might produce some issue of value for himself. Now he had found it in the growing rift between the President and the ensconced powers of the Republican Party. The national committee, generally a group of people more conservative than Dayton or York, was becoming more and more irritated by York's unwillingness to accept—and at times, even listen to—their advice. The President's major offenses against them—the denunciation of "big business and big money" in the celebrated Detroit speech, and the recognition of Castro—had been only the most obvious reflections of York's independence. There had been dozens of other political appointments, public works projects, and special-interest legislation that the committee had wanted and the President had refused to support.

As York became more of a pariah with party regulars, Dayton more and more became their confidant and fair-haired boy. His political antenna told him that the York Administration was going to be greatly slowed—perhaps totally stalled—due to this increasing establishment distaste for the President. Without Republican support on the Hill, little legislation of any significance seemed likely to pass—although York was developing an interesting and possibly effective working relationship with the Deomcratic leadership in Congress.

This morning, Dayton had been sent to the Oval Office by the party establishment to issue a warning and report back York's reactions. It was a sensitive task, for Dayton had not wanted to reveal his pro-establishment position to the President—not just yet, anyway. But when Len Buhler, the party chairman, suggested that the vice-president take on the mission, Dayton quickly agreed to do it; he felt he could not risk offending the powerful Buhler at this point.

Dayton entered the Oval Office and York rose from his desk to shake hands. He towered over the vice-president, but there was nothing intimidating about him today. His smile was bright and his handshake genuinely warm. "Brownie! We don't see each other often enough just to talk. How are you?"

"Fine, Mr. President." They spoke briefly of Dayton's recent trip to the West Coast. Then the vice-president said, "I have something specific to discuss. I have been talking with Len Buhler and other members of the committee, Mr. President." He paused, then said softly, "They need you, Mr. President."

"Need me? What does that mean?"

"They need you on their side, not working against them."

York frowned. "By that, I assume that they need me to approve that horse's ass Ed Morningside to be ambassador to Italy—which is something I won't do. And they need me to sign that bill with all the pork-barrel projects in Arizona—which I won't do. And they need me to let all that water-development garbage go on in Wyoming. That's what they need, right, Brownie?"

"Those are all points they have discussed, yes. You just can't run the country, Mr. President, without keeping your bargains."

"Those were never my bargains, Brownie. They were the party's bargains."

"But you are the party."

"No, I am not. I happen to be President, but I am not the party. I haven't much liked what the party did to me from the moment old Peg Ironwood started shooting me down after the convention. I haven't liked the debts I was saddled with—sending that son-of-a-bitch Gellatin to India, for example."

Dayton spoke gently. "You really aren't big enough to buck the whole system, Mr. President. You can't change something that's been going on for two hundred years. You can't change politics."

"Maybe I can't, but I don't want politics to change me completely, either. I know how the system works. Buying votes, trading lame horses, patronage. I was never meant to be a horse-trader, Brownie. I was never meant to sell snake oil. I don't believe in it."

Dayton looked at York in surprise. The man was even more naïve than he had appeared to be. He understood nothing at all about the pragmatics of politics. He wanted to substitute his own private values for the demands of party politics, congressional politics, national politics, presidential politics. He wanted to make the Presidency an extension of his own personality. It was, Dayton knew, impossible. The system, the mechanics, the expediencies of the Presidency did the molding of the man, not the other way around.

"What is it the party thinks I should do differently?"

"There is one thing above all others at this point."

"What?"

"Fire Tom Matthews at Health, Education, and Welfare. He's running the department as if it's his own. He's not producing what the Republican leadership on the Hill wants."

"Matthews is doing fine. He's cut the budget; he's

got morale up over there where everyone's been in the pits for fifteen years. Why him?"

"He's just not the right guy for that job."

"Because he's black?"

"No . . . only partly."

"That's it entirely."

"No. But Matthews isn't the kind of guy the party people are comfortable with. He's rough and outspoken. He just doesn't do what he's told to do. He doesn't fit. The Hill people are embarrassed by him."

"He's doing things the way he believes they should be done. He's tough. He's honest. Christ . . . leave him alone."

"Look, Mr. President, he's alienated half the Republicans in Congress already. That testimony before Ways and Means was devastating. He practically told John Bloodgood to go screw himself in front of the whole country—John Bloodgood! The ranking *Republican* on the committee! Matthews can't get away with that—no matter what color he is."

"Bloodgood was baiting him, Brownie. He hates that whole H.E.W. operation. Matthews had to hit back or he'd have looked like a fool, letting his entire department be ridiculed."

"But he couldn't throw down the gauntlet to Bloodgood like that. That son-of-a-bitch controls half the appropriations in Congress! You can't sell him down the river in public like that, no matter how he insults you."

"Tom Matthews is about a thousand times smarter than John Bloodgood ever thought of being."

"You have to get rid of him, Mr. President. The longer he stays, the less you're going to get from the Hill."

"I'm not going to let him down."

"This party is going to crack right down the middle. You can't let your own personal likes and dislikes get in the way of running this Administration. The Presidency isn't *yours*. You have to *give* something or you'll never get anything."

York shrugged. "I have to go with what I feel. I can't run everything through party P.R. I can't start making a thousand changes in my personality. I have to do what I believe to be right, Brownie."

"That's right for a Boy Scout, bit it's naïve for a politician. You can't run the U.S. government that way. It isn't built to be run on high principles and good deeds. It is a machine. Machines can't tell truth or goodness from all the dirty tricks in the world. A machine responds only to efficiency. For you, Mr. President, to try to run this country on personal principles and individual ethics is worse than naïve. It borders on the criminal. The President of the United States is not an individual; he is an institution."

Dayton found himself shaking his finger at York, and he was surprised that he had let himself get so emotional on the subject. He knew he was right, but now he pulled back quickly. "I'm sorry, Mr. President. I've gone too far."

York said with a touch of sadness, "I have a feeling you might be a lot more right than I am, Brownie. But I don't see how I can back down. I can't fire Tom Matthews—not when I believe he did the right thing."

Dayton stated flatly, "Well, it's going to cause a lot of trouble, Mr. President. You really should reconsider. Uh . . ." he paused, frowned, then went on—". . . the other specific suggestion is that you might want to begin working with a committee—call it a management steering committee—from Republican headquarters."

"A committee?"

"Uh, well, yes. There is a general feeling that if you discussed more of your decisions with some of the more, uh, experienced members of the party, things might go better."

York sighed again. "I don't think so, Brownie. Not yet, anyway." The President rose again and towered over him. The vice-president saw a quizzical frown on York's face. York took his hand, held it firmly for several seconds, then shook it once, hard. He said, "You'll probably make one hell of a President someday, Brownie. You are about as efficient as any man I ever saw."

* * * * *

Chapter 24

The President's trip to Louisville was scheduled hurriedly and without fanfare. The press complained about the short notice, but it was a fairly insignificant event—a fund-raising ceremonial for Ira Bunker, a retiring Republican state senator, a friend of Gus York for years and a much beloved Kentucky curmudgeon. This would be York's first visit to the city since the election, and he was distressed to learn the banquet for Bunker was scheduled to be held at the same hotel where the assassination attempt had occurred. He insisted that it be moved elsewhere.

"Goddammit! A man has a right to some superstitions if he wants," York said to Morley. "It's not exactly as if I won't walk under a ladder, now, is it? I mean, something damn frightening did happen there."

"I know, Mr. President, but they have everything set up: bunting, posters, and the whole works."

"They need me there worse than I need to go. I want to give old Ira a nice send-off, but I'm not going to do it unless it's in another hotel."

The event was moved. York arrived in Louisville late in the afternoon. A cluster of reporters and television crews met him as *Air Force One* rolled to a stop at a runway far from the main passenger terminal. York stepped out of the plane and his smile was dazzling. He seemed relaxed and he fielded questions from the press happily.

York's speech later on was warm and moving. "Ira Bunker is not a certifiable genius," he said. "But he has what we used to call 'coon-dog smarts.' He could figure out exactly what he needed to do to keep that coon up the tree with a minimum of effort and a maximum of efficiency. Ira Bunker is a mountain man and he has the stiffening of a thousand mountaineers in his spine. This man is what Republicanism is all about—roots and rocks a million years old, the good and ancient motives of men who want to control their own destinies. This man is what we used to call a rugged individualist. He was born in the hard-scrabble dust of mountains. Those hard-knob hills have been his home. That is what he is made of, my friends . . . mountain rock . . . mountain rock, my friends."

York paused a moment, then added softly, almost as if he were surprised to hear himself say it: "And so am I. So am I."

The crowd rose to its feet. He was more Kentucky's President than anyone's. York raised his open hands in triumph, then waded into the crowd to shake hands. Towering above everyone, he laughed and shouted greetings until his face was flushed and gleamed with sweat. Milly stayed at the head table and watched, a pleased smile on her face.

An hour later, in the limousine on the expressway to the airport, York was expansive. "I haven't felt better since before the campaign began. I'm really glad we came back here."

He turned to Milly and was about to say something more when he saw a pickup truck hurtling across the fifty-foot grass strip separating the east- and westbound lanes. "Look out!" he bellowed. The truck's headlights bounced crazily as it crossed the divider. In the split-second before it struck the presidential limousine, the headlights filled the car with such fierce light that Milly shrieked in fear and Morley covered his eyes with his hands.

When the truck hit, the sound was thunderous. The vehicles locked bumpers. They rolled over twice together, crashing against each other down a bank in a loud shrieking of metal. When they stopped at last, the truck lay on its top, the wheels spinning. The mangled limousine lay on its right side. Headlights and taillights beamed in crazy beacons.

Troopers and Secret Service men sprinted to the wreckage. Someone sprayed foam over it. No sound came from either vehicle. The truck driver had been thrown out at first impact. His body lay by the highway, spreadeagled in death, one leg at a grotesque right angle outward from his knee, his head oddly flattened.

The rear door of York's limousine was open, mangled on its hinges. Two Secret Service men peered in fearfully; one climbed inside. They removed York first. The President's head hung loosely on his chest; his limbs were limp. They carried him a short way up the bank and laid him on the grass. Mikkelson made a calm swift check of his spine, neck, and skull. "He might be okay," he said. A large knot was growing on the President's forehead. He began to moan as his eyes fluttered open.

Mikkelson said, "His pulse is good." He looked into his eyes. "Doesn't seem to be in deep shock."

They pulled Milly from the wreck. She was conscious, though she could not stand by herself. She saw York lying on the grass and she shouted, "Is he dead? Is he dead?" And she began to crawl frantically toward him.

"No! No!" yelled Mikkelson. "He's all right, Mrs. York. Stay where you are!"

She sank to the grass, and a trooper wrapped her in a blanket.

Morley climbed out under his own power, but he limped badly when he tried to walk. Miraculously, no one in the rear of the car had been seriously hurt, but both Secret Service agents in the front seat were dead, crushed when the full weight of the speeding truck slammed the limousine engine back against them. The windshield and interior dripped with their blood.

Ambulances arrived. Attendants loaded the injured President into one, Milly into another. Morley went with Mikkelson in the Secret Service car.

At the hospital an hour later, doctors gave their verdict: no fractures; a minor concussion; and a large lump on the President's forehead. Milly had a sprained wrist, nothing more. Morley had a twisted ankle.

The accident occurred at eleven-fifteen P.M. By two A.M., a hospital spokesman addressed an eager gathering of reporters: "The President can expect soreness for the next few days and perhaps a slight headache. But he is really in no worse shape than someone who took a bad fall skiing."

It turned out that the truck driver was just that—a truck driver. But a very drunk truck driver. A quick autopsy indicated that he had an alcohol content of .31 in his blood, enough booze to befuddle three normal men.

By eight A.M., York insisted on leaving Louisville. "What a jinx town this is!" he said. "Let's get home."

The party had the look of harried survivors when they boarded *Air Force One*. York moved slowly because of his bruises and Milly wore a small black sling to support her wrist. Morley struggled on crutches.

Air Force One was no more than five minutes into the air when the President moved to the seat beside Morley. His voice was tense. "Why didn't we know this was going to happen?"

Morley was bewildered. "What?"

"Why didn't that goddamn computer give us some warning? Where was the prediction?"

Morley said, "The damn thing doesn't work yet, Mr. President. They have it programmed, but they can't seem to get anything you can depend on consistently. It's mishmash."

York glared. "I want it to work, Andy. Make it work. Goddammit! I don't want to be worrying about freak accidents and lunatics every time I leave the White House. I mean it."

"Yes, sir."

"Find out today." The look York gave Morley was one of desperation.

Ten minutes after he returned to the White House, Morley swung himself awkwardly along on his crutches to the CIPHER suite.

Appleton tried to explain. "Brandeis has been tinkering with it for days. I don't think he's got anything useful yet. We haven't correlated enough data."

Morley said coldly, "You didn't use it at all before the Louisville trip?"

"We tried, but it didn't produce anything we could understand."

"The President is madder than hell. It damn well *better* start giving out something we can understand. Or one helluva persuasive memo about why it *doesn't!*"

Morley hobbled on his crutches out of Appleton's office, his face ashen with fatigue.

Appleton called Brandeis, and when the wan little man appeared, he said, "Go over all the readouts for yesterday to see what they say about the accident."

Brandeis blinked his bright eyes. "I am doing that. I've been doing tests with a series of different combinations of psychics. It's still very unclear. But there's one combination that seems to relate to the accident."

Appleton went with Brandeis to the computer panels. Brandeis explained: "Until today, we've been getting nothing but junk. No patterns that hang together. But watch." Brandeis pushed a set of buttons, then dialed numbers. The machine produced a running tongue of paper covered with figures. "That's the usual gibberish," continued Brandeis. "Now watch this. It's only five sources of input."

The readout roll was covered with a neat set of words, precise and orderly. Appleton read the list: "blood . . . trucks . . . wheels . . . midnight . . . highway, road . . . violence in this day . . . auto accident . . . airport road . . . collision . . ."

The combination of words came from five sources: two psychics, one in San Francisco, the other in Amsterdam; a clairvoyant in Amarillo, an astrologer in San Diego; and a parapsychologist at Duke University. Suddenly a chill rushed through Appelton's body. He shuddered involuntarily.

"Cold?" asked Brandeis.

"God, yes!" The chill felt oddly alive, like fingers of ice on his body. It lasted for five seconds or so, and when Appleton spoke there was a tremor in his voice. "You mean this stuff was in the computer yesterday? We just didn't know how to break it out?"

"It was there. Apparently some of these people are in better connection with the President's vibrations than others," said Brandeis. "We have to find which ones."

Appleton studied the computer writings. To know after the fact what the signals referred to was interesting but useless. Could they have picked out these five isolated sources earlier and reacted to the warning? He turned to Brandeis. "Can we double-check this stuff?"

"We'll have to sort back over the last month and see if there's any consistent correlation between the five and what actually happened to the President," Brandeis replied.

"How long will it take?"

"Maybe four or five hours."

Brandeis punched up the information, rolling out the previous month's predictions of the five occultists. By nine-thirty he had the full list, and Appleton compared the readouts to events in York's life; the five had actually come close on a dozen occasions. Yet it was still basically random and uneven. Not once did all five totally coincide on an exact event, and their patterns of accuracy were off just enough so that they could not be one hundred percent dependable. Brandeis departed and Appleton summoned Morley.

An hour later, after examining the material, Morley scratched his head and spoke briskly: "Christ! We can't tell from this stuff whether he's going to be constipated or have a visit from the pope! We'd be picking through this like barnyard crap for days and days trying to extract something worthwhile."

Appleton agreed. "It's hopeless. So what do you want to tell him?"

"We can't tell the President the truth—that we think it is a hundred percent bullshit. But somehow we have to stall him. Maybe hold out some hope, but explain to him that it just isn't perfected yet. It's too sophisticated a problem."

"Will he buy that?" asked Appleton.

Morley took a silver flask from his jacket pocket. "Sorry about this. I can't get through this night without a touch of the poison." He gestured at his ankle. "Pain, all the time, pain." He swallowed twice from the flask and offered it to Appleton, who declined.

Morley shrugged. "Sweet whiskey, wild whiskey." He belched lightly.

Appleton realized that Morley was more drunk than he appeared at first. "Do we tell him anything about the readings from these five?"

"I think not. He'd be enraged if he knew there had been a hint of that accident and we didn't do anything about it." He looked closely at the Secret Service agent. "It is just the wildest chance that these five came up with the same forecasts at the same time. Isn't it?"

"Absolutely. Total random chance." Appleton recalled the chill he felt when he first saw the warnings. He added, "I *think* it's blind chance."

Morley went on: "So if it is blind chance and we start trying to act or react every time a few of these kooks come up with the same readings, we'd end up as cracked as they are, wouldn't we?"

"But what about the President? What are you going to tell him?"

"I'm going to tell him the machine is spouting gibberish, that the program is probably all wrong. I'm going to tell him that we're bringing in another crowd of experts to get it on the right track."

Appleton groaned. "Jesus."

Morley grinned and his eyes widened with an exaggerated look of villainy. "So Brandeis probably gets his ass kicked down to a programming assistant in Social Security."

Appleton said angrily, "He has worked hard. He couldn't have done more than he did."

"He didn't predict York's accident, did he? That's failure. He's out."

Appleton grabbed Morley by the collar and yanked him forward in his chair. "You drunken slob, you've kicked my ass all over the White House and probably wrecked me for good. But I'm not going to let you do it to that innocent little dummy. Pick on someone your own size, Morley, you bastard."

Morley sat perfectly still, gazing hard at Appleton. The Secret Service agent released him and turned away. Suddenly Morley loosed a burst of cackling laughter. "You've got balls, Appleton!" He took another swig from the flask and sank back in the chair. "Help me back to my office. I have to sleep on this."

"You don't have a hell of a lot of choice." Appleton almost carried him, along with his crutches, to his office.

Appleton returned to the CIPHER suite and once more examined the readouts predicting the President's accident. He was again seized by an unearthly chill. Reflexively, he swiveled his head to see if there was someone in the room behind him. He was sure he felt a presence. But the place was empty. Appleton filed the readouts and hurried out into the night.

* * * * *

As Albert Sauvart, Le Bombardier had traveled to Louisville on the press plane. He had taken the trip to learn more about York's security system. At the press conference, he noticed that York stood behind a lectern on which a presidential seal was affixed. It was a circular piece of plastic with a rim about two inches deep. As he examined it during the questions and answers, Le Bombardier wondered if he might be able to secrete his plastique inside sometime while the seal was not in use. If so, the President and the Secret Service would, in effect, be carrying the instrument of York's death with them wherever they went. The idea appealed to Le Bombardier, as much for its efficiency as for its irony. When York had finished the conference, Le Bombardier watched as a Secret Service agent carefully removed the seal and placed it inside a locked case, taking it to the banquet room where the President would speak. That night it was on the rostrum there, too. Le Bombardier was so fascinated with the idea that he scarcely heard the President speak.

* * * * *

Chapter 25

Milly knocked at the door of the Lincoln Bedroom. There was no answer and she turned to the marine sentry in the hall. He had the face of an anxious cherub, pink and smooth, peering out of the stiff collar of his dress blues. "Is he in there?" she asked.

"Yes, ma'am, he ain't come out." The voice was high-pitched and tense.

She knocked again, harder. The President's valet stood there, too. He had been roused by the young marine and then had summoned Milly to report that York was bellowing inside the locked bedroom. "Dreams, Miz York, bad dreams, so bad maybe he's hurting himself," said the valet.

There was silence behind the door. Milly asked the marine to bang the door with the bayonet he carried at his belt. The sound reverberated like shots. A moment later the doorknob slowly revolved.

York stood there, tousled and blinking against the bright light of the corridor. His pajamas were wet with sweat around the neck and armpits, and his face had a dull gleam. The smell of whiskey was strong. He spoke in a monotone: "Milly, what do you want? What time is it?"

"It's three-thirty, Gus. They . . . they said you were yelling in your sleep."

"I thought I was out cold."

"Will you let me come in, darling?"

York held the door open for her. Before he closed it, he said gruffly to the marine, "Son, I don't want you or anyone bothering Mrs. York again just because a man has a nightmare. She needs her sleep." He looked at the valet. "You, either, George."

The marine flushed scarlet. The valet bowed his head and said, "Sorry, sir. We thought you were in trouble."

The room was chilly and she pulled her robe tighter around her. She had not been asleep when the valet knocked; she, too, was restless and depressed. The night before, she and York had participated in the annual lighting of the Christmas tree on the South Lawn. It was a pretentious and oddly unnatural ceremony led by an Episcopal bishop, a man who preached with the effervescence of a game-show emcee. Milly had pushed a switch to turn on the lights, but instead of feeling the "soaring gladness and shimmering hope" the clergyman prattled on about, she felt only a lump of futility in her chest. The hundreds of bulbs on the tree cast a greenish light over everything. They turned York's face a ghastly ashen hue. That had made her mood dark, but the overwhelming cause of her mood was the state of their marriage. Gus had become, once again, impotent. She could not be sure that it was as debilitating and total as it had been during the campaign. They had not even been in bed together for more than a week now. He had told her that he was too restless, and that he wanted to sleep alone in the Lincoln Bedroom so he would not disturb her.

At first, she had taken this at face value. But thinking back, she had realized they had not made love in nearly a month. Twice they had lain together naked and embraced, but he had pleaded fatigue. She did not doubt him then. But now she was beginning to think the situation was more serious.

She spoke gently to him as he crossed the room to a chair. "Were you dreaming, darling?"

His voice was harsh. "I don't know. I dream so damn much I don't know when I'm sleeping or awake anymore."

"Gus, I love you. Can't I help?"

"I don't know if you can."

"Let's make love, darling. Let's be together. To-night. It's always so much better when we make love."

His face was sad. "Oh, Milly, I know that. I love you. I don't want to hurt you. But I . . . I can't. I have this deadness inside me and chaos everywhere outside. It's like a kind of paralysis."

"You've been drinking more than you should."

"A little whiskey never hurt in a case like this."

"What are you dreaming about?"

"They're all nightmares, Milly. People rushing me, trying to get me. I try to run away in heavy sand, thick air. I can't yell for help." He paused. "I dream about Gussie a lot. He's talking to me through water. I wake up trying to dive in after him, trying to swim. And it's all a swamp, ooze as thick as wet concrete . . ."

She pulled him from the chair and led him to bed. They lay down and he suddenly hugged her so fiercely that her ribs ached. "You are my love," he said. Then he relaxed and soon he was breathing evenly and deeply. Milly lay with her sleeping husband cradled as if he were her child. Her eyes filled with tears. She felt an immense weariness, but she could not sleep. She lay staring for hours at the ceiling. At last, it slowly grew gray, then white, as morning came.

Just before seven the phone rang, frightening her. York did not move. She picked up the receiver and heard Morley's rapid speech: "Is the President there? We've got one hell of a problem."

She woke York gently, caressing his stubbled face with her cool hand until he opened his eyes. He took the phone and listened for a moment. Then he hung up and slowly sat up in bed. "The damn Iranians are rioting. The Russians seem to be helping the left-wingers take over. The Cabinet is going to meet in an hour." He rubbed his face with his hands and shook his head. "I don't know if I can face this."

She said, "Please, darling. Please try to relax."

He turned and hugged her. "I love you."

He showered and dressed, and when he left, Milly wept for a few moments, then reached over and dialed the phone. When Morley answered, she said, "Andy, you've got to come talk to me—now. I think Gus is in trouble." At first he protested that the Iranian crisis was too pressing. Milly insisted; the alarm in her voice was real.

Morley arrived almost immediately. "I can't spare more than ten minutes, Milly. What is this terrible trouble?"

"I think he may be approaching a nervous break-down, Andy. I think he ought to take a vacation, a rest somewhere without any of these pressures."

"My God, we can't just fold up the Presidency of the United States. The world won't stop. What makes you think he's in such bad shape?"

"He doesn't sleep at all anymore. He has nightmares constantly. He looks as if he's half-dead. He's discouraged, confused."

"Milly, you're exaggerating. You haven't been sleeping that much yourself, have you?"

"Well, no."

"Gus is tired. I won't fool you, though. There is

some emotional upheaval at the root of it. He's insecure about the job. The national committee is badgering the hell out of him. He's been very upset by the things that have happened—the assassination attempts, the accident. And he's still obsessed with that damn zero-year idea that he's going to die in office. He feels he's sinking in quicksand. That damn Crystal Ball computer of his, full of psychics and star-gazers—that's a symptom too. . . ."

"What are you talking about?"

Morley stared at her. "He never told you? He never talked about trying to forecast the future with a computer?"

"No."

Quickly, Morley told her of the project, and Milly's heart sank. "You mean you know all these weird things and you still don't think he's in terrible trouble?" she said to Morley.

"Not really. I mean, he seems perfectly capable of going on."

"Capable of going on?"

"By that I mean he isn't in danger of being removed from office for, uh, for mental disability. He's just tired, and the extra pressures, the damn obsession with the zero-year phenomenon, have got him down a little. It will pass. We need him in office."

"Who is 'we'?"

"What kind of question is that? 'We' is the country, the party, the world. For God's sake, Milly! *You* need him there, and I need him there."

Milly's voice sharpened. "Just a minute! *I* don't need Gus York to be President, for God's sweet sake. I want him for *myself*. I want him the way he was. And whoever said the country is so desperately in need of him? He's barely keeping his head above water in the polls. And the party? Come on, Andy, you just told me how much they dislike him. Andy, the 'we' who needs Gus York in office is *you!* No one else really needs Gus York to be President but *you."*

Andy looked at his watch. "Milly, I can't stay here and debate the morality and the opportunism of my motives. The Cabinet is meeting in four minutes. I'm telling you, Gus is all right! I agree he needs a rest—but only a vacation, not a hospital treatment. You're exaggerating this whole thing."

Milly began to speak, but Morley hurried across the room. "I'm sorry, I just can't spare another minute."

The door slammed. Milly felt a despair as palpable as pain. She could think of no way to escape the prison that the White House had become.

* * * * *

Chapter 26

York rubbed his neck and squinted at the chandelier above the coffin-shaped table where the Cabinet convened. The vague pain at the base of his skull had come to be a familiar companion. The haggling and haranguing going on at the table were also familiar. The schism in the Cabinet lay between the party establishment led by Slaughter of Defense and Vice-President Dayton and the more moderate minds of Matthews of H.E.W., Morley, and York himself.

The uprisings in Iran were serious enough in themselves since they threatened to exacerbate, even more, the unrest and anarchy that had held the area since the overthrow of the Shah. But the fact the Russians were probably involved could turn it into a crisis as desperate as Khrushchev's attempt to ship Soviet missiles to Cuba in 1962.

Dayton spoke up. "We have to show power—bring them to a face-off. We simply cannot be meek and let it happen without a reaction."

Matthews of H.E.W. remarked sarcastically, "Our destiny *would* be ours to control if we had a better source of energy than oil from countries that are run like banana republics."

Slaughter of Defense said, "That's beside the point.

We have to scare the shit out of the Russians. Send in Phantom jets, strafe the rioters, show those bastards that we won't let them cut off our oil."

"We don't know for sure the Russians are behind it," said Morley calmly.

"Goddammit!" Slaughter said. "They *are* behind it! Our intelligence says they've even got a command post in Teheran. Those rifles the lefties are using are Soviet-made."

York was having difficulty concentrating, totally on the grand strategic elements of the situation. He looked at the freshly shaven faces around the table. They belonged to men accustomed to power, to dealing with the fate of thousands of human beings as coldly and impersonally as scientists dealt with white mice.

Matthews said, "I think we should hold off with force—or even a show of it—until we know for certain that the Russians are actually using force in Teheran, too. If they are just advising the rebels, we can't really justify going in with rockets."

"The hell we can't!" the Defense secretary shouted. "The American economy is at stake here! You get those left-wingers in and they'll turn off that oil in a second!"

York spoke at last, though it took great effort. "How can we move in and stamp out a revolution that might be what the people want? They have a right to their own choice of government."

Slaughter stood up abruptly. His voice was hard with anger. "Goddammit! Why do I feel like I'm arguing with a bunch of hard-core Democrats whenever I sit down at this table? I don't think Kennedy and his crowd of knee-jerk lefties were as far out as some of you are." He took a deep breath and turned to York. "Mr. President, I can't go on like this any longer. I'm being undermined every time I make a decision. I don't think this country can survive the philosophy this Administration stands for. I have thought about this for weeks, Mr. President. It is not a decision made in haste or anger. I have no choice. My resignation will be on your desk by lunchtime."

York said sadly, "Ed, think it over. That's all I ask. Think it over." The ache at the base of his neck was a bright throb.

Slaughter was already at the door. "I have my principles, Mr. President. You do not stand for them!" He closed the door with a slam that resounded like a shot. The men at the table were silent.

York licked his lips and rubbed his neck. "I'm sorry I let it get out of control." He turned to Vice-President Dayton. "Brownie, can you talk to him? See if you can persuade him that his resignation now is going to create a terrible rift in the Administration."

Dayton said, "Mr. President, I don't think Ed Slaughter should come back. He disagrees with you too much to be of any real use. And, frankly, I'm wondering about myself, too." He paused. "I don't think you can run this country—let alone Iran—with your consistent refusal to use power that we have at our command. We are contributing to chaos, to anarchy, Mr. President, if we don't bring our power into use!"

Matthews of H.E.W. spoke up. "You're talking about an *image* of power. Why not some kind of resolution in the Congress, maybe something in the U.N. Security Council?"

Dayton was irked. "That's pure paperwork. Nothing changes. Nothing happens. We need something to scare them!"

York stood up and turned to Morley. "Andy, you draft a resolution for Congress. Something tough, but don't threaten anything we can't do." He hesitated, then said softly, "I don't want military force. Not yet. We'll talk about some other options after we see what happens."

Morley and Eddie Hanson followed York back to the Oval Office. Morley said, "The Slaughter resignation is going to be rough, Mr. President. He's going to make one hell of a noise. The whole Reagan–Connally crowd is going to line up behind him. It's going to be bad."

"I can't help it, Andy. We just can't start slamming in with all that hardware on a bunch of people who, maybe, are just fighting to get what they think they need."

"I agree. But that son-of-a-bitch has a million connections. He'll kill you."

York slumped in the chair at his desk and loosened his tie. The intercom chime sounded. His secretary said, "The vice-president would like a moment or two with you, sir. He's here."

"What's on the schedule?"

"The Spanish foreign secretary in fifteen minutes, then lunch with the trade delegation from Japan, then . . ."

"That's enough. Tell him to come in." He looked at Morley.

"Stick with me on this."

"Yes, sir."

Dayton strode in. His face was grim. "Mr. President, I don't want to beat around the bush. You know as well as I do that Slaughter's quitting is going to exacerbate the split in this Administration. It could wreck us. We have to come up with a compromise on this Iranian situation."

York gazed at him steadily. "What compromise are we talking about? I'm not sure there is any middle ground. I don't want to upset the natural balance of events over there. You know as well as I do that we can get along—not badly—without oil from Iran. Sure, it hurts. But it isn't a national crisis, and it sure as hell isn't something we should be dropping bombs over!''

Dayton's voice was soothing. "Mr. President, it's as much what happens in the *future* as what happens now that is at stake in this. A show of force—now—will make an impression everywhere around the world that will last for *years*. It isn't only the specific situation in Iran that matters. . . .''

York was adamant. "It's *their* country, for God's sake. I want to wait to see what happens.''

Dayton's eyes narrowed slightly. "Mr. President, you are being called a populist President these days. That manifesto of the common man and the Cruise missile settlement, and the recognition of Castro—all this has put you in a very liberal light. For a Republican it is practically unprecedented. And a lot of people in the party think it is not particularly appealing.'' There was an edge in Dayton's voice.

"I guess you are probably one of those people. Right?''

"Wrong, Mr. President. I agree with you that the party needs a new face—a new *soul,* for God's sake. The party of Richard Nixon was an abomination, and the party of Jerry Ford was a joke. You wouldn't be sitting here now, Mr. President, if that weren't the case. No, I'm not entirely set against you. I just think you've crossed over the line too far sometimes. You know how I've felt. I've made no secret of it.''

"You've been quite open.''

Dayton went on smoothly, "But I'm wondering about the hypocrisy involved in all this ostensible concern for the common man and another practice you've put into effect. There's a direct contradiction in principles, Mr. President."

"What do you mean?"

"I'm talking about CIPHER. For all your talk about the rights of the little man, CIPHER flies in the face of everything you say you stand for."

York was confused. "I don't follow you. It's just extra security—for you as well as for me."

"True enough. But you must realize that in order to make that system work, you also have to violate the civil rights of dozens, maybe hundreds, maybe thousands, of people every time you make a trip or a speech. In fact, CIPHER is an 'enemies list' exactly as Nixon's was. These people are, by definition, deemed political criminals simply because their names are in that computer. It is absolutely arbitrary, absolutely unjust, and an absolute violation of their rights, Mr. President."

York was silent. "But it's all an abstraction, symbolic. Having their names in that computer doesn't circumvent their freedom," he said at last.

Dayton said coolly, "Of course it does. It's an invasion of privacy. There is harassment, too. When the police of New York City or Chicago or Paris just happen to take a relatively hot suspect in for questioning or put a gumshoe on his tail for a couple of days while you're in town—that is a documentable violation of his civil rights under the Sixth Amendment. He is being harassed, in the interests of *your life!*"

The two men stared at each other. Morley had listened quietly. Now he cleared his throat and said calmly, "No one ever claimed it was going to stand up in a Supreme Court case, Brownie. It is strictly expedient. It takes some shortcuts, yes. I weighed the values involved and decided that the President's life was the number-one consideration." He continued: "You know, of course, that CIPHER was set up and working before the President even knew it existed. It never even came to his attention in any detail until after the assassination attempt in New York."

Dayton shook his head. "I'm not trying to get you to shut down CIPHER. I think it's one hell of a system. Necessary—in fact, invaluable. All I'm doing, Mr. President, is pointing out an element of hypocrisy that arises between your public image and a private reality."

York felt the pain building in his head again. "I sense a warning in there somewhere. Can that be?"

"No. The warning I gave you is about the Administration splitting over Iran. I'm just pointing the other out to you as a matter of guidance."

Morley said, "Okay. I think we got the message. Thanks."

The vice-president left the Oval Office.

York said wearily, "Exactly what message was that, Andy?"

"He just wants you to know that he knows something about you that you might not want spread around. He wants you to know that there are some cracks in your armor that give him some power over you."

"Cracks in my armor." York puffed in exasperation. "From the minute I got this job, I thought there were more cracks than there was armor." York shook his head in bewilderment. "They never knew what they were getting when they nominated me. And, son-of-a-bitch, Andy, neither did *I*."

"I've got this memo from Len Buhler at the national committee. He wants to create what he calls a management steering committee—five people including Buhler and Brownie Dayton—to advise you. What it really would be is a clearing house for policy decisions.

They'd want to tell you what to do instead of suggesting. But I'm wondering now if maybe you shouldn't consider letting them form the committee."

York frowned. "Dayton mentioned it a couple of weeks ago. I said no."

"You could use it as a sounding board. At least give them an entrée to the decision process. It might soothe them a little, get some of the more rabid right-wingers off your back."

"It's strictly advisory?"

"Absolutely. The only power they have is the power you give them."

York closed his eyes in resignation. "I'm so damn tired and confused half the time, Andy, that I guess I'd welcome someone to help do some thinking for me. Let's do it."

* * * * *

Chapter 27

York lay in the Lincoln Bedroom, locked in and alone, as he wished to be. The silence in the room was profound, but his mind rushed about as if it were filled with fierce windstorms and bursting bombshells. He lay still, trying to relax, trying to calm the chaos in his head. The days following Christmas had been hectic, and more than once he had found himself wondering if he had *any* capability at all to handle the job of President. He turned on his side, restlessly, and curled his knees up toward his stomach. He squeezed his eyes closed and tried to sleep.

Suddenly a bark rang out, sharp as an explosion, an abrupt and shocking sound. York bolted upright, peering blindly into the dark. The sound had risen from a corner across the room. It was a man's cough.

But there could be no man in the room. York had locked the door himself from the inside. A young marine was on guard outside, and there were Secret Service men all through the White House. The gates were manned by uniformed sentries.

Another sharp cough shattered the silence and York bellowed in panic, "Who's there?! Goddammit! *Who's there?!*" Was it all an illusion?

He peered warily toward the corner and he sensed faint movement there. He cried out again, "Who's there?!" There was no reply.

He was frightened, but he rose from the bed and began to move slowly across the room. Again, he detected a rustle of movement in the corner, and after a half-dozen steps he could see that there was indeed a dim figure seated in a wingchair there. York's throat tightened. The man sat perfectly still, his feet planted flat to the floor, his hands motionless on the chair arms. He wore a black suit, white shirt, a black ribbon tie. His face was grayish-white. York could not make out the features clearly. He spoke to the figure again, this time in a low, trembling voice. "What do you want?"

No reply came, and York moved closer. Now within twenty feet, he could see the man's features were gaunt and ghostly. Suddenly the mouth opened wide, a taut black hole in the face, and a single terrible cough exploded in the still room. York cringed.

Now he noticed the man's eyes. They were crimson, bright as fresh blood, the only spot of color on his whole person. They gazed at York with such intensity that he could not look directly at them.

The room seemed suddenly to grow colder, and York shivered. But he no longer felt the wild panic that had coursed through him before. Perhaps this was a spirit come to visit him, to speak to him, to help. He had heard of such things as a child. Visitations from beyond, the dead returning to advise the living.

York said softly, "Have you come to help?" He could see the man's features clearly now. The visitor had a long, slightly bulbous nose, thick arched eyebrows, full downturned lips. A curl of ash-black hair lay over his forehead; his ears were long and large. Now the mouth moved stiffly, and a single word came forth:

"Tippecanoe." Could this be real?

Now York knew him. The man in the chair was William Henry Harrison, the first of the zero-year Presidents to die. York knew his face well, for part of his obsession with the zero-year phenomenon had been to learn all he could about the Presidents who might have been his fellows in this cursed union of zeros.

Harrison's hand, white as ice, shifted on the chair arm. His lips moved. "From the grave I greet you, from death I wish you well." His voice rattled like the hollow roll of a snare drum.

York tried to make his mind slow down so he could accept and understand the strange thing happening here. But he experienced a powerful sense of disorientation. He wanted to talk to William Henry Harrison, but another wave of cold swept over him and he was so chilled that his teeth began to chatter. He could not speak. He could scarcely think.

Harrison said, "We all die. Some soon, some late. I died late in my life, soon in my Presidency." He paused. The crimson eyes fixed on York, and Harrison went on: "I recall death when it came. Comforting, yet not welcome." He paused. When he spoke again the snare-drum sound was gone and his voice was that of a normal man, excited, dramatic: "Sir! I wish you to understand the true principles of the government! I wish them carried out! I ask nothing more!"

Even in his confusion, York recognized these as the last words Harrison uttered in delirium just before he died in 1841.

But now Harrison's voice returned to the hollow drum rattle. "We have two things in common: death and the Presidency. I welcome you to both. The Presidency is unknowable to all but forty men in all of time."

York felt his face contort, his body grow spastic in its

shivering. He tried desperately to concentrate on Harrison's words. He felt disembodied, no longer anchored to himself. This wasn't real!

Harrison said, "Come and see with me what death is and keep the zero line intact." He rose slowly from the chair. He was emaciated and his clothes were draped on him as though on a rack of bare bones. He moved so slowly that he seemed weak, harmless. Yet the menacing scarlet eyes were fixed on York as the apparition advanced toward him in the gloom.

The snare-drum voice said, "Come and see, come and see." He was within a yard of York. He reached out a hand. York tried to recoil, but he could not move. Harrison's hand touched his wrist. It was dry and rough, scaly and cold as snow. It tightened on his wrist with the strength of a hawk's claw. York tried to pull away. Harrison's hand tightened its grip. Then his figure grew dimmer, as if a shadow had fallen over him. The terrible eyes began to turn dull; the fierce grip of the hand slowly vanished.

York stood alone. He was still shivering and his heart was pumping wildly. The figure of the dead President had disappeared. Quickly York returned to the bed and covered himself. His shivering slowly eased. Though he was exhausted and confused, he felt that he could trust what he remembered of the frightening visit. But was it real—a true visitation from the grave? Or a dream? A hallucination brought on by his own anxiety, by his own fatigue? He lay there, fighting to make sense of it. But then he must have slept, for the next thing he knew the room was radiant with the light of a bright winter morning and the nightmare had faded.

He rose, feeling oddly refreshed by his brief sleep. He decided that he would tell no one, not even Milly, about the ghost of President Harrison. Dream or not, he did not want to alarm anyone any further about the state of his mind.

* * * * *

A presidential trip to Europe in February seemed likely enough that Le Bombardier took the Concorde to Paris and spent December 20 and 21 examining the neighborhood of the American embassy on the chance he might be able to plant plastique somewhere in the vicinity. On December 22 he visited London to investigate the possibilities of arranging an assassination near the embassy there. On December 23 he returned to Washington. The trip to Europe was satisfying for its food and the welcome change of scenery from the banal winter landscape of Washington; but, otherwise, it was unfulfilling. Le Bombardier had not discovered a foolproof locale for the killing of President York in either of the two European capitals. Yet he was not discouraged, for as the time drew closer to the trip, there would be a chance to explore specific possibilities. Le Bombardier had contacts in Paris with expatriate Russians and a defector or two who would be delighted to help him. He preferred working alone, but they could be enlisted if an idea seemed particularly propitious.

At LaGuardia Airport, he boarded the shuttle and returned to Washington. On the way he read *The New York Times* and the *Washington Post*. Both papers featured front-page stories on the continuing conflict in the York Administration over the resignation of Defense Secretary Slaughter and his insider's reports of the Administration battles going on over the uprising in Iran. This issue interested Le Bombardier peripherally in that he was curious how it might affect York's schedule.

The next day he returned to the White House to attend a morning press briefing by Eddie Hanson. After an extended and heated series of questions over new developments in the Slaughter/Iran story, the briefing cooled. Someone asked what the Yorks would be having for Christmas dinner, and Hanson made a note to dig up that momentous information from the White House kitchen. He reminded the reporters that the Yorks would be at Camp David for Christmas and that those members of the press wishing facilities there would have to put their names on a list.

"What's he going to do New Year's Eve?"

Hanson made a note to find that out, too. Then he said, "One thing I can tell you, the President is going to be active as hell. He's got those meetings in Hawaii with the Japanese prime minister over the trade balance at the end of January. He's thinking of going to Europe in February. We have a full legislative program in the works and ready for Congress when it reconvenes on January 20. Until the State of the Union message, he'll be tending to business around here."

The New York Times man said, "You have anything new, Ed, on the legislative programs? Anything more specific?"

"Only what's been given out."

"Nothing more?"

"No. The only official statement from the President is that he is confident he'll be getting all the support he needs on the Hill this session."

The New York Times man snapped, "Support? Tell us how he's going to get any more Democrats behind him when he can't even count on Republicans."

Hanson smiled and quipped, "They aren't made of

stone. We'll melt 'em with kindness."

"What kind of kindness?"

"Booze and beautiful girls with bare asses," Hanson joked. "That's off the record."

The assembly guffawed. The session went on in a desultory way. Most reporters drifted off to file stories. The man from the Chicago *Tribune* said to Hanson, "Jesus, Ed, except for that routine stuff on Iran, there's about as much news here as there is in the White House Christmas card."

Hanson grinned. "Why not do a story on the Christmas card?"

"Haven't you got *anything* new on the legislative program yet?" asked the man from *Time*.

"You already got the big handout on it, Jack. There is nothing new."

"But it's all generalities."

"Some people think the Declaration of Independence is, too."

"Okay—how about an advance copy of the State of the Union? That ought to be real meaty. 'Anchor on the ship of state holds firm despite stormy seas and winds of evil.'"

"It'll be about as meaty as the Christmas card—that's a promise." Hanson added quickly, "Off the record."

As the meeting broke up, Albert Sauvart went to his acquaintance from the Washington *Star* and asked, "The State of the Union? And when is that?"

The man looked in his appointment book. "January 23."

Feigning ignorance, Le Bombardier asked, "It is where?"

"In the Capitol, the House of Representatives chambers. The entire government is there. It's mainly ceremonial, however. Not much news, usually. A tradition."

Le Bombardier wandered off idly, as if the information were of only slight interest to him. But he was very excited. He had at last found a time and a place. . . .

The day after Christmas, Le Bombardier joined a group of visitors on a guided tour of the Capitol. He endured patiently the monologue about the origin of the marble and the significance of the statuary. He listened, without hearing, to a lecture on the history of the building. At last the guide took the group into the chamber of the House of Representatives, and Le Bombardier saw for the first time this elegant cavernous room.

The guide continued speaking about ancient debates and long-dead politicians who had walked the carpeted floors of this grand old chamber. But Le Bombardier heard nothing. His concentration was totally engaged by the physical layout of the room—how far the visitors' galleries were above the floor, the arrangement of the rows of seats, the distance between the press gallery and the podium where the President would speak. This last seemed to be about one hundred fifty feet at the closest. This fact troubled him, but his face remained bland.

When the tour was over, Le Bombardier returned to his room and began to make calculations on a sheet of paper. A series of algebraic equations rapidly jotted down told him what he needed to know. The pulse of the remote radio signal had to travel over one hundred fifty feet, a far greater distance than any he had tried before. His calculations indicated that it was doubtful that the equipment he now possessed could produce the necessary electronic impulse in the tiny detonator batteries at that distance.

The triggering device needed further work. Also, he

would have to examine the podium to find how large a charge of plastique would be required and where he could hide it. There was much to do, but at least Le Bombardier now had his time, his place, and a comfortable period of four weeks in which to make his preparations.

* * * * *

Chapter 28

The January 3 headline on page one of the New York *Post* was simple and explosive:

Boys in the Band:

FIRST LADY'S
MANY LOVERS

Inside was the first of a series of articles chronicling the love life of the band singer Milly Waters. The stories ran for a full week and began with her brief fling with Jimmy Booth, the blue-eyed trumpet player, and ended with her long affair in Chicago with Bob Venturi before her marriage to Gus York. The facts, as gathered and artfully assembled by the *Post,* documented a string of steamy affairs with a variety of musicians. The prose was lurid and explicit, describing liaisons in seedy motel beds, in the back seats of cars, in dressing rooms of the roadside dives where the bands and friends of Milly Waters had performed. The article quoted fifteen men who claimed to have slept with Milly at one time or another.

A former saxophone player, now long out of music and running a bowling alley in Queens, said, "Milly Waters was a loving, lovely woman. She knew what men wanted and she seemed to like the same thing herself. We did it in the back of the bus on the road."

A trombonist now working in a Broadway theater recalled, "She and I hooked up for maybe a month once when we were doing a bunch of gigs in Illinois and Indiana. It was the best road trip of my life."

A drummer was "pretty sure" he had slept with her a few times in 1958, probably somewhere in the Midwest, because he remembered snow on the ground.

A piano player who now ran a nightclub in Minneapolis reported a period of two months during which he and Milly were lovers on the road.

Mercifully, Jack Karos, the drunk she had married briefly, was dead.

Bob Venturi had cited sexy chapter and steamy verse about the months they had lived together and summed up "dreamily," as the *Post* put it: "She loved to make love more than anyone I knew. She was not a tramp, but she was as sexy and as sex-oriented as any woman I have known before or since." Venturi's quote—*"She loved to make love"*—was used as the identifying kicker headline for the series.

Ultimately, the rest of the press had to deal with the story. With exquisite good judgment, *The New York Times* ran just one story—on page forty-two—which briefly chronicled the skeletal outlines of the *Post*'s reporting, and reported national reaction. The networks, too, dealt mainly with reaction rather than the story itself. *Time* did an essay on morals and mores— "The 'A' for Adultery"—which said: "Mrs. York certainly had a right to her perceptions, her own proclivities as a woman in her youth. Yet her position as First Lady puts her high on a pedestal, and even though she has every right to her privacy, to her own vision, and to her own history of love and love affairs, she is bound to be judged differently from other women. It is unfair, unjust, hypocritical, and cruel to judge her darkly for these revelations. Yet almost everyone will—and there lies the harsh truth of life around the Presidency. Even your past does not belong to you, and certainly not your present, and probably not your future."

Milly was angered by the articles, but she was also badly hurt. An accusatory pall seemed to hang over her, as if she had been caught doing something unclean. Yes, she had had affairs with some musicians she genuinely liked. She had enjoyed being footloose on the road. She had thought it normal. But, of course, it wasn't. She had lived in a kind of no-man's-land, adrift in society without the usual constrictions of being known, being watched, being judged by a community. Until now, she had never stopped to think that her young life had been so out of the ordinary. Until now it had not been a problem, because no one cared. However, as First Lady, it seemed that to have lived anything but the most banal and predictable life was a violation of the public trust.

Gus was aware of her affair with Venturi, her brief marriage, and some other romances. He was enraged by the *Post* stories. He summoned Morley and bellowed, "Goddamnit! I want those bastards punished. I don't care how we do it—libel suits, anti-trust suits, I.R.S. investigations. I want that goddamn publisher and every one of these bastard writers ruined!"

Morley had calmed York at last. He reminded the President that bringing in the F.B.I. or the I.R.S. was precisely what Nixon had done, and no matter how wronged Milly had been, one could not use such tactics against them. "What we have to decide, Mr. President, is whether to respond to those stories or not."

"Damn right, we respond!" cried York. "I will not have Milly's name dragged around this country like this! It's nobody's business what she did when she was twenty-five years old!"

Morley remained calm. "It's all part of being in the White House spotlight. You can't keep people from prying. They'll dig up every scrap of dirt they can find."

"Why didn't they plaster *my* affairs all over page one? Why Milly?!"

"They pander to what they see as the public's appetite for sensation. They sell papers with Milly. With you—what the hell, Mr. President, you are a man, a former football star—you're *supposed* to have lots of women. It's macho. It makes people comfortable, makes them rate you better. Milly, a woman, the President's wife with a string of affairs behind her—no one's comfortable with that, Gus."

"Well, I'm comfortable with it! She's *my* wife! It's nobody's business!"

York and Morley went to see Milly in the Princess Room. She had canceled her appointments for the day. Her secretary, Bitsy Rogerson, had made one quick visit to tell her that there would be no appointments for the next day, either, if Mrs. York wished. Bitsy waited for an answer at a safe distance across the room, as if the *Post*'s revelations had somehow made Milly contaminated. She scuttled away quickly after Milly snapped that she wished to have exactly that—no appointments.

When York and Morley entered, Milly said coldly, "I have no idea how I'm supposed to feel about this thing. I certainly don't feel guilty, although I think everyone would be a lot happier if I did. I don't feel remorse. I do feel violated and I do feel anger—a *lot* of anger. I would welcome some kind of public platform where I could humiliate the people who wrote that story." She paused, then closed her eyes in pain. "But Bob Venturi . . . how could he do this?"

Morley said softly, "They paid him twenty thousand dollars, Milly."

She opened her eyes wide.

"All of them were paid, Milly," explained Morley. "We had it checked. We may use it in some of our own material on the story."

"Our own material?"

"Yes, Milly, we probably are going to have to respond somehow sooner or later. The other papers and the networks, all are clamoring for some reaction. Eddie issued a flat 'no comment.' Said that he wouldn't dignify such claptrap with a reply. But I think we should come up with some kind of an official reaction."

"Well, about half of it is true, about half of it they bought lies. No one's given me a list of all the people who claimed they slept with me. But I can remember, if they can't. There have been nine, counting Gus."

Morley cleared his throat uncomfortably. "Well, we, uh, should probably try to, uh, clear your name, you know," he said quietly.

"Clear my name?! Of what?!"

"Uh, well, of being, uh, wanton, you know, uh, well, wanton . . ."

York snapped, "Wanton! Milly doesn't need her name cleared of anything. She was—she is—a healthy, normal, loving woman. Dammit! Just because she had a few affairs before she was married . . ."

Milly glared. "So I made love to some men I liked or loved or thought were attractive. What is that?"

Morley said, "Uh, well, you do seem rather, uh, smeared by those stories. Don't you think?"

"No, I don't. *I* have been violated. Those peeping Toms digging around in my private life! Why can't we sue those people for invading my privacy, for destroying it? Why can't we *hurt* them some way?!" She began to weep.

A phone rang and Morley picked it up. He listened,

then held a hand over it and said to York, "Buhler, Dayton, and the steering committee want a meeting on how to handle this at six o'clock. Okay?"

York nodded. "Okay."

Milly interrupted: "Now, wait a minute. Don't I have something to say about how this is handled? It's *my* privacy they wrecked."

Morley said into the phone, "Mrs. York would like to have a say in the decision. . . . Yes. I suppose that is true. Okay, I'll tell her." He hung up and told Milly, "Buhler thinks it might be uncomfortable for you to be there while we're discussing the articles. It might get a little, uh, steamy. The reactions are angry, we understand. There have been hundreds of telegrams and calls to the White House. They are, uh, very negative, Milly. Very negative."

"I'm going to be at that meeting," Milly said. "It is my life that's being discussed, and I am going to be there!"

The meeting began at six sharp. Buhler, the party chairman, held a kind of magnetic center in the room, yet it was Dayton who opened the conversation. He spoke smoothly. "In truth, Mrs. York, your life is not entirely yours. You are not just any woman. You are the wife of the President. The country expects— probably even deserves—something extra from you, some kind of example to follow."

"I'm not a national monument. I'm no Joan of Arc. God knows I wasn't when I was twenty-five years old. I fell in love. I went to bed with the men I loved. I did what was natural. I did what felt right! That's not a bad example in itself!"

Dayton said, "We're not old fogies. We know that you were being yourself. But you have to face the realities of politics and, uh, the *expectations* of today.

You have to be what people *want* you to be—not necessarily what you want to be yourself!"

"And what do you think they want me to be?"

"They want you to deny all these things. They want you to say there is no truth in them. They want you to be pure—or, if that's not possible, to say you're sorry."

"Pure! What does that mean? Who's pure? And exactly *what* am I sorry about!?"

Len Buhler's voice was heard at last, a low, drawling purr. "You have to do it for the Administration, Mrs. York. It's a public relations problem. We can't project an image of being a bunch of people who condone or encourage this sort of thing."

"What sort of thing!?"

"Uh, extramarital affairs. Uh, adultery, ma'am."

York spoke up angrily: "Why the hell do we have to do that? We're the government, not some kind of keeper of morals."

Dayton spoke again. "We have to seem as if we are foursquare for the right things, Mr. President. You just can't have a wife who has done all these things. . . ."

Buhler interrupted. "Mrs. York, perhaps it might have been wise for you to have told us about those, uh, little moral detours. We might have been able to handle this better if we were forewarned."

Milly said, "You mean like forewarning you that I have a criminal record or a history of insanity or a drinking problem?!"

"Something like that." His bulging eyes were fixed on her and they did not seem to blink at all.

Milly's voice rose. "For God's sake, I was being a woman, being myself! Whose business is that?" She began to weep.

Morley said uncomfortably, "I still think we have to

have some kind of a statement. Maybe deny the whole thing."

Dayton said, "I agree. We just can't let this go without taking some kind of a stand. It's too damn important."

They were talking to each other, ignoring Milly and York.

Buhler cleared his throat. "We can't deny it if it's true," he said softly.

Milly rushed from the room. Tears streamed down her face, almost blinding her. She wanted to run away, but the White House held her, as confining as a penitentiary. When she did get to a rear door, a Secret Service man moved quickly behind her. She ran onto the South Lawn and found herself in a downpour. Rain soaked her hair, her clothing, and in a moment she began to shiver. Gus York came up quickly behind her. He enfolded her in his arms and led her upstairs.

The following morning Eddie Hanson issued a statement from the White House press office that Buhler, Dayton, and Morley had drafted. It said: "The stories about Mrs. York's early life were exaggerated, tasteless, and a shocking violation of privacy. Her behavior those long-ago years is not a subject that can be dealt with objectively now. Mrs. York regrets that such distasteful episodes have been brought to the public's view. She expresses her wish that the subject be dropped since it is painful, pointless, and taken utterly out of context. It is clearly a matter of her own private life many years before she became a public figure of the magnitude and dignity of the First Lady."

Neither Milly nor the President saw the statement before it was released. When they read it, they were appalled. She said, "It sounds like I'm apologizing for my whole life. It sounds like I'm ashamed. It sounds like I'm a reformed prostitute. How could they do this to me?"

"No wonder they didn't clear it with us. They knew we wouldn't approve it." He paused, then picked up a phone. "Give me Eddie Hanson." When the press secretary answered, York's voice cracked with anger: "I want a full-scale press conference set up at two o'clock—today . . . yes, *goddammit*, today! The subject is Mrs. York's private life, and I will be there in person."

He slammed down the phone and looked at Milly. "Okay?"

She nodded. "Thank you, darling." She spoke softly. "I'll be there, too."

At two o'clock, York stood at a podium in the Green Room before two hundred fifty reporters and a full battery of network cameras. Morley had tried frantically to talk him out of appearing, but York would not listen. Now he spoke in a low, grim voice, his eyes fixed in a cold glare on the assembly: "I am here to speak about my wife. She has been put through an ordeal of prurience and ugliness that is disgusting. The release, given to you this morning by my own press secretary, was never seen by me . . . or by my wife. We would not have approved the wording.

"Milly is not ashamed of her life. She does not remember those years as being distasteful or shameful. She does not feel that sex is distasteful or shameful. Nor does she feel that she has anything to explain, to clarify, or to apologize for. She is a courageous, honest woman, and she wants to speak to you in person. Here she is."

Milly walked to the microphone. Her dark hair was

freshly brushed and she wore a white cotton shirt and a pleated wool skirt. Her face was tranquil and her voice was strong. "My private life twenty years ago is no more the business of the press or of the people of this country than my private life today. There are many things I do not want millions of people to know about me. If you wanted paragons to come and live in this house, then you have elected the wrong people. We are human beings, Gus and I, ordinary human beings. We have shared a lot of happiness and some grief. We like being together. We are in love.

"I have never apologized to him for my life before we met. And I certainly have no intention of apologizing to you. I am not ashamed. I do not feel guilty and I do not feel that I must try to fit some impossibly perfect image of womanhood that is invented to satisfy a public relations problem. That, by the way, is the way one of the White House advisors so coolly labeled my life: 'A public relations problem.'

"There are strains between Gus and me that were never there before we moved to the White House. Perhaps the 'public relations problem' is the biggest one of all. But I love Gus and I'm not going to let a public relations problem destroy our private relations." She paused. "At least I'm going to *try* not to."

She turned to York, hugged him and kissed him, leaving a slight mark of lipstick on the corner of his mouth. Surprised, he responded with a dazzling smile. Then they left the room.

The press buzzed for a moment. Then two or three people began to clap, and, soon, everyone rose in an ovation to the empty lectern where Milly had stood.

But the White House press was not typical of the nation. Milly's press conference was shown repeatedly on news programs that night. More than 150,000,000

Americans watched her and listened to her, and by morning a flood of telegrams and phone calls swamped the White House. Milly's remarks were repeated, analyzed, enlarged on for several days more. Not until a week later did the grand tide of reaction recede enough to allow an accurate counting of the pros and cons. The score against Milly turned out to be roughly three to one.

It was, as Morley wryly put it, "not exactly a mandate for adultery."

* * * * *

Chapter 29

Le Bombardier had attended the startling press conference. He had found it laughably melodramatic, this American obsession with sex combined with this weird insistence on flawless behavior in their leaders. Hypocritical, naïve, unsophisticated, he thought to himself. He had watched the President in fascination. Despite the strength of his words, the staunchness of his defense of his wife, the man had looked to Le Bombardier weary and surprisingly sad, a man who might actually welcome death.

The next day Le Bombardier returned to the White House, introduced himself to a young woman correspondent from CBS, and told her that he wished to do a letter from Washington about television coverage at the White House. He asked her if she perhaps might introduce him to some producers and cameramen from CBS who covered the President every day. To her, Albert Sauvart seemed an obsequious and unprepossessing man, ill at ease and in need of help in this alien land. She said that she herself could spare little time. Albert assured her that he did not wish to take the time of a famous correspondent, that he would rather talk with a floor producer or a cameraman, one of the behind-the-scenes technicians who did so much to make American television so superior to all other broadcast outlets in the world. He smiled meekly, and she agreed to help.

At noon, Albert Sauvart was speaking to a lanky, middle-aged assistant producer for CBS, an expansive and self-important sort of fop who was flattered to be interviewed, spoke rapidly and enthusiastically for more than two hours about the technical miracles of American television and his own indispensable role in the same. Le Bombardier seethed on the inside, but on the outside Albert Sauvart smiled, ducked his head, and took slow, careful notes.

When the interview was over, they shook hands, and Albert Sauvart stumbled slightly against the assistant producer. When they parted, Le Bombardier had the man's wallet.

That night Le Bombardier transferred a Polaroid photograph of himself wearing aviator-frame spectacles and a graying wig, razor-cut in a stylish coif, onto the identification card of the assistant producer.

Two days later, on the morning of January 10, Le Bombardier left his room in the guise of Albert Sauvart. He was carrying his large, shabby briefcase. He took a taxi to the Arlington Marriott Motel across the Potomac. He engaged a room at the busy registration desk. Once in the room, he took from his briefcase a stylish blue blazer, fawn trousers, Gucci loafers, a blue button-down shirt, and a regimental necktie. He dressed carefully, then placed the wig on his head and donned the aviator-frame spectacles. He took a taxi to the Capitol and entered the House chamber through the press and TV entrance. He showed his new identification to the guard there. It was not yet nine o'clock.

"Morning," said Le Bombardier in a nasal Midwestern accent.

"Morning," said the guard.

"I have to run a check on camera angles from the podium. We might put one behind the Speaker's rostrum," said Le Bombardier. "I'm early enough, right?"

"There's no one in there yet," said the guard. "Christ, you never saw a congressman on the floor before noon yet, have you?"

"Not upright, anyway."

They laughed.

Le Bombardier pushed open the thick walnut door and walked onto the floor of the House of Representatives. The chamber was empty except for three young pages who paid no attention to him. He squatted behind the podium, held up his hands as if he were sighting toward the back wall of the chamber. He strolled around the low barriers to the wall behind the Speaker's rostrum. He pretended to examine the wall, sighting angles toward the floor. He returned to the podium and knelt under it, making sure his actions went unobserved. Le Bombardier quickly took out a jackknife, honed that morning to the sharpness of a razor, and in a moment he had sliced and pried up a section of carpet six inches long. It was loose enough to slip in a lethal pancake of plastique loaded with tiny detonating batteries. Properly placed, the explosion would rip upward, hitting York's legs, bursting into his groin and stomach.

Le Bombardier got to his feet and looked up to the galleries to his right, where Albert Sauvart would be sitting on the night of the State of the Union address. It was one hundred fifty feet away. Would the radio signal be powerful enough to work over that distance? There was still that problem to solve.

When he left, he said to the guard, "I don't know if

it's going to work. The camera has to be concealed up there, and I don't know if it's worth it. I'll have to come back again. A week or so from now, maybe."

"Why not?" said the guard.

"Are you here mornings all the time?"

"For the next two weeks, I got the same shift."

"I'll see you again, then," said Le Bombardier. He strolled out of the Capitol into the biting January sunshine and returned to the Marriott Motel, where he again became Albert Sauvart.

That afternoon he rented a car and drove down the Chesapeake Bay to a deserted beach. He removed a canvas bag from the car and dug out a wad of plastique. He molded it around a piece of wiring, batteries, and spark-charges. For the first test the plastique was the size of a golf ball. He set it in a depression in the sand and placed a bit of driftwood next to it. He strapped around his waist the thick cummerbund-like strap which contained his radio-activator.

He walked a hundred feet away, knelt, and turned the dial on the cummerbund. A faint humming sounded and, after a split-second delay, the plastique exploded with a powerful thud. Le Bombardier walked to the spot of the explosion. The driftwood was reduced to dust; a hole two feet deep was blasted in the sand.

Le Bombardier now molded a hunk of plastique around another detonator device and moved about two hundred feet away. He turned the dial again. Nothing happened. He removed the radio belt to adjust the signal, tinkering with the minuscule tubes inside. It took him half an hour to increase the intensity in the tubes. He knelt, turned the dial again. A shriek burst out of the radio, then the plastique erupted in a geyser of sand.

The distance problem was solved, but Le Bombardier was very concerned about the screech when he turned the detonator dial. He tried various adjustments, but he found that to generate the necessary triggering impulses from this distance—the same distance he would have to operate from in the House chambers—the radio emitted a shriek. He worked another hour on the equipment and set off two more explosions. He was able to reduce the noise, but a low screech was still audible, and there seemed no way to correct this flaw. It was a critical problem, for Le Bombardier would be sitting with press people at his elbows as the President spoke. If they heard this strange howl just before the explosion, they could easily make a connection. He concentrated, trying to visualize the setting, the details of the scene in the House chambers on that night. Suddenly he smiled. Yes, there was for this, too, a solution—one so simple, so natural, and so foolproof that he might easily have overlooked it.

The only essential element of preparation that remained to be accomplished was the actual planting of the plastique beneath the podium. A week later, Le Bombardier repeated his routine, registering at the Marriott Motel as Albert Sauvart, leaving as the television producer and taxiing to the Capitol, where he greeted the same guard and displayed the same forged credentials. He poked about the House chamber for a bit, then knelt beneath the podium and concealed beneath the carpet a piece of plastique roughly the size of a man's shoe heel.

As he left, Le Bombardier spoke to the guard. "No chance of putting a camera up behind him. We'd have to tear up half the wall to hide it in there. It's not worth it."

"No," said the guard. "I never thought it was."

"The State of the Union is only two days away, anyway. There's no time. I don't know why they made me waste my time," Le Bombardier went on.

"That's bosses for you," said the guard.

* * * * *

Chapter 30

The month of January had gone badly for York, worse than any so far. Reaction to Milly's press conference continued to be relentlessly negative. Resigned Defense Secretary Slaughter continued his fierce tattoo of abuse and criticism of the Administration's "indecisive leadership." To many he seemed to be right; the situation in Iran was still not clear, and York was not certain that the Russians were involved. Thus, he continued to fight off demands within his Cabinet and the steering committee to begin air raids against the left-wing rebel forces. And, thus, he seemed woefully indecisive.

But the worst of all was Tom Matthews. York had defended him constantly against attacks from the steering committee, and then suddenly he had been forced to resign as Secretary of H.E.W. In an incredibly embarrassing series of revelations, Matthews proved to have not one, not two, but *three* mistresses on his H.E.W. payroll. None was qualified to do the job she held. One was a former prostitute, the second was an unemployed stripper, the third a pornographic-movie actress. To make matters even worse, the trio of harpies was discovered by the staff of Congressman Jim Bloodgood, the ranking Republican on the House Ways and Means Committee whom Matthews had publicly humiliated in the fall.

York had remained cool toward Morley for a time because of his role in approving the abortive press release about Milly. Yet he found that he could not function without him. Buhler and the steering committee constantly squeezed York, cornered him, tried to trick him into doing their bidding on every issue. He had to have Morley to withstand their pressure. A week after Milly's press conference, York said, "Andy, I can't forgive you for going behind my back on that press release. But I also can't seem to hang onto the handle of this job without you. I have to have you with me. So let's clear the air and forget the damn thing."

Morley spoke in his usual brisk staccato: "Mr. President, for what it's worth, I was wrong. I thought you and Milly were too strung out to be able to think clearly then. I thought Buhler and Brownie and I could see through to the realities. And maybe we did, at that. But we should have talked to you first. Whatever they said, I was wrong not to talk to you."

"Okay, then. It's finished." York shook his head. "I'll tell you, I am so damn tired these days, Andy, I can hardly decide what to eat for breakfast. I feel like something's got hold of me and is sucking all my energy out. Like a damn tapeworm."

Morley was sympathetic. "Gus, you and Milly have to get away. Not just a two-day fishing trip, but a good long rest. Two weeks, maybe, in the Caribbean. After the State of the Union, okay?"

York closed his eyes. "I can't even make a decision about that, Andy."

In the Lincoln Bedroom York had slept alone with his nightmares every night since Milly's press conference. Despite the strength and warmth of his support for her that day, he had been, as usual, unable to make love to her that night. Angered, ashamed, confused, he had risen silently and stood dejectedly by the bed. Milly had tried to comfort him, but he replied, "Okay, maybe it is temporary again. But I can't take it, lying here with you, knowing I'm such a sorry specimen, such a damn *failure*."

She had been alarmed. "*Please* don't talk that way, darling. You aren't a failure. You're tired. The job is killing. We must be together, Gus; we must help each other." But he could not make himself stay with her.

For two weeks now, he had spent each night by himself. There had been no further visitation from William Henry Harrison, but York lay in conscious anxiety that the man might return. The memory of the steely claw-hand of death on his wrist had not left him.

York kept a bottle of whiskey on the bedtable and swigged at it through the night in the hope that it would knock him out so that he could sleep without dreams. Now on the night of January 21, he lay in a liquor-induced stupor, neither soundly asleep nor fully awake. Suddenly a fearsome rattle filled the room. A chill washed over York and he bolted upright, straining to see into the gloom. There was a rustle of sudden movement in the chair where the Harrison figure had sat. A hand—was it a hand?—rearranged itself on the chair arm. York whispered tremulously, "Is something there?"

A sound, a sort of trembling whine, seemed to reply, but York couldn't understand. He felt himself drawn out of bed. He crept closer until he could see more clearly a rigid, sharp-angled body seated in the chair. The ashen face seemed hideously emaciated. As he moved closer, it took on the look of a mummified Abraham Lincoln, though the eyes were a fierce and living crimson. Suddenly the mouth flew open, a vast yawn in the sparse beard. York assumed the figure would speak, but what leaped out of its throat was a crazed, howling babble.

York cringed. Now the figure unfolded itself to its great height, stood and, still howling, began to advance on York. "President Lincoln?!" York cried. Then a sharp explosion rang out. Could it be real? York saw blood streaming from the howling Lincoln's chest and head. It covered the chair, covered the floor. . . .

York shouted, "No!" He covered his eyes with his hands and sank to his knees. He knelt for several minutes. He realized that the howling sounds had stopped. The room was silent. He uncovered his eyes.

The chair was empty and clean. York went to it, touched it. He stood puzzled. Then he heard another rattling sound behind him. It came from a large antique wardrobe. York felt weak with fright, but he went to the closet and slowly pulled open the door. It was full of hanging clothes. The rattling grew louder. York saw a man's boots and legs beneath the clothes. He stood paralyzed in horror as the hangers grated and the clothing was pushed aside. York gasped as he recognized the face of James Garfield peering at him from the closet. Blond-bearded and grinning, his skin was taut and white, his eye sockets empty as a skull.

The mouth opened wide and a single piercing shriek split the air. Terrified, York covered his eyes with his arms. He felt as if his mind was whirling dizzily, but that his body was dead and heavy as stone. What the *hell* was happening to him? Now silence fell again and York saw the closet was empty. He staggered to the bed.

A moment later, an hour later—he did not know—he heard shrill, squeaking sounds. Peering into the gloom, he made out the gleam of a moving wheelchair. The wheels made shrieks as Franklin Roosevelt, caped and grim, the patrician features on his face bony and gray, moved toward him. In F.D.R.'s lap, barking in relentless hyena yaps, was the Scottish terrier Fala, his teeth grown long as a tiger's fangs. Roosevelt's eyes, bright red, were fixed on York, and the chair rolled closer.

York heard something behind him and turned to see the figure of John Kennedy gliding toward him as if it were afloat. York saw a head wound glistening but the chalky face of the young President remained still and beatific as he drifted closer. Now a bull-like bellow thundered from another corner of the room and York swiveled his head. A thick-chested man with angry hollow eyes stood there, tranfixed, his hands clasped across his breast where a massive wound was bleeding heavily. This figure had the visage of William McKinley and when it began to move toward him, York shouted, "No! Go away!"

Suddenly the apparitions were not so easy to see. They floated dimly about. Fala's bark and the squeak of FDR's wheels diminished. Soon everything seemed obscured by dark and drifting smoke. York felt his eyes closing. When he lifted his head again, sunshine filled the room. No sign of the night's dementia remained.

The next day York managed to function with surprising normality. His mind was preoccupied from time to time by the apparitions of the night before, yet he was outwardly rational and attentive.

Late in the afternoon he and Morley met with Buhler, Dayton, and the steering committee. The vice-president had just returned from a five-day trip through the Far East, and for half an hour he spoke about his visits to Tokyo, Peking, Bangkok, and Australia.

When Dayton finished, Len Buhler said, "Mr. President, don't you think we should put a paragraph about the trip in the State of the Union address tomorrow night?"

York said, "Absolutely."

Buhler fixed his bulging eyes on the President and

drawled slowly, "One other thing we might want to add, also." His voice seemed vaguely menacing. "That would be the new appointment at H.E.W. It's been two weeks since Matthews quit. You know that Malcolm Hingham at General Electric is expecting the call from you. Why not do it today and put it in the speech tomorrow?"

York grimaced. "Damn, I don't want to see that man a member of the U.S. Cabinet. What does he know about health *or* education? And he sure as hell doesn't know anything about welfare because he refuses to admit it should exist."

Buhler's voice was hard. "You made a serious mistake with Matthews, Mr. President. He was your man. Hingham is our man. He runs one of the biggest corporations in the country. He knows big management, big organizations. He is also one hell of a big contributor to the party."

York's face was pained. He spoke softly. "I know all of that, Len. You and Brownie and the others have never let me forget it."

Dayton said, "Why don't you announce it in the State of the Union? It would have one hell of an effect. It's dramatic. It's good political theater."

Morley spoke up sharply: "Brownie, that appointment is going to catch machinegun fire from the press. *The New York Times* and the *Post,* the *L.A. Times*— they're going to massacre us if Hingham gets the job."

Buhler was firm. "We owe him."

Morley sighed. "I know. But if we have to appoint him, let's do it where there's less of a spotlight than the State of the Union."

Buhler shrugged. "Okay. But we have to get it done within the next two, three days. It shouldn't be put off." He paused. "And neither should the appointments of John Stabler as undersecretary of the Treasury and Joe Ray Coolidge as ambassador to Spain."

"Goddamn!" cried York. "Talk about fools! Those two!" He gazed down at his desk, breathing heavily. Then he looked up wearily. "We're finished? I'm suddenly very tired."

That night his dreams were filled with Buhler's heavy face, ranting and attacking him. York tossed and shouted. Then suddenly he was awake and aware, once more, of a strange sound in the room.

This was a man's voice humming, low and even and monotonous. York sat up and saw a figure near the foot of his bed. The man had ash-colored hair, beetle-thick brows, a long straight nose and a firm jaw. He was tall and broad-shouldered, striking in his powerful and patrician looks. York knew him. It was Warren Gamaliel Harding.

Like the others, his eyes gleamed crimson out of dark cadaver sockets, but Harding seemed less sinister than the others. Indeed, there was almost a sense of amiability.

The humming stopped and Harding gazed at York. His red-bead eyes were fierce looking, but his voice was flat and neutral. "I will be on the square with you," he said.

York did not speak. Harding's monotone seemed to drift about the room, wafting off to a corner, then back to a near wall, then down beneath the bed. "I have bloviated. I have made politician's wind, empty oratory, many times. Bloviation is a politician's best friend." The voice came from everywhere but the moving mouth. "I am foursquare for America and foursquare in our brotherhood, the Presidency. I am on a voyage of understanding from the grave."

Harding's handsome, ravaged face seemed to slip in

and out of focus, as if there were dark water moving between him and York. But York felt a genuine kinship with the man. Harding had doubted his abilities as President, too. He had been nominated at an angry stalemated convention similar to the one that had selected York. Harding had accepted the nomination, but he had asked, "Am I a big enough man?"

Now Harding's voice wafted off to a corner. "A Presidency is short. Mine was shameful. Too short. I was cursed. The curse of the zeros."

York spoke tentatively. "Am I? Cursed?"

Harding paused, as if the question was difficult to answer. At last, he said, "No. There is no zero curse. No. Yours is the curse of ordinariness and honesty. It is deadly, too."

"But not a curse of the zero year?"

"I think not. I have been on the square with you . . . I want to be on the square with all the world. . . ." The ghostly ventriloquism went on, but York found the words hard to hear. His mind wandered. Soon he lay back and dozed. When he opened his eyes, the room was silent and empty, gray with morning light.

York was soothed by Harding's visit, especially by his denial of the zero curse. He showered, then stood before the bathroom mirror to shave. His face was ashen, and he looked old, far older than he felt this morning. There was a tremor in his hands. He decided he had best use an electric razor; a nick or two on his face would scarcely do on this night, when the State of the Union had to be presented. The buzz of the shaver was an irritation and soon produced a small flickering headache.

York rang for George, his valet, who had laid out his

clothes in the dressing room. York's trembling fingers made the shirt buttons difficult to manage and George said gently, as if to a child, "Here, let me do it, Mr. President." The little man frowned in concern.

When York breakfasted with Milly, he felt better. He said, "Something good is going to happen. I know it."

She looked up, surprised. Her eyes were haggard, her skin pale. "Did you sleep well?" she asked.

He hesitated. "I had dreams—a dream. But I feel as if I did sleep all night."

Milly cupped her forehead in her hand. "I didn't sleep at all. I twitch and jerk and worry so. I have this terrible sense of futility. I . . ." Her face twisted and her eyes filled with tears. "I'm so damn unhappy . . ." Her voice rose to a squeak and was choked by sobs. She covered her face with a napkin.

York knelt by her chair and gently took her face between his hands. She looked at him and he saw in her eyes something close to panic. "Milly, things will be fine. After the speech tonight, darling, we'll sleep together. We'll make love, we'll . . ."

He stopped. There was no sign of hope or belief in her eyes. She shook her head slowly.

York kissed her. "Cancel your appointments, Milly. Try and sleep. Get the doctor to give you something." She nodded and he went to the Oval Office.

Two hours later, after a grueling meeting with the National Security Council on the situation in Iran, York hurried to the swimming pool. He quickly undressed, dived in, and began a steady churning stroke, his arms rolling lazily over his head. He felt protected by the water, comforted by the power of his stroke. The figure of Harding returned to his mind now, orating as he had the night before, and York again had a surge of camaraderie. He swam for ten minutes in the oddly comforting company of Warren Gamaliel Harding.

When he climbed out of the pool, Morley was waiting with a towel. York dried himself and said, "Andy, I have a couple of last-minute things I want to stick in the State of the Union speech. Nothing complicated—two or three sentences."

Morley cleared his throat. "Uh, well, the speech has been typed and already distributed to the press, Mr. President. The, uh, steering committee . . ." He let the sentence drift off.

York said, "It's nothing all that substantial. Just a paragraph—something with a little more inspiration than we have now."

"We all agreed it would be low key, calming."

"Well, I'm not going to call on the country to man the barricades. It's just something to liven it up a little. I'll put it on paper when I get to the office."

The State of the Union message had been a group effort involving Morley, Buhler, Dayton, and York for the first draft. This had ultimately been cleared through the full five-man steering committee and had then gone through three more polishing drafts by Morley. It was bland and avuncular. It began with a mildly congratulatory dissertation on the traditional self-reliance of the American people, then proceeded to a patient, almost plodding recital of the state of the nation and the state of the world. No bugles, no drums, no shouts of triumph or cries of despair.

"I just want to put in a few phrases that have a little more spice," said York.

"It's up to you. Just don't forget that the press is

depending on the copy they have as being basic gospel."

"Just a few words." The President went to the locker room to dress, and Morley sprinted up the stairs toward his office.

* * * * *

Chapter 31

Back in his office, Morley poured half a tumbler of Jack Daniels and sipped it slowly. He was concerned about York. His oscillations in mood—high, low, high, low—seemed a classic case of manic depression.

Until now, Morley had convinced himself that the problems were temporary, that York would snap out of it naturally once he adjusted to the pressures of the Presidency. Now he was beginning to wonder. York had been so adamant in his attempts to prove that he could be his own man, act on his own principles—and this, of course, had failed. The steering committee was more successful every day in keeping York from acting outside the "sphere of interest of the Republican Party," as Len Buhler the chairman put it. York was a creature of the committee now, and though he fought and felt humiliated by it, he could do little to stop it.

Morley poured himself another drink. It was noon, what the hell. He was aware that he was drinking close to a fifth every day. But he rarely felt drunk and he was convinced that whiskey was only fuel to supply the enormous amounts of energy he was consuming.

The phone rang and Morley heard Appleton's voice. It crackled with tension.

"We've got a problem here, and I need your advice. I don't think you should delay."

"What is it?"

Appleton hesitated. "I don't think I should talk about it on the phone."

"For Christ's sake, this is an internal White House line! Have you gone totally paranoid?! Now, what *is* it?!"

"It's the Crystal Ball."

"Appleton! I can't screw around with that jack-o'-lantern smoke today. I thought I told you to ignore that!"

"I know. I want to ignore it, but, goddammit, there are so many warning signals here . . . I . . . I . . ."

Morley sipped his whiskey. "What kind of warnings?"

"Those five sources are together on this—totally together! They see bombs, explosions, blood, violence . . ."

Morley decided he had been right the first time. "Appleton, pull the plug on that machine and forget about it."

"You won't even let me show it to you?"

"No!" Morley hung up the receiver with a crash.

Appleton put the phone gently in its cradle and looked up at Brandeis.

"He doesn't want to hear about it," he said.

"These readouts are way out of the median," said Brandeis. "We've never had such consistent deviations from the safety factors. Every one of the five is on some kind of danger-code fluctuation."

Appleton said sardonically, "We happen to have fifteen hundred others. What the hell are *they* saying?"

"The usual. Random discrepancies, no pertinent or consistent patterns."

Appleton again examined the readouts on his desk. The wild flare in the readings from the five was frighteningly clear. When he had first seen them an hour earlier, he had felt the same crazy chill he had experienced before when these predictions had proved so accurate. That had been *after* the fact of the accident in Louisville. This, presumably, was *before* the fact, and the question was how to protect York against . . . against what? The predictions referred to blood and blasts of dynamite, bombs, radio-triggered explosions, hidden violence. But where? When?

Appleton figured the most likely time and place had to be tonight when the President was on the way to or from the Capitol. Somewhere on the route in the limousine. And how? A dynamite-laden car might crash into York's car. A motorcyclist might roar up and toss a grenade. Appleton concentrated on the possibilities. They were, of course, endless. In the White House or in the Capitol, there should be no danger. Security at the House chamber was more than adequate. No one would attempt an assassination there, no one could . . .

A chill washed over Appleton once more as he recalled that in 1954 in that very same chamber there had been a massive assassination attempt by a group of Puerto Rican fanatics. They had fired pistols from the visitors' gallery and wounded five congressmen. What was to stop that from happening again tonight?

Appleton picked up the phone and dialed Morley's extension again. No, said his secretary, Mr. Morley was with the President and would be with him for at least an hour, until at least four this afternoon. Yes, she would leave a message, another urgent message from Mr. Appleton.

* * * * *

Le Bombardier appeared that same day at the White

House press section and picked up an advance copy of the State of the Union message. He studied it for a few moments, reading each paragraph swiftly. It would take about thirty-five minutes if York finished it—which he would not. The only question was how far into the speech he would get before Le Bombardier used the plastique.

He went to his acquaintance from the Washington *Star* and spoke in the self-deprecatory manner of Albert Sauvart: "I have what will be a poor idea, I am sure, but let me say it. I am interested in how politicians respond to other politicians in the United States. By that I mean, what are the rules of courtesy and what are the rules of honesty?"

The *Star* man said brusquely, "You're right! That doesn't sound like a very good idea, Al. I don't know what you're talking about."

"Let me try again. My English is slow and my mind is sometimes, too. Take, for an example, this speech of the State of the Union. Where, exactly, in it do you think the politicians of the Congress will respond with applause? And will that applause be loud and very genuine, or will it be only sham applause—done only for the sake of politeness?"

"I'm still not sure what your idea is, Al, but if you want me to show you where the big applause will be in this speech, I can do that." He quickly scanned Le Bombardier's copy of the speech, placing a small "x" at eight or ten points and two large "X's"—one on the second page of the speech, perhaps two minutes into the address, and the other at the end.

He looked up at Le Bombardier. "It's very bland stuff, Al. The only news in it is this announcement on page two where he says because Americans are so self-reliant he is going to cut the budget by two billion dollars. That will get a good loud blast, I think. Then a few little ones, a ripple here and there. Then a nice firm round of clapping at the end—that's pure courtesy. The one on page two is pure enthusiasm. Is that what you wanted?"

Le Bombardier nodded enthusiastically. "Ah, yes, my friend. I could not have asked for a more precise answer. *Merci.*"

These had been approximately the points that Le Bombardier himself had decided would draw applause from the floor of the House—applause noisy enough to drown out the whine of his detonator radio signal. It would be a simple matter of reading along as York gave the speech. Then at the precise moment after he uttered the words which produced a burst of clapping and shouting, Le Bombardier would turn the dial. At least, Le Bombardier thought, the last sound to be heard by the fortieth President of the United States would be that of people applauding him.

*   *   *   *   *

Chapter 32

York hunched over his desk, scribbling rapidly on a yellow legal pad. He leaned back in his chair to ponder, scratched out words, re-edited slowly, thoughtfully. Morley entered quietly and the President said, "Give me three more minutes. I'm just polishing up this little paragraph for the speech."

"Okay." Morley paused. "Len Buhler and the vice-president are waiting outside. Do you, uh, want to mention this to them?"

York did not look up. "No. I can still do a few things on my own, dammit."

A few moments later, York jabbed a final brisk period at the end of a sentence. He pressed the intercom button to his secretary. "Maudie, I have something for you to type. There's no hurry. Just sometime this afternoon. Tell Len and Brownie to come in."

Morley studied York closely. His eyes were oddly shiny and his face alarmingly pale. Yet he seemed in control of himself. The meeting with Buhler and Dayton lasted an hour. When they left, he seemed exhausted.

"Andy, I just have to get some rest. Maybe I'll take a nap."

"You don't have any appointments until the speech tonight. We leave for the Hill about eight-thirty—more than four hours away."

"I'll just doze here for a while. That should help."

Back at his own office, Morley's secretary gave him a stack of messages and told him that Appleton had called again—it was most urgent. Morley decided he would make a quick visit to the CIPHER suite. He was impressed—and more than a bit surprised—that Appleton, consummate professional that he was, should be so extremely upset by the Crystal Ball readings.

When Morley arrived, Appleton was gazing again at the psychics' readouts. He said, "I can't take the responsibility for this stuff anymore. I keep telling myself it's pure superstition. Then I get chilled again and I think maybe it *is* real, maybe there *is* danger."

Morley said sharply, "We've proved that it's the purest unreliable dreck. Why do you keep clinging to the possibility that it's true?"

Appleton looked up sadly. "I don't know. I can't believe I'm actually trying to peddle this black magic around the White House."

"You're the one who labeled this whole thing a Halloween prank when I ordered you to do it. Are you some kind of convert to the occult now, or what?"

"Look, I'm in a terrible bind. If I cry "Wolf" and nothing happens, I'm the stupid star-gazer who thought you could read the future in a computer. But if I ignore it and something happens . . ."

"Okay, let's just say we *do* take it seriously. What would you have us do about tonight?"

Appleton did not hesitate. "First I would institute an End Around, then . . ."

"What's 'End Around'?"

"It's using a fake limousine from the front of the

White House with a full motorcycle escort, Secret Service cars—the works. But don't have the President ride in that one. He goes to the Hill in a pool car, a Chevrolet or something. Bring him in the back of the Capitol. It's simple."

"So tell Mikkelson to institute an End Around."

"You know better than that. He'd want to know why I was telling him. He'd laugh out loud if I told him the reason was a computer full of black magic. *You* tell him. He won't ask you why."

Morley paused. "Okay. I'll tell him. But I'm not doing it because of these pointy-eared electronic Merlins. I'm doing it because it's a good precaution, anyway—and York will like it. He's damn nervous these days."

"The other thing I'd like is to set up a full extra-credentials check outside the House chamber."

"How would you do that?"

"Issue a new tag or button or ticket to get in tonight. Send them around to the embassies, deliver them by courier to the congressmen for their families. Mainly, they're for the people the Secret Service might not recognize—foreigners and relatives, and, of course, the press."

Morley said, "There's no time for that."

"We could get most of them out. It's only four-thirty."

"Then what?"

"Anyone who didn't have the new credential or wasn't someone absolutely identifiable with other credentials, we would check their names and physical features through the assassin profiles in CIPHER."

"You mean check every congressman's family? Every embassy official? The *press?!*" Morley's face grew redder, and his voice grew loud. "Good God,

Appleton! You'd have the whole damn world down on our backs. They'd want to know *why* all the special precautions. The *press!* My God, they'd be after us with questions for *weeks!"*

"You'd rather risk his life than be embarrassed by a few questions?"

"Who the *hell* says it's risking his life? Half a dozen gypsy card-readers? Come on, Appleton, be sensible."

Appleton swallowed. "Okay. Maybe I'm getting whacky myself. Maybe it's not risking his life." He had come to doubt his judgment over this thing, perhaps even his sanity. Clairvoyants, psychics, precognitive kooks . . . God! That he had actually become an advocate of these screwballs struck him as both ludicrous and tragic. It reflected perfectly the absurdity of the disasters that had befallen him in the past year.

Morley said crisply, "I'll tell Mikkelson to do the End Around trick with the limousines, but I can't do more. It's too late. And that damn machine is too unreliable. And do *not* bother me about it again!"

Appleton shrugged. "If I were in your place, I'd probably be saying the same thing. I'm going to run an extra series of security checks, though, on everyone who does have a credential for the speech tonight. We can at least be sure that some Iranian press attaché isn't also in the computer for bumping off a sheikh somewhere."

"You should probably be doing that, anyway," said Morley coldly. "It's a hell of a lot more practical than standing here whining about bat squeaks in a computer."

Morley left and Appleton began the computer cross-check of people cleared to attend the State of the Union address. He was particularly careful with those from foreign embassies, missions, and from the press, areas where dangerous strangers were likely to infiltrate the audience. He began to check these names, perhaps four hundred of them, back and forth across CIPHER's massive reservoir of assassins, terrorists, lunatics, and political fanatics. It was all he could do.

* * * * *

Chapter 33

It was almost six when Morley finally read the paragraph that York had written for inclusion in the State of the Union address. When he finished it, he gasped in surprise and read it once again, frowning. He pulled a book from his shelves and meticulously compared the typewritten script of York's version with the book's printed text. He took two quick swallows direct from his bottle of Jack Daniels and rushed toward the Oval Office.

When Morely flung open the door, York was slumped in his chair, his eyes closed. He looked up at the sound of the door opening to see Morley standing before him. His face, always flushed, was a bright crimson and his eyes bulged behind his glasses. The President said in alarm, "Andy! What's the matter?"

Morley spoke in a tightly controlled voice. "Mr. President, I have just read your addition to the State of the Union message and . . ." He hesitated.

York detected the fragrance of whiskey. "And?"

Morley swallowed hard. "Where did you find it?"

"Find it?"

Morley spoke loudly, almost angrily. "Where the *hell* did you get it, Gus?!"

York fired back, " I got it out of my mind, for God's sake. Where else would I get it?"

Morley took a deep breath. "Do you know what this paragraph is from—word for word, comma for comma? For Christ's sake, Gus! Do you *know where it's from?!*"

"What do you mean?" York paused, then said flatly, "Andy, how drunk are you?"

Morley snapped, "I'm not drunk at all." He pointed to the paper in his hand. "This whole damn paragraph of yours, Mr. President—it *isn't* yours!" He read aloud from the paper: ". . . 'a patriot's duty is to stabilize America first, to prosper America first, to think of America first, to exalt America first. . . . We must strive for normalcy to reach stability. . . .'"

"I know what it says. I wrote it!" York was grim.

"No, you didn't, Gus! I don't know what's going on in your mind, but that whole paragraph is from the *inaugural address of Warren G. Harding!* Word for word, what he said in 1921!" He paused, then said angrily, "For God's sake, it's one of the most famous inaugurals in history! The 'America First' speech—any political science sophomore knows it. If you had to steal something, why not something a little more mysterious? And why, for God's sake, Warren G. Harding?"

York stared at Morley. His throat was dry now and he felt a curious lightness in his head. He had worked over those words, edited them, sculpted the sentences. Hadn't he? If a man could be so far gone . . . He said softly, "I don't believe it."

"Gus, I looked it up as soon as I read it, just to be sure. It is *verbatim!* What the hell is going on?"

He looked closely at the stricken President. York's face was slack with shock. "You didn't know it, Gus, did you? You *really* didn't know it!" Morley paused. "But how the hell did you get it the way it is—letter perfect?"

York swung his swivel chair around and gazed out the tall windows. Twilight had fallen. The darkening rose garden was empty. A uniformed White House guard stood beneath a light across the driveway. York shook his head slowly from side to side in somber disbelief. He spoke weakly. "I had no idea it was Harding's. I thought it was mine."

"What is going on?"

York continued to gaze into the garden. "I don't know, I don't know." He sighed, then turned the chair back. "I've got to think. Pour me a drink, Andy, and leave me alone. I'll be all right. I'm just very confused. My memory must have been playing tricks on me, that's all."

Morley poured some whiskey. He said, "Gus, you *have* to go through with the State of the Union. We can't cancel it now unless we have something damn serious to explain it. Something medical." He paused. "Do you want to do that? Tell everyone you're sick? Do you feel all right? I mean, do you feel capable . . ." Morley did not continue.

York was shaken. He sipped the drink and swallowed with a grimace, setting the glass on the desk with a sharp rap. "That's no medicine for me." He looked at Morley. "My mind *feels* all right, if that's what you mean. I don't know if it *is*. But, yes, I can go ahead with the speech. I've read it a dozen times. Maybe we could shorten it a little. . . ."

Morley shook his head. "The press has those advance copies. If we cut a lot out, they're going to ask why."

York nodded. "Okay. But leave me be now, Andy. Please."

"I don't know if I should leave you alone, Gus." He hesitated. "I'll look in on you in a half-hour. Okay?"

"No. Don't come in unless I call for you. I want to think this thing through."

Morley left reluctantly, closing the door with a gentle click, as if he were departing from a hospital room.

York turned again to the windows. The twilight had become night. His mind was overwhelmed with chaos. He closed his eyes and let the storm rage. He could comprehend nothing as long as it went on. He could only wait. He switched off his desk lamp.

When Milly opened the door ten minutes later, the Oval Office was blacker than the January night outside. The figure of York was silhouetted against driveway lights outside the window. She was alarmed. "Gus? Are you all right? Andy told me you might need me."

She hurried to his chair. "Gus! Can you hear me?"

He lifted an arm slowly and said, "Leave me be, Milly. I can't talk about it. You can't help. I'm sorry."

She knelt by him, looking at his shadowy face. His jaw muscles were taut as piano wire; they moved steadily as he ground his teeth. His hands were clenched in tight fists on the arms of the chair. His body seemed coiled to a breaking point.

"Darling, what is it?" Milly's voice broke in her anxiety.

His voice was forced out between clenched teeth. "I *can't* talk about it, Milly! Go! Go!"

But she continued to kneel by his chair. "Please, darling, tell me . . . what has happened?"

He shook his head once, a savage twitch. She reached up and placed her hand on the back of his neck. She whispered, "Gus, darling . . ."

In a movement so swift that she had no time to react, he slapped her cheek with his open palm. The blow sent her sprawling on her side. Tears sprang to her eyes as she lay on the carpet. He rose awkwardly from the chair. Tears glistened on his face. "God, oh, God. Milly . . . Milly . . ." He leaned over her, but she recoiled in fear and scrambled to her feet. He turned back to the window. His voice was rough now. "Please *leave, Milly!* Get out! Can't you see . . . you have to!"

She went to the door and looked back. He was silhouetted against the window, his head turned warily to watch her. His body was tense, his shoulders stiff, his hands again tightened in fists held ready at hip level. He seemed cornered and fierce. Milly left without a word.

* * * * *

Chapter 34

It was almost six-thirty. Appleton stared at the computer as if it were a crouched dragon that might spring at him. What more could he do with it? The cross-checks turned up nothing alarming, yet he felt he had to keep trying to wrench something meaningful, something useful, out of this damn infernal machine.

Brandeis appeared at the door of his office. "Maybe we could get new data from the five. Maybe interview them again to get more specifics."

Appleton shook his head. "Forget it. No one will believe it." He sighed. "Let's put through the list of people with credentials for tonight, one more time. Match photo features with facial features of all the known troublemakers who might be here tonight. We've got the whereabouts of ninety-nine percent of our assassins nailed down all over the world. Check them all together. Again."

"That'll take an hour or more," Brandeis said. "The President will be leaving for the Capitol by eight-thirty. That's only two hours away."

"Do it," said Appleton. Then he took a deep breath and dialed Mikkelson's extension. He said, "It's Appleton. Can I see you? I've got a crisis you have to know about."

Ten minutes later in Mikkelson's office, Appleton said, "I cannot believe I'm actually in a position where I have to make this kind of occult claptrap sound sensible, but, goddammit, I do." He explained the alarms coming from the five psychics. Before he had finished, Mikkelson was glancing at his watch, and when he was done, Mikkelson said harshly, "I've got maybe eight minutes before I have to check out the detail, Appleton. Are you through?"

"Not quite. I think we should delay everyone going in until we run a check in the computer on their credentials . . . every press guy, every diplomat, every wife, every . . ."

"Every congressman?" Mikkelson interrupted. "Every Supreme Court justice? Every joint chief of staff? Every member of the Cabinet?"

Appleton swallowed. "No, obviously, not the guys who we recognize—just the ones we aren't sure of."

"The press will howl like wolves," said Mikkelson. "The foreign bunch will attack us for using police-state tactics. The . . ." He paused and looked angrily at Appleton. "Son-of-a-bitch! You want me to put my job on the line with this Triple AAA security check. You wouldn't have the galleries filled by midnight if we did this."

"It won't delay things that long. Just send each name that's doubtful to me via walkie-talkie. I'll check it in the computer. We've got the list cleared. All we have to do is check each name of the ones going in against the clean list. It'll take five seconds per name—no more."

"People are going to wonder about all the cloak-and-dagger stuff. It's going to be so *obvious* that something is wrong." Mikkelson shook his head vigorously. "*If* we had a real threat of some kind—a letter-writer like that bastard in Louisville or something—we could justify it. But we have nothing but a bunch of occult bullshit."

Appleton spoke quickly: "But you're doing End Around with the limos."

"Morley ordered that." Mikkelson looked up quickly. "How did you know about it?"

"Because I told Morley about the Crystal Ball readouts and he agreed to tell you to do it."

Mikkelson nodded. "Morley knows what he's doing. If he told me to lay on that credential check you're talking about, I'd do it . . . but he didn't, Appleton, and I'm not going to do it on my own."

Appleton sighed. "Okay. I tried."

Mikkelson smiled smugly. He looked at his watch. "I'm late now."

"You're a horse's ass, Mikkelson," blurted out Appleton. "You cut me out of this job, and I hate your guts. But I think I'd be saying the same thing you're saying if I were in your shoes."

"And I'll tell you something," said Mikkelson, poking a finger into Appleton's chest. "I would *not* be saying the same thing you're saying if I were in *your* shoes. You are acting like a nuthouse escapee, Appleton, trying to sell me crystal-ball shit when it comes to the President's life. You ought to be ashamed of yourself."

Appleton, as much as he might have wanted to, could not bring himself to disagree.

* * * * *

Chapter 35

York at last was able to calm the violence in his mind. But now it was replaced by a sense of futility so profound that it seemed to have a cosmic texture of its own, a reflection of some eternal mortal helplessness that was too old and too immense for mere human comprehension.

York switched on the desk lamp and a ghostly cone of silver shone on the polished surface. He began to write quickly on a yellow legal pad. He was finished in a minute and he pushed the intercom for his secretary. His voice was thin and weary. "Come in, please, I have a little typing for you, Maudie."

She entered and spoke cheerily. "Mr. President, have you been sitting in here in the dark? My mama used to say sitting in the dark made you lose your hair before you're twenty-five."

Her cheerfulness was like a ray of sunlight in the blackness. He spoke stiffly: "Maudie, can you read that okay? My handwriting's getting more scribbly all the time. Type it on White House stationery."

She scanned it quickly, then looked up, stunned. "Mr. President! No!"

He nodded quietly. "No questions. On official stationery—no copies, and don't tell anyone." She started to protest, but he held up his hand, and she left quickly.

York gazed into the gloom for a moment. Then he began to scribble on the pad again. He paused from time to time as he wrote.

The intercom buzzed and Maude told him Milly wanted to see him. York snapped, "Not now. I'm busy." He switched the intercom off, then dialed Maude's number on his phone. When she answered he said sharply, "You didn't show her that letter you're typing, did you? *No one* is to see it."

"I didn't show her."

"Morley, either?"

"No." She sounded on the verge of tears as he slammed the receiver back into the cradle. It couldn't be helped. This was essential. A man had to show some strength, some resolve in his life.

He turned to his yellow pad. His face became more serene and the pen flowed more quickly. It was eight-ten. In half an hour, York would leave for the Capitol.

* * * * *

Le Bombardier was at the Capitol by eight-thirty. He wanted to enter the House chambers with a crowd. He climbed the marble stairway to the press gallery and hesitated at the top to watch as a uniformed guard casually checked other people's credentials. There was no Secret Service agent in the vicinity as far as he could tell. This did not surprise him. Here, the President would be considered as safe as if he were in his own bed in the White House.

Le Bombardier wore the seedy blue blazer, a wilted shirt and tie, baggy checked gray trousers, and narrow scuffed black shoes. His hair was, as always, oiled and combed down flat; steel-rimmed spectacles framed his eyes. He waited until he saw a reporter from the Chicago *Tribune* he had interviewed once and then said in his French accent, "Hello, my friend. We together shall see the President reveal the state of the nation."

The *Tribune* man looked up quickly and said morosely, "I doubt this will reveal the state of anything."

"Ha-ha! We shall see."

Le Bombardier and the *Tribune* man went past the guard together, chatting as they showed their White House press badges. Le Bombardier's forged credential passed easily. He stood at the top of the gallery stairs and studied the scene below. The chamber was crowded. The aura of history and tradition was almost palpable. Though Le Bombardier had tried occasionally to imagine the splendor of the scene, he had not fully appreciated the supreme theatricality of killing the President in these august surroundings. It was magnificent, inspirational. His eyes blinked innocently behind the schoolmaster's spectacles. His tapered hands moved nervously in and out of his jacket pockets, touched his necktie, adjusted his pocket handkerchief, checked his fly. Behind the crude and nervous mannerisms of this bumpkin French reporter, Le Bombardier experienced an almost sexual rush of triumph as he realized exactly how splendid had been his choice of time and place.

He descended the steps slowly and took a seat on the aisle. The detonator-transmitter was in the cummerbund strapped around his waist. The plastique waited to do its ghastly work beneath the podium one hundred fifty feet away. Le Bombardier felt nothing but anticipation for the events to come. He had telephoned Jamie in San Francisco and told him that he would be home the next afternoon. Le Bombardier licked his dry lips. He had been tending to business too much. He needed passion, abandon, sex. But he could not be misled now by such thoughts. He needed every bit of concentration. He glanced at his watch. It was eight-thirty-five.

* * * * *

Chapter 36

York entered Milly's room a few minutes before they were to leave for the Capitol. He said sadly, "I'm sorry, darling. You must trust me and love me. It won't be long now, not long."

He looked so haggard, so stricken, that Milly's anger vanished as she became alarmed again. But she remained grim and silent. She was patting makeup on her cheek where a faint bluish tint had appeared from the slap. There was no perceptible swelling, but the idea that she had to go through this masquerade, hiding this unprecedented treatment from her husband, had first made her frightened, then angry, and now it left her simply morose and confused. She could not bring herself to sympathize with him—not right now. That this terrible job had turned Gus, loving Gus, into a brute was something she could not assimilate. It was an absurd act, an aberration so wildly beyond the normal that she was unable to think about it clearly. She had already decided that she would leave the White House in the morning. She thought it entirely possible that she would never return. Gus could stay if he wished, but the poisons of the Presidency were something she could no longer tolerate.

She said to him, "I can't forgive you now, Gus. I

wanted to talk a while ago. Maude said you were too busy." She swallowed to keep a sob from breaking through. "I can't take this rejection."

Tears welled in York's eyes, but he left the room without another word. A few moments later, a marine guard escorted Milly out a side door of the White House to the car. It was a small black Chevrolet. Neither York nor Morley was there yet, so she climbed into the back seat alone.

Morley arrived moments later. He reeked of whiskey, and Milly said, "Andy, with you drunk and me about to burst into tears and Gus acting like he's some kind of maniac, what is the state of the nation, anyway?"

"Grim," replied Morley. "I just hope we all get through this night in one piece."

"Why are we going in this car?"

"Economy."

York arrived a moment later, stuffing a thick envelope into his inside coat pocket. He sat heavily on the cushions of the car and snapped, "Let's go." He seemed unaware that the car was not a limousine. They sat in strained silence as the car rolled past the Ellipse and up a circuitous route to the Capitol. At the Capitol, the car was waved through a barricade manned by three uniformed guards, then pulled up to a door at the side of the building. Half a dozen Secret Service agents waited as York, Milly, and Morley climbed out, then surrounded them in a protective pocket as they entered the Capitol.

Appleton again examined the sheets from the computer and looked at Brandeis. "Nothing suspicious after that guy at the Algerian embassy?"

Brandeis shrugged. "We checked three times now, and every time it comes up clean. No one with an invitation for the speech has even a remote connection with any assassination profile."

Appleton sighed. "Let's forget it." He switched on the television set by his desk and looked at his watch: eight-fifty-five P.M. Brandeis returned wearing his overcoat.

Appleton asked, "Aren't you going to watch the speech?"

"No. I'm going now. I've got to get home in time to see 'Starsky and Hutch' when the speech is over. Good night." He put on his hat and left.

Appleton stared blankly at the commercial on the set for a moment. He picked up the phone and dialed his apartment. When he heard Suzanne's voice, he sighed in relief. "That's exactly what I need. Contact with a human being."

"Are you all right, *chéri?*"

"Yes, just tired of holding conversations with a computer all day."

"Are you coming home?"

"After the speech. I'm watching it on television."

"So am I." Appleton watched as the interior of the House of Representatives appeared on the tube. He heard the avuncular tones of Walter Cronkite: ". . . the fortieth President of the United States is expected to arrive momentarily. The chamber is packed with all the power and personalities of the American government, foreign dignitaries, their guests, the world press . . ."

A camera panned down the rows of chairs on the floor, then swung slowly across the upstairs galleries. Appleton saw Milly York and Morley in front-row seats. Cronkite said, "There is the First Lady, Millicent York, and the President's number-one aide, Andrew Morley. They both look quite serious, even grim. Nevertheless, this speech is not considered one of the more important points of President York's Administration. . . ."

The cameras continued to pan, moving across the press gallery. Suzanne spoke casually into the phone, "Oh, there's Albert Sauvart."

Appleton said absently, "Who?"

"Sauvart. A seedy Frenchman, a journalist. Never mind."

Appleton gazed at the televised panorama for another moment. Suddenly he spoke loudly into the phone, "What was that name?"

"Sauvart," answered Suzanne. "Albert Sauvart."

"I don't remember his name," said Appleton tensely. "Hold on." He went into the computer bay as Cronkite was saying, "The President should begin his walk down the aisle any moment now."

Appleton pressed the selector button to check through the name Albert Sauvart. He had spent so much time examining and re-examining the names of foreign dignitaries, and particularly the press, that he had practically memorized the list. Sauvart, he did not remember. In ten seconds, the computer answered his question—there was no Albert Sauvart cleared to attend the State of the Union address.

Appleton clamped his jaw tight as he dashed back to the phone. On the TV tube he saw the camera sweep across the assembly on the floor of the House and come to rest on President York entering at the rear of the chamber. Appleton shouted into the phone, "Where is Sauvart sitting, Suzanne? What is he wearing?"

"He is in the fifth or sixth row up, I think, from the balcony rail. On the aisle next to the stairs in the center. He is wearing a blue blazer, I think. He has very oily, slicked-down hair. He wears wire-rimmed spectacles."

Appleton was short of breath. He gasped into the phone, "You know him from the embassy? A journalist?"

"No, I don't really know him. He has been in a few times. He is a freelance from Aix-en-Provence. Small papers."

"I'll talk to you later!" He hung up and quickly rang the duty officer in the Secret Service office at the other end of the White House. A young agent named Brown answered. Thank God it wasn't one of the older agents, Appleton thought, or he would have to argue to get what he wanted.

"Brown, get Mikkelson on the walkie-talkie at the Capitol, and hook me up with him!"

"Yes, sir," said Brown.

A moment later Appleton's phone receiver crackled and a voice said, "McCarthy, here."

"It's Appleton. I want Mikkelson. Now! It's a Condition White!" The code word for a definite presidential assassination attempt cracked like a thunderbolt.

"Jesus!" said the voice.

Appleton spoke slowly. "Tell Mikkelson there is a man in the press gallery who is an impostor. He is extremely dangerous."

Appleton glanced at the television set. York was now striding down the aisle, his progress impeded occasionally by congressmen moving in to shake his hand. Cronkite said, "The chamber is standing, applauding the President. It is not an extremely enthusiastic welcome. This has been a year of ups and downs for President York and . . ."

Mikkelson's voice crackled in Appleton's ear: "What the hell do you mean, 'Condition White'?"

"There is a man in the press gallery, unidentified on clearance readouts."

"Where is he? What's he look like?" Mikkelson's voice was crisp and authoritative.

"In the fourth row or fifth row up from the balcony. On the aisle next to the center steps. Blue blazer, necktie. Oily hair, steel-rimmed spectacles."

Appleton heard Mikkelson's voice snapping orders to his agents. "They're on the way," said Mikkelson. He paused. "Now what the hell are we going to do with this guy?"

"Grab him! Get him out of there as quick as you can!"

"Who is he?" said Mikkelson.

"Claims to be a French reporter."

"What's wrong with that?"

"He doesn't check with any of our clearance runs."

"Okay," barked Mikkelson. "We'll watch him." Appleton heard the sound of a walkie-talkie in the background reporting to Mikkleson. "They see him," said Mikkelson. "He's sitting still. Nothing suspicious. We'll watch him."

"You can't hustle him out of there? We don't know what the hell he might have with him."

"You got your TV on? Look at it. It's too late to cause a commotion."

Appleton watched the President walk to the podium. The Speaker of the House and Vice-President Dayton stood above him. The applause was receding. Cronkite said, "The Speaker of the House will introduce the President of the United States."

Appleton kept the phone at his ear and sank into his chair to watch. He had done what he could.

* * * * *

Chapter 37

Le Bombardier spread the mimeographed copy of the speech on his knees as soon as York entered the chamber. An asterisk marked the place on the second page where he expected the President to receive sufficient applause to drown out the whine from his detonator-transmitter.

The Speaker of the House gave a brief, cool introduction of the President. A polite rustle of applause traveled like a breeze through the assembly and quickly faded. York did not look up at the crowd. His eyes were on the sheaf of papers he held in his hands.

Le Bombardier glanced at the printed speech before him:

"My fellow Americans, I speak to you in a time of relative serenity, a time when no American boy is fighting in a war . . ."

Le Bombardier's eyes fixed on these lines expectantly. But the President remained silent. The chamber was becoming tense now, waiting. York hesitated longer. Each moment seemed interminable. The audience shifted restlessly. York continued to stand with his head bowed, silent.

Le Bombardier waited nervously, too, yet the suspense of the situation acted as a tonic to him and he felt as if his perceptions were becoming more lucid as each second ticked past.

At last, the President began to speak. His voice was tremulous and hoarse. He read from the papers before him and did not raise his eyes.

"I have failed you. I have fallen short. I know this to be true."

His voice was as inflectionless as a schoolboy reciting a poem. Le Bombardier looked up quickly. Across the chamber in the V.I.P.'s gallery, Milly York frowned and leaned forward in her seat. Andrew Morley drew a hand across his eyes, glanced sharply at Milly, then back to York.

The audience remained silent, waiting, puzzled.

York went on: "I was raised to believe that there is a *right* thing to do and a wrong thing. It is unsophisticated, it is simplistic, but doing the right thing makes a man like me feel that he is true to his heritage . . ."

He paused again, took a breath, and seemed to fight for control. Then he reached into his pocket and brought out the letter his secretary had typed on White House stationery. He took a pen and scribbled rapidly. He held up the letter before the assembly, before the television cameras, and for the first time he looked directly at his audience.

"You are my witnesses . . . these friends here, the nation out there. This is my resignation from office. As of this moment, I am no longer your President."

A great sigh rose in the chamber, followed by a low babble of surprise. Le Bombardier experienced a sharp pang of anxiety. The noise was not loud enough yet to serve his purpose . . . *but* . . . the man was no longer the President of the United States!

Milly rose in her seat, her eyes wide in disbelief. York glanced up at her as he held up the letter of resignation. He brushed at his eyes and a tight smile appeared briefly. He gazed at her for several seconds.

Le Bombardier's mind raced over the nuances of this shocking occurrence. York no longer President! The plastique was less than a yard away from him, ready to blast upward into his body at Le Bombardier's whim. Yet, the man had been totally transformed in a matter of seconds. He was only a man now, no longer an institution. Le Bombardier pondered the question. He had contracted to kill the President of the United States; this was merely Augustus York, a man who had failed at a job and then resigned. Le Bombardier could kill the man in the next split-second, if he wished. Yet, what would it mean? Would it, in fact, even fulfill his contract? Would the death of a mere citizen named York meet the terms of the agreement? He had risked much already, had taken every intricate step in his assassination plan except the one final act of pushing the detonator switch. His expertise and his courage had been put on the line; he had withheld nothing. His businessman's mind told him that he had given full return for the money paid so far. He felt justified in keeping the first payment he had received for "preliminary procedures." It had been a hard job. He also felt that the terms of the agreement were no longer valid. He had been hired to murder a President of the United States named Augustus Alvin York. This was no longer possible. The contract was, in fact, void. There was no point in risking his own life by taking the life of the man at the podium. It would be foolhardy, dangerous—and absolutely unbusinesslike, and Le Bombardier was, above all, a professional.

Le Bombardier removed his slim fingers from the radio switch and sat back, relaxed.

York began to speak again: "I will tell you why I

have resigned." He paused, then spoke gently, as if he were explaining a complex and subtle idea to children. "I have been haunted. I have become increasingly convinced that a curse of death hangs over my head as long as I am President, and I have been frightened."

Morley sat forward in his chair, his face glum and thoughtful. Milly was weeping quietly, but a certain radiance had begun to show in her face.

"It is a foolish thing, I know that. But it has become an obsession that I cannot shake. It grew from the roots of my boyhood in the mountains, where there were ghosts all around and all of us knew of someone who had been cursed and was suffering or was dead because of that curse.

"The death of Presidents elected in years ending with zero has occurred seven times. It's a coincidence, a capricious bit of numerology. In cold moments of logic, I know this. But I have come to believe it is something more sinister, something deadly—and I cannot rid myself of the belief."

He looked up at the audience. "Even now, I cannot rid myself of that belief. And as I stand here, I feel great relief—yes, and even a sense of accomplishment—in that I have broken the zero curse with my resignation: I have left office alive. Presidents never need fear the zero curse of death again. The skein is broken."

He paused, then went on quietly: "I am an ordinary man. I do not want to lead the life of an institution, a monument, an idol, a *target*. To me, the Presidency is not as important as my life. Or as my wife." He looked again at Milly and this time his smile was radiant and relaxed.

"There are men in American politics who can withstand—who may even *require*—the tension, the pressure, the power of the Presidency. I have failed at that. I commend you to the next President, Browning Dayton. He will be everything that I have not been. Thank you."

He gathered up the papers and moved around the side of the podium. Milly rose, her face glistening with tears. She brushed past Morley and ran up the stairs to the corridor. Morley followed more slowly. Now the chamber roared with sound and chaos. Reporters rushed up the steps past Le Bombardier. The floor was filled with people milling in confusion. As York descended from the rostrum, the crowd parted to make way for him. He walked slowly up the aisle alone.

Vice-President Dayton and the Speaker of the House conferred at the Speaker's podium, an elevated platform behind York's lectern. The chief justice of the Supreme Court joined them. As York reached the end of the aisle, Milly ran to him. They embraced, then disappeared through the door into the corridor.

Le Bombardier rose casually now and began to climb the steps with the crowd. The radio equipment was a comfortable weight around his waist. He regretted slightly that the expertise that he had invested would not be used tonight, but there would be another time for it. At the top of the stairs, he reached for the brass handle on the door. A strong hand grasped his left elbow tightly. Another encircled his right wrist. A voice spoke flatly: "Mr. Sauvart, come with us."

Le Bombardier quickly looked to his right and left. The Secret Service men were grim; their grips were powerful. Suddenly Le Bombardier twisted his right wrist violently. It came free and he instantly reached the switch beneath his shirt and pushed it. The high whine of his radio was followed instantaneously by a thunderous blast in the chamber below. A billow of black smoke burst from beneath the lectern. A spray of slivers showered the audience. There was a single piercing scream. A page lay on the floor, one leg a shredded mass, blood gushing from his severed arteries.

Le Bombardier wrenched his other arm free and burst out the door. In the corridor, a guard came at him, but he chopped a blow at the man's throat and he went down. The corridor was crowded with people. A Secret Service agent shouted, "Stop him!"

Le Bombardier shouldered through the crowd, knocking people down. A guard drew a pistol.

"Don't shoot!" shouted the Secret Service man.

Le Bombardier reached the stairway to the ground floor. It, too, was jammed with people. He threw his shoulder into a row of backs at the top. People tumbled before him. Le Bombardier clambered over fallen bodies. But he could not get through. A Secret Service agent landed on his back. Even before he felt the swift blow to the base of his skull, Le Bombardier knew that he had been brought down.

* * * * *

Chapter 38

Appleton stalked his office restlessly. He was drained to the bones, weak, occasionally even dizzy, but he could not sit still. As he paced, he listened absently to television commentators nattering on about York's resignation. The door opened and Morley came in. He was carrying a glass of whiskey. His eyes were pink and he staggered slightly. He spoke abruptly: "What're they saying?"

It took Appleton a moment to realize that he was talking about the television commentators. "Haven't you been watching them?"

"No. We've been getting Milly and the President— uh, Milly and Gus—on their way. They didn't want to spend one more night in this haunted house. We shipped them off to a beach house my family has on Cumberland Island off the Georgia coast. No one around this time of year. Just big waves and sand dunes. It's been a hell of an ordeal."

Appleton said, "I can only imagine it."

Morley snapped, "No, you can't. No one can. What are these assholes saying about him?"

"Shock and regret. What will the Kremlin do? Can the nation stand a shock like this? Is York a hero or a coward?"

"Which way are they leaning?"

"Hard to say. A little of both."

"Which way are you leaning?"

"Also hard to say. He was not one of my favorites."

"You weren't one of his, either. Maybe Dayton will do better with you. I dropped him a memo tonight about how you set up that assassin tonight. Told him you deserve something better than this. He'll probably ignore it since it came from me."

Appleton said, "Thanks—I guess." Suddenly he felt a sob rise in his throat, involuntary and surprising. He swallowed hard. His eyes itched.

Morley looked at him strangely, then drank deeply from his glass. His voice was blurry and harsh, but he posed like a man playing Hamlet as he shouted:

"Age, and the deaths, and the ghosts . . .
Hosts of regrets come and find me empty.
I don't want any thing
or person, familiar or strange.
I don't think I will sing
anymore just now
or ever. I must start
to sit with a blind brow
above an empty heart."

Morley cackled wildly. "John Berryman! Drunken, suicidal son-of-a-bitch! He should've been the poet laureate of this goddamn star-crossed Administration!"

He laughed again and sat heavily in a chair. Appleton began to weep. Tears, the first he had felt in forty years or more, burned as they rolled out beneath his shaded spectacles. They dripped off his chin onto his houndstooth-check jacket, his button-down shirt, his black knit necktie. He did not cry very long, but he felt very calm when he was done. He left the office a few minutes later.

As he walked down the corridor, he heard Morley shouting alone in the CIPHER suite. It sounded vaguely familiar to Appleton, but he couldn't place the source: *"Battalions of the accursed, captained by pallid data . . . some of them are corpses, skeletons, mummies, twitching, tottering, animated by companions that have been damned alive . . ."*

Morley's voice went on and on, fading as Appleton hurried down the corridor and disappearing as he stepped outside. Appleton devoutly wished this to have been the last time he would ever be in the environs of the White House. He knew it would not be the case. He could do nothing else, *be* nothing else but a bodyguard to American Presidents. He had no choice, no alternative, no way that he could change. It was his life: he could not escape his life. He realized that he had been weeping over his own helplessness far more than over the events of the lunatic night just past. He adjusted his dark glasses and hailed a taxi to take him home to Suzanne.

York stretched and walked to the tall French window facing the sea. The sun had just appeared. The sky and the sea were turning pink; the beach sand was the color of peaches. He heard the far-off clatter of the navy helicopter as it rose from Cumberland Island and returned to the base at Jacksonville. Aboard it was the entire cadre of Secret Service men dispatched from Washington to guard him. York had sent them back; he wanted no further reminder of the perils of the Presidency. The nightmare was over, daylight was at hand, there was nothing more to fear.

He turned to Milly. "Do we sleep first? Or do we celebrate?"

She smiled stiffly. Her face was pale. "I can't believe we've made our escape. This must be what it feels like to leave Devil's Island alive." Tears welled in her eyes and she quickly wiped them away.

The helicopter clatter faded to silence. Birds sang. A wild turkey made its odd, sharp chirrup off in the woods, and the breeze blew flecks of foam off the surf. Milly moved to York's side by the window and put an arm over his shoulder, a gesture as comradely as it was loving. She looked up at him. Her eyes were bright. "I'll tell you what I'd like to do before we either sleep *or* celebrate."

"What?"

"I want to go swimming. . . ."

York's reflexes were slowed, his mind still muddled from the tumult. He gazed at her silently, puzzled, unable to comprehend her meaning for a moment. Then his frown disappeared and he smiled. He began to laugh. He took off his shoes and his socks. He wriggled his toes, laughing.

An hour later, they were still frolicking in the roaring morning surf, two naked people, their bodies wet and glistening in the sun. From time to time their laughter could be heard rising over the detonations of the waves.

* * * * *

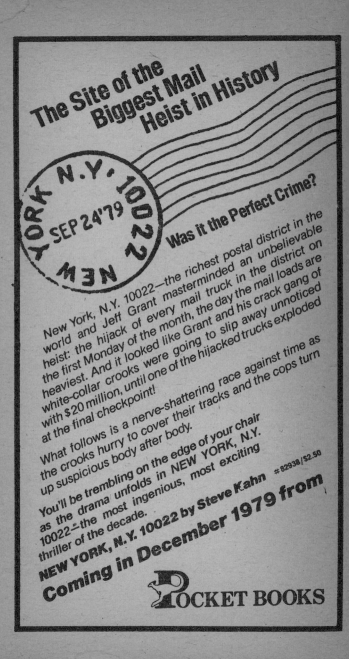